"FOR THIS, WE NEED JIM KIRK AND HIS CREW . . ."

Starfleet had apparently made up its mind; Kirk yielded, but not graciously. "Very well, Admiral. Go ahead."

"Your orders are to proceed to Nimbus Three, assess the situation, and avoid confrontation if at all possible. Above all, you've got to get those hostages out safely."

An unpleasant realization struck Jim. "What about the Klingons? Have they reacted?"

"No, but you can bet they will."

"Klingons don't negotiate," Jim said. "They annihilate. They're liable to blow up the hostages just for the chance to revenge themselves on the kidnappers."

The admiral's smile thinned to a grim line. "I know. That's why you've got to get there first, Jim."

Look for STAR TREK Fiction from Pocket Books

Star Trek: The Original Series

Star Trek: The Next Generation

STAR TREK V
THE FINAL FRONTIER

A novel by J.M. Dillard

Based on the screenplay by
David Loughery

Story by William Shatner & Harve Bennett
&
David Loughery

POCKET BOOKS

New York   London   Toronto   Sydney   Tokyo

An *Original* Publication of POCKET BOOKS

POCKET BOOKS, a division of Simon & Schuster Inc.
1230 Avenue of the Americas, New York, NY 10020

STAR TREK is a Registered Trademark of
Paramount Pictures Corporation.

This book is published by Pocket Books, a division of
Simon & Schuster Inc., under exclusive license from
Paramount Pictures Corporation.

ISBN: 0-671-68008-0

First Pocket Books printing June 1989

10 9 8 7 6 5 4 3 2 1

For George, Dave Stern, Kathy,
and especially Irwin and Geraldine

Special thanks are due Dr. Carol Williams,
an astronomer at the University of South Florida,
and George at Simply Computers in Tampa

Prologue

THE WATCHER CALLED SOFTLY at the door of the stone chamber.

T'Rea rose from her bed—nothing more than a double layer of thin handwoven fabric spread across the hard floor. She had lain awake, expecting the summons, for some time now. On the floor beside her slept her young son. He stirred fitfully as T'Rea stood and pulled her neatly folded cloak from a nearby ledge, but he did not wake.

T'Rea slipped on her cloak in the darkness, aided by the bright starlight entering through the open window carved from black rock. She navigated carefully around the shadowy, still figure of her son, then moved with soundless steps to the door. It stood slightly ajar; T'Rea pushed it open farther, and went out into the cavernous hallway.

Lean and dark-haired, the Watcher waited in the flickering torchlight. Beside him stood T'Sai the adept, the woman T'Rea had long suspected would replace her. The hood of T'Sai's robe had been raised, shadowing her face, but T'Rea recognized her carriage.

T'Rea knew what would come next. She felt an almost physical stab of pain at her betrayal, but her training as a kolinahr adept was consummate; no shadow of emotion crossed her face. She could almost hear the words before the Watcher spoke them, but there was nothing to do now save to listen and endure it.

"The kolinahru have reached a consensus," the Watcher said. His eyes were opaque, as cold as the night wind on the desert. "A decision has been made."

Without me, T'Rea finished silently. The faces of T'Sai and the Watcher, Storel, told her that the decision had gone against her. She was already stripped of her title and power. For that, she felt pain . . . but what gripped her heart was the fear that her child might be taken from her. Remarkably, her expression remained serene.

T'Sai lowered her cowl, revealing a pale, sallow complexion framed by black and silver hair. "I am now High Master of the kolinahru," T'Sai proclaimed in a voice that was strong and free from any taint of T'Rea's shame. "You are High Master no more. But we will grant you this: Upon your death, your spirit will be enshrined in the great Hall of Ancient Thought." Her voice dropped as she switched to the familiar form of address. "It is enough that thou art dishonored in life; we will not dishonor thee also in death."

"What more?" T'Rea asked. T'Sai would understand what she meant; there was the question of banishment from the desert mountain retreat of Gol.

The new High Master returned to the more formal pronoun, the one the kolinahru reserved for strangers, outworlders . . . and heretics. "If you wish, you may remain on Gol. But you may not live as one of us; you must remain apart."

"And my son?" T'Rea struggled to keep the anguish from her voice.

"He may remain with you."

T'Rea closed her eyes.

"With one provision. The boy is most talented in the mental arts. Such untrained power is . . . dangerous. He must be instructed by the kolinahru in the proper use of his power . . . and in the proper Vulcan philosophy."

In a way, this was a slap in the face to T'Rea, an intimation that her methods of training the boy were suspect, her philosophy improper. Yet had she been in private, she would have smiled. Let the kolinahru do as they wished to indoctrinate the boy with "proper" philosophy. He was already too much hers. He was barely eleven seasons old—not quite five years old, in Terran terms—yet he had already mastered the elementary mind rules customarily taught to children thrice his age. The child was a prodigy, as intellectually gifted as his father, as telepathically adept as his mother, and T'Rea had taken full advantage of his gifts. She had offered her knowledge to him as freely as she would an adult initiate.

For the boy would be a savior of his people.

He was his mother's only child, and much beloved. T'Rea had borne him in secret and had kept news of the child's existence from his father. She named the boy Sybok, an archaic word that conformed to the pattern of male given names but was rarely used; it meant "seer," "prophet." In private, she often called him *shiav,* a term from a long-dead religion, which had no counterpart in the modern Vulcan tongue: "messiah."

He was only three seasons old when T'Rea, High Master and adept of the highest degree, received illumination and began to speak out against the imbalance of Surak's teachings of nonemotion. In her role as High Master, T'Rea often entered the Hall of Ancient Thought and consulted the *katras,* the spirits, of the enshrined Masters; thus, she had received illumination and the understanding that, in order to receive spiritual knowledge, one must transcend logic. To be truly free, the adept needed to find the balance between reason and emotion.

From the most ancient Masters, she had learned also of the existence of Sha Ka Ree.

Her scholarly training was in history, specifically prehistory, with a focus on Vulcan's earliest religions. The boy was brilliant, and she had shared as much as she could of her knowledge with him, telling him of the old beliefs: of warrior Vulcan deities, fierce and loving by capricious turns, satisfied with nothing less than blood sacrifice . . . and of the ancient legend of Sha Ka Ree, the Source of all creation, the paradise where all gods and goddesses of Vulcan and alien pantheons merged into the One.

And of the *shiav* who would come to unite all religions and all peoples, and lead them to the Source, to Sha Ka Ree.

Sha Ka Ree is no legend, T'Rea had told him. She had written an academic paper on the subject and had saved it for Sybok to read when he was a little older. The paper had caused her to be the recipient of much ridicule; it had been one of the major factors in her downfall as High Master. *I tell you, child, that it exists,* she had said. *And you are the* shiav, *the chosen one. One day you will lead others to Sha Ka Ree, but now it is too soon to speak of this to anyone.*

Where is it? the child had cried, enthralled. *Tell me, and I will take you there with me!*

T'Rea had smiled mysteriously. *When the time is right, my* shiav. *When the time is right.*

After her illumination, T'Rea had restricted her consultations to those Masters who had lived before the pacifism of Surak caught hold of Vulcan and transformed it. Shortly after publication of the paper on Sha Ka Ree, word had spread among the adepts that T'Rea had abandoned her ethics and was actively pursuing the study of mind control—not of self, but of others.

She thought she had been careful. Neither she nor the boy displayed emotion in public . . . yet, in retrospect, this confrontation had clearly been a matter of time.

In the dim, shadowed hallway, T'Rea gave her answer to T'Sai.

"I accept," she said. The new High Master nodded and, along with the Watcher, withdrew into the shadows.

T'Rea stepped back into the room and gently closed the door. She had known this was inevitable; yet her pain was not lessened by it. She let it fill her soul, then rested her forehead against the warm stone of the door and wept silently, bitterly.

She turned to see her son sitting up, staring owlishly at her in the starlight.

"What is it, Mother?"

She sighed. He was too brilliant, too empathic, too telepathically gifted to be put off by a simple denial that there was anything wrong. Better to be truthful now.

"I have been silenced for my heresy, *shiav*. I am no longer High Master."

"They cannot do it!" the boy cried.

"They already have." T'Rea went over to him and sat down. *"Shiav,* they mean to train you as a kolinahru."

"I will not do it!" The boy's eyes seemed to sparkle with hate.

"You will. But you will not allow them to change what is hidden deep within your soul. And you must never forget your destiny."

"Never!" the child swore passionately . . . and then his voice began to tremble in a way that wrenched her heart. "Will they make you go away, Mother?"

"No." The thought brought T'Rea a grim momentary satisfaction; the kolinahru were embarrassed by her. Rather than let her go out into the world to preach her heresy, they preferred to let her remain among them and keep silent. "I will remain here with you."

In the starlight, she saw the outline of Sybok's

narrow shoulders against the dark wall as they rose and fell in a sigh of relief.

T'Rea hesitated, oppressed by the weight of what she now had to say. "Child, there is something I must share with you. I have had a vision from the Masters. It is the only way to win your heart, to be sure that the kolinahru can never corrupt you."

He clutched at her with a child's desperation, catching hold of the fine white fabric of her robe. "Share the vision . . . only do not go away. I swear to you, Mother"—his childish voice rose higher—"I swear to you by the Masters, I will take you away, to Sha Ka Ree, where we can be happy together."

She stroked his hair and laughed softly—her heart was not in it, but she wished to reassure the child—then took his hands in hers. "I will not leave, Sybok. I will *not leave*. And I pray that someday, we shall see Sha Ka Ree together, not in a vision, but as it truly exists."

"I will take you there, on my life, I swear it!" the child cried.

T'Rea smiled sincerely this time, touched by his loyalty. "Dear *shiav*, that is a promise I only hope you can keep. And now I must do something that will be hard, something I have learned from the ancient Masters. It will ensure your loyalty forever. Only then can I share the vision to you."

"I am ready," the boy said.

She released his hands and put her fingers against the warm flesh of his temples. "Share your pain, Sybok. . . ."

Chapter One

A STORM GATHERED on the desert horizon.

J'Onn paused in his work to stare beyond the wavering black bands of heat at the growing cloud of dust. Normally he would have headed back for the ramshackle shelter that served as home and waited the storm out there; today he did not care if the dust cloud swallowed him whole.

He looked back down at his work, at the small auger sunk into the scorched ground in a pathetic attempt to find water. This hole, like all the others, was barren; there was an utter lack of moisture in the soil. J'Onn no longer thought of it as such. To his mind, soil supported life, but this bleak, parched sand supported nothing—not his life, not Zaara's.

After Zaara's death the night before, he had wandered out to the field—once fertile, now no more than an extension of the desert—and begun to dig. Now the sun was overhead, and the field around him was dotted with hundreds of holes, many of them a few years old, made in happier times when water was not such a precious rarity. But most had been made during the gentle insanity that sustained J'Onn through the night and well into the day.

It was afternoon now, and the sun shone with unforgiving fierceness. The ground was hot enough to blister the skin beneath the fabric of J'Onn's ragged clothes as he knelt next to the auger, but he registered no pain. It was madness to work during the worst part of the heat, madness not to take cover from the duststorm . . . and he was mad, mad with grief and anger.

He had been half mad with frustration even before Zaara's death. Until the Great Drought, the land had been . . . not, in honesty, bountiful, but rather a place of sparse beauty. He and Zaara had made themselves a life—a hard one, lacking comfort, but a life nonetheless. For them there had been no alternative. On their home planet, Regulus, in the Romulan Empire, J'Onn had embezzled money from his employer and been caught. The choice was simple: execution or exile on Nimbus III.

Like thousands of other petty criminals, J'Onn became a homesteader on Nimbus III. A once-fertile planet situated near the Neutral Zone, Nimbus had achieved the dubious distinction of being claimed by three mutually hostile governments: the Romulan and Klingon empires and the United Federation of Planets. At that time, Nimbus had possessed enough natural resources (timber, some fossil fuels, and a scattering of useful minerals, including dilithium— all quickly harvested) to be worth squabbling about. The dispute was finally settled by a Federation diplomat from Altair: Why not permit all three governments to develop the planet? This, of course, necessitated legislation that—theoretically, at least— would enforce peace between the settlers: no weapons of any type were to be permitted on the planet. Accordingly, Nimbus was given the rather grandiose subtitle, "The Planet of Galactic Peace."

For several years, the concept almost worked. And then, while the three governments were drawn into arguments over details, the settlers—most of whom, like J'Onn, were "volunteers" who had come to escape execution or imprisonment—had decimated the forests, exhausted the mines, and destroyed the ecosystem by farming with the aid of chemical toxins that had long ago been outlawed elsewhere in the galaxy. In less than twenty years after the agreement was signed, Nimbus III was a desert, and the starving homesteaders fashioned homemade weapons and began to fight one another for the dwindling resources.

In a blindingly short time, there was no more water for irrigation. The crops failed, and Zaara seemed to wither with them. There was no money for her medical treatment. Because of J'Onn's crime, she could not return home to her family for help unless she divorced and renounced him. That she would not do, though J'Onn pleaded tearfully for her to do so.

She had died last night, hours before dawn, and J'Onn had stumbled outside, dazed by grief, unaware

11

of himself or his surroundings, only of his loss. It was midmorning before he came to himself and saw the dozens of fresh holes he'd apparently drilled the night before in his feverish search for water. By then the obsession had hold of him, and he could not stop. With both Zaara and the land gone, there was nothing left. He was vaguely aware that he intended to drill until he found water or died of heatstroke. Considering the harsh afternoon sun, he reasoned he had an excellent chance of accomplishing the latter. He had already stopped perspiring. J'Onn ran a hand across his forehead; it felt cool and dry. His thoughts were beginning to drift randomly. Soon would follow disorientation, convulsions . . . death.

J'Onn let the auger slip from his hands and closed his eyes. Already the delusions had started; he imagined he heard a sound in the far distance, in the direction of the storm. A low rumble, like thunder before a rain.

He had not heard thunder in a very long time.

Oddly, the thunder failed to reach a crescendo and then fade. Instead, the rumble grew steadily, unmistakably louder, as if it were moving closer. Mildly curious, J'Onn opened his eyes.

A rider emerged from the storm.

He rode astride a native creature that Federation settlers jokingly referred to as a "horse." For some reason the term had caught on, though the beast resembled no Earth animal J'Onn had ever seen. Granted, it was a quadruped, but larger and shaggier, with a twisted horn jutting from its snout.

J'Onn was not frightened of horses; he knew the creatures, though homely, were quite docile. But the sight of the rider made him gasp and struggle to his feet.

The stranger rode like one possessed, spurring his steed onward. His face was covered against the dust-storm, and he wore a white cloak that caught the wind and flared out behind him like the wings of an avenging angel.

Or a demon.

The rider thundered closer. Clearly, his destination was the very patch of ground where J'Onn now stood.

A thread of awe and fear penetrated J'Onn's grief. Because of them—or perhaps because of the force of experience, which had long ago taught him to expect ill of strangers—J'Onn scrambled for the weapon lying next to him. A handmade pipe gun, with stones for projectiles. It was not reliably lethal, but it was the only protection he had.

At the same time that he fired a warning shot in the intruder's direction, J'Onn asked himself, *Why am I protecting myself? I wish only to die.*

Yet habit was strong. J'Onn clutched the gun protectively as the rider reined his mount to an abrupt stop several feet away. Behind him the storm continued its slow but inexorable approach.

The beast stamped its feet while its rider uncovered his face to remove his breathing device. He and J'Onn studied each other tentatively. The stranger's face, half hidden inside the hood of his white cloak, was distinctly humanoid, male, adult; the eyes were shadowed, yet somehow J'Onn perceived that they were extremely intelligent, full of a strange, disconcerting brilliance.

Still clutching the pipe gun, J'Onn gaped at the

apparition before him until at last the rider spoke. The language was Standard, a tongue that J'Onn had mastered before coming to Nimbus.

"I thought weapons were forbidden on this planet," the rider said. He said it easily, with good humor rather than reproach, then swung down from the saddle to stand directly before J'Onn; he was tall and well muscled. J'Onn should have shot him then, but something held him back.

With a powerful arm, the stranger gestured at their barren surroundings. His voice became soft, full of knowing sympathy. "Besides, I can't believe you'd kill me for a field of empty holes."

J'Onn stared out at his land. The stranger was right; there was nothing left of his farm now except a parched field of dry wells. And in most places the soil had become too soft and shifting even to serve as a proper burial site for Zaara. "It's all I have," he answered feebly.

He had meant to sound strong and defiant, but the stranger's kindness stole away the last reserves of his strength. J'Onn collapsed under the weight of his grief, his exhaustion, his fear. He was dimly aware of the stranger approaching him and gently taking the pipe gun from his hands . . . and of the sound of his own sobbing.

"Your pain runs deep," the stranger said.

"What do you know of my pain?" J'Onn cried. It was both an accusation and an admission.

The stranger did not move, but J'Onn felt cool fingers brush his cheek and rest lightly on his temples. "Let us explore it together."

The stranger, again without stirring, seemed to

come closer, until he loomed vast in J'Onn's field of vision. The sun-scorched land with its pathetic holes, the storm ominous on the horizon, even the memory of Zaara's death—all were obliterated, swallowed up by the incandescence in the stranger's eyes.

J'Onn was mezmerized by those eyes, but even so, in the back of his mind lurked mistrust. His culture was rich with ancient legends of magicians who wielded untold powers to control weaker minds, and here, without a doubt, was one of them.

Yet, try as he might, he could not be afraid of the stranger. The brilliance seemed full of nothing more than kindness and love.

The stranger spoke again, his voice as soothing as a caress. "Each of us hides a secret pain. It must be exposed and reckoned with. It must be brought forth from the darkness into the light."

"No!" J'Onn cried with sudden anguish. As the stranger talked, the image of Zaara, lying dead upon the hard narrow cot that was their bed, struck him full force. He could see her last few moments of life again, could hear her gasping for breath, unable even to speak his name, her eyes full of misery and concern for him. For him! She had chosen to be loyal to her husband, and the decision had destroyed her. J'Onn trembled under the weight of Zaara's quiet suffering, under the weight of his own guilt.

The sensation of a cool touch upon his forehead.

"Share your pain with me," the stranger said, with such tenderness that J'Onn wept. "Share your pain and gain strength from it."

J'Onn ceased struggling. The horror of what had happened to Zaara—the look on her face when she had been forced to leave her family, the expression in her eyes when she died, the drought that had rendered the land barren, the shame of banishment from Regulus . . . in short, the utter ruin that was his life—all of this misery washed over him, engulfing him with sorrow until he could bear no more. He cried out and sank to his knees in the hot sand.

And when he thought he could stand no more, the pain eased, as if gentle, invisible hands had reached in and lifted it above him. The events that had caused his grief did not disappear, but now he saw them with another's eyes, eyes that were objective, yet sympathetic. J'Onn could face them now with a strength he recognized as not his own but the stranger's. Even the memory of Zaara's death was tolerable now, as if it had happened twenty sols ago instead of hours ago. J'Onn saw the part he had played in her misfortune . . . and knew with unshakable certainty that it had been Zaara's decision to stay.

A strange peace descended on him, a peace born of the stranger's wisdom. J'Onn realized that his eyes were squeezed tightly shut; he opened them and gazed with gratitude and awe at his benefactor. Euphoria replaced pain.

The stranger had been standing several feet away; now he reached a hand forward to assist J'Onn to his feet. His grasp hinted at great physical strength.

"Where did you get this power?" J'Onn whispered, when at last he could speak. "I feel as one reborn."

The stranger released his grip on J'Onn's hand; his face was still hidden in the shadows of his hood. "The power was within you, J'Onn."

The stranger knew him by name, a fact that impressed J'Onn but was certainly no more marvelous than the miracle the man had just performed. If not an angel or a god, then the stranger was at the very least a holy prophet. Overwhelmed with gratitude, J'Onn struggled to express himself. "I feel as if a weight has been lifted from my heart. How can I repay you for this miracle?"

"Join my quest," the stranger said.

"What is it you seek?"

"What *you* seek," the stranger replied earnestly. Next to him, the horse snorted and stamped impatiently, startling J'Onn, who was so hypnotized by the stranger that he had completely forgotten about the animal. "What *all* have sought since time began—the purpose of existence, the ultimate knowledge. But to find it, we'll need a starship."

J'Onn smiled, still giddy from the relief of his sorrow. Had the stranger professed himself to be a murderer on a rampage, J'Onn would gladly have followed. As it was, his heart was filled with near-unbearable joy at the sound of the stranger's words. To know at least the meaning of his bleak, unhappy life . . . and to find a starship! It would mean freedom from this accursed desert! But Nimbus was isolated, far removed from any trade routes. And after the Great Drought came, all exports had ceased, and the homesteaders could no longer afford to buy expensive imported goods. No sane person came to Nimbus—at least, not voluntarily. No trading vessels bothered to make the journey, least of all, the starships.

"A starship?" J'Onn asked hesitantly. "There are no starships on Nimbus Three."

Although he could not see the stranger's expression,

he got the impression his question was met with amusement. "Have faith, my friend," the stranger answered. "There are more of us than you know."

The rider threw back his hood. He was ascetic-looking: hollow-cheeked, unshaven, uncombed, yet there was a handsomeness to his rugged, even features. Unshadowed, his eyes were startling, full of a piercing brightness that J'Onn found awe-inspiring and slightly frightening.

And then J'Onn saw the ears. Regulus was governed by Romulans; J'Onn could perceive the subtle differences between them and other Vulcanoids. He let go a gasp. "You . . . you're a Vulcan."

The stranger gave one slow, grave nod. And then he did something that J'Onn had never seen a Vulcan do before.

He smiled and threw back his head and laughed.

Chapter Two

A STARK AND FORBIDDING MONOLITH, El Capitan rose out of the forest and into the clouds. At the campsite near the banks of the Merced River, in the shade of tall pine and cedar, Dr. Leonard McCoy peered through binoculars at the mountain's face. El Capitan reared straight up to form a right angle with the forest floor; it was nothing less than a massive wall of rock, and from where McCoy stood, its sides seemed smooth, offering little or no purchase.

Only a fool or a madman would attempt to scale it.

The doctor raised a pair of binoculars to his eyes and scanned El Capitan until he found what he was looking for: a lone human figure pressed against the rock, hugging the side of the mountain. From this distance, Jim Kirk appeared the size of a mosquito.

McCoy swore under his breath. Kirk had managed

to make his way a few hundred meters up, and he was doing it—against the doctor's loud protests—with no equipment, no ropes, no grommets. If Jim's grip should weaken at an inappropriate moment . . .

" 'You'll have a great time, Bones.' " McCoy mimicked sarcastically. " 'You'll enjoy your shore leave and be able to relax.' " He lowered the binoculars; without them, Kirk became a barely distinguishable speck on El Cap's face. "You call this relaxing? I'm a nervous wreck."

True, Jim's suggestion had been a good one. Yosemite was the ideal location for shore leave, possessing a wild, remote beauty that filled McCoy with humble reverence. He hadn't been to Yosemite since he was a boy, and it moved him to find that it had not changed: it was every bit as vast and breathtakingly majestic for the adult as it had been for the child.

Yet here he was in the midst of this rugged paradise, unable to relax and enjoy it, and for that he was honestly angry at Jim. The Federation Council had finally granted Kirk what he had wanted all along—a demotion to the captaincy and the *Enterprise,* or at least her namesake, back under his command. You'd think the man would be glad, but his demeanor aboard the ship was withdrawn, irritable, brooding. McCoy figured shore leave would solve it. And it did, to an extent, but now Jim's attitude had become reckless. The day before, the doctor had taken him white-water kayaking. Jim had refused to wear a life preserver until McCoy put his foot down. And then Jim had intentionally sought out the most dangerous rapids, in the process nearly drowning himself and

McCoy, who had followed in his own kayak in a rescue attempt.

Kirk was not only unapologetic about the incident, he was belligerent, angry that McCoy had interfered. Shortly thereafter, he had announced his intention to climb El Capitan without benefit of safety equipment, and had the nerve to seem irritated that the doctor was upset about his decision. Only the most experienced mountain climbers attempted El Cap, and those who did so generally used equipment. Only the finest climbers in the world went without, and all of them, as far as McCoy knew, insisted on a wide-dispersal electromag cushion at the mountain's base, in case the worst happened. More than one person's life had been saved by the cushion when rocks, or muscles, gave way.

Jim wouldn't hear of it.

Here was a man, McCoy reflected, who had just gotten what he wanted most out of life—his ship, his command—and he seemed determined to destroy it . . . or himself.

The most frustrating thing of all was that Jim denied it, refused to discuss it; in fact, suggested that the doctor was being paranoid and was himself sorely in need of R-and-R.

Which, God knew, McCoy would not deny. They were all in desperate need of shore leave—including the new ship, which had been slapped together so hastily that nearly half the crew had stayed behind to make her spaceworthy. And they had all been drained by the events surrounding Spock's rescue: the death of Kirk's son, David Marcus, the loss of the old *Enter-*

prise, the harrowing ordeal of standing before the Federation Council and awaiting a verdict.

Yet, to McCoy's mind, none of those events explained Kirk's current actions. It was almost as if Jim was thumbing his nose at death. Not just the kayak incident, not just this mountain-climbing business . . . there were subtle things as well. Such as the way Jim paused a bit too long when setting logs on the campfire, as if daring the fire to burn him.

McCoy wanted none of it. He'd been through enough, thank you, after the mental stress he endured as the carrier of Spock's *katra,* and the torment of the ritual of *fal tor pan,* which separated his consciousness from the Vulcan's.

"Just keep this up, Jim," he said softly, "and if I'm not careful, I'll end up talking to myself."

He was just about to raise the binoculars again when he caught sight of Spock heading back toward the campsite. The Vulcan wore levitation boots and was navigating slowly through the trees a couple of meters above ground that was thickly carpeted with dried pine needles. McCoy remembered Mount Seleya all too well and figured Vulcan had its share of mountains far higher and more formidable than any Earth had to offer. It wasn't all that surprising to him that, when Jim professed his desire to tackle El Capitan, Spock showed little interest. More than anything, the Vulcan seemed quite taken with the trees and had spent the entire morning examining a grove of ancient giant sequoias from their massive gnarled roots to their towering uppermost branches. Spock had politely invited McCoy to join him, but the doctor had begged off, leaving Spock and Kirk to examine aerial phenomena by themselves; he preferred to seek excitement closer to the ground.

The sight of Spock gave him an idea; he gestured vigorously for the Vulcan to approach.

Almost three hundred meters above them, Jim Kirk balanced on a ledge no more than a few centimeters wide, his body pressed against the cool stone surface of the mountain. There was a narrow crack in the rock just above his head, and he reached cautiously up, probing. The gap was just wide enough to admit the middle two fingers of his right hand, up to the first knuckle; he inserted them securely, drew in a deep breath, then exhaled.

Concentration was critical. A single instant of distraction, a hesitation, one tiny slip, and death would be the inevitable outcome.

He honestly enjoyed mountain climbing, just as he had enjoyed white-water kayaking, and perhaps for the very same reason: because it forced him to *not* think.

And there were many things he wanted to avoid thinking about: the grief he still felt over the loss of his son, David, and the fact that Carol Marcus still wanted nothing to do with him. He could only assume her silence was an accusation, a laying of blame.

And then there was the different but no less keenly felt loss of the *Enterprise*. The new ship was no substitute, though at first he had been exhilarated to have a ship, any ship, to command.

But this ship wasn't the *Enterprise*, regardless of the name emblazoned across her hull. To begin with, not a damn thing aboard her worked. The real *Enterprise*, even when crippled, had given her all and kept trying. The new ship couldn't even synthesize a passable cup of coffee. It was simply a metal hull.

He had no son, no Carol, no ship. He had been attracted to Gillian Taylor, and he had hoped—hell, maybe he had only hoped for a distraction from his grief over David . . . but Gillian was far too absorbed by her work at the New Cetacean Institute, and the challenge of repopulating the humpback whale species.

At a time in his life when he should have been happiest, Kirk felt empty. Rudderless.

James T. Kirk, hero at large. You can save the galaxy from destruction, but you can't put your own life in order.

Jim stopped himself and forced his mind back on the mountain. At eye level, he found a slight depression in the rock—not enough for a firm grip, but enough for what he needed. He rested his left hand in it and, gripping with the two fingers of his right, pulled himself up.

The act was at once exhausting and exhilarating; Jim paused for a moment to let his rapid heartbeat slow and to take in the phenomenal view of the Merced River as it cut a path through the tall forest beneath him and of the aptly named Half Dome on his right. A shame McCoy was not here to enjoy it with him, but then, knowing Bones, he'd probably complain that the sight was conducive to attacks of vertigo.

There was a sudden soft *whoosh* next to him. A hawk, Jim thought at first, and instinctively he tensed, struggling against the onrush of dizziness and fear, and leaned into the mountain. The disorientation lasted only two seconds before he reclaimed his balance.

"Greetings, Captain," Spock said. His hands were clasped behind his back, in a typical fashion. It took a moment for Jim to remember the Vulcan had brought along a pair of levitation boots on the camping trip.

He was tempted at first to curse the Vulcan for almost causing him to fall, but, as Spock would have pointed out, only Jim's own fearful reaction could have done that. Besides, arguing would only cause more distraction, and so he swallowed his anger and relaxed against his place in the rock without allowing himself to forget exactly where he was. "Spock," he said, deliberately casual. "What brings you to this neck of the woods?"

"I have been monitoring your progress," Spock said.

Kirk's lips twisted wryly. "I'm flattered. Twelve hundred points of interest in Yosemite, and you pick me."

It was a very broad hint to get lost; the Vulcan, as usual, failed to catch it. "I regret to inform you," Spock said, "that the record time for free-climbing El Capitan is in no danger of being broken."

Jim was unconcerned by this revelation; he frowned in his renewed attempt to concentrate.

"I'm not trying to break any records, Spock. I'm doing this because I enjoy it. Not to mention the most important reason for climbing a mountain . . ."

Spock tilted his head, curious. "Which is?"

Jim smiled as he intently studied the rocky surface just above his eye level. "Because it's there." He found the crevice he was looking for and reached up to probe it with his fingers. It was sound.

"Captain," Spock said, "I do not think you realize the gravity of your situation."

A few years ago, the Vulcan might have committed such an atrocious pun in all innocence; but lately Spock had devoted himself to understanding and— God help the rest of them—occasionally attempting Earth humor, with painful results for all concerned. Kirk groaned. As he did, his feet slipped; only his firm handhold saved him from falling. Beneath his feet, a small avalanche of rocks were dislodged and tumbled to the valley below. Alarmed, Spock hovered closer, but Jim found his footing again.

He glared over at Spock, no longer good-humored about the interruption. Another distraction like that, and . . . "On the contrary. Gravity is foremost on my mind. Look, I'm trying to make an ascent here. Why don't you go pester Dr. McCoy for a while?"

"Dr. McCoy is not in the best of moods," Spock confessed.

Spock's observation was quite accurate—and becoming more so by the second. From his safe vantage point in the forest below, McCoy had witnessed Kirk's near-accident with a wrenching spasm of fear that left him breathless. Once the doctor was sure Jim was all right, his terror subsided, leaving anger in its stead. McCoy's grip on his binoculars tightened; he swore under his breath.

"Goddamn irresponsible . . . playing games with life . . ."

He hoped—foolishly, of course—that the near-tragedy would bring Jim to his senses, that the captain would latch on to Spock and take the safe way down. But from the looks of things, Jim was going to be pigheaded as usual and keep climbing.

And the doctor was unable to shake the premonition that something awful was about to happen.

Furious, terrified, mesmerized, McCoy peered through the binoculars.

Hovering next to the captain, Spock continued. "Besides, I have come here at his insistence."

Kirk frowned. "McCoy put you up to this?"

Spock appeared unmoved by Jim's indignation. "He is concerned, as well he should be. Attempting to scale El Capitan without benefit of safety precautions is somewhat reckless."

"So is distracting someone attempting to scale El Capitan," Jim countered, but Spock, if he heard, ignored the remark and continued.

"Concentration is vital. You must become one with the mountain."

"That's very philosophical. Spock, I appreciate your concern, but"—he let the irritation creep into his tone and turned his face and thoughts back toward El Cap; there was a deep crevice several centimeters above his head that looked sound. Jim slipped his left hand in and tested it—"if you don't stop distracting me, I'm liable to become one with the—"

The narrow ledge beneath his feet began to crumble. Jim tried to hold on with his left hand, but couldn't get a solid enough grip in time. With a sickening awareness of what was about to happen, he lost his balance . . . and fell.

It was one hell of a dizzy ride. The stretch of mountainside that had cost him painstaking hours to climb now hurtled by at lightning speed. Jim thrashed and put his left hand out to try to catch hold of a ledge, a rock, anything—but the stone surface was maddeningly smooth; he succeeded only in bruising and scraping his hand. By this time he had somehow managed to get turned upside down, so that he was falling head first.

He would land in the forest of cedar and pine and juniper below, probably bouncing off a tree or two before it was all over. He was not all that far from the campsite and McCoy—who no doubt was watching, horrified.

Oddly, Jim didn't feel that frightened. Even in the thrilling, disorienting throes of the fall, he was calmed by the thought that Spock and the doctor were nearby.

He heard the sound of boosters firing, then felt something clamp tightly on his right ankle and jerk, not at all gently, upward.

Spock.

Jim struggled to raise his head and peer up at his rescuer. Without releasing his grip on Jim's ankle, the Vulcan said dryly, "Perhaps 'because it is there' is insufficient reason for wanting to climb a mountain."

The sudden release of tension made Kirk giddy, and the fact that he still dangled upside down made the blood pound against his ears. A part of him had actually enjoyed the fall and found it exhilarating. He grinned weakly, grateful for the Vulcan's intervention. Spock *had* been a distraction, but the ledge had crumbled on its own. The fall had been no one's fault. "I'm hardly in a position to disagree, Mr. Spock."

There was a thrashing in the forest, like the sound of a wild beast on a rampage. Jim turned his head and watched McCoy tear through low branches and underbrush. Dangling from a strap around the doctor's neck, a pair of binoculars swung from side to side.

Jim felt suddenly like laughing. Maybe it was the upside-down perspective: McCoy looked like a crazed, wild-eyed mountain man. "Hello, Bones. Mind if we drop in for dinner?"

But the doctor was as furious as Jim had ever seen him and would not be placated. He indignantly brushed stray twigs and pine needles from his plaid flannel shirt and glowered at Kirk. "That's right, turn it all into one big joke. What the hell do you think would have happened if Spock hadn't been there?" His voice shook.

"For God's sake, take it easy, Bones. I'm all right."

"What would have happened?" McCoy demanded, as if Jim's life depended on the answer. He gestured accusingly up at the mountain.

Jim didn't want to surrender his sudden good humor. He lifted—or rather, lowered—his hands and shoulders in a sheepish gesture. His palms grazed the rocky ground. When McCoy folded his arms and intensified his glare, Jim answered: "All right, I would have been killed. Does that satisfy you? But I wasn't. Spock caught me."

Spock lowered himself and Kirk gently to the ground. Jim righted himself on the rocks and pine needles and sat, trying not to be too obvious about massaging his bruised right ankle. The backs and knuckles of his hands were skinned and bloody. He'd be sore as hell tomorrow.

"Dammit, Jim!" McCoy exploded. "What's *with* you? Yesterday you tried to kill us both in the rapids —don't deny it! And today you throw yourself off the side of a mountain. Are you really all that anxious to meet your Maker?"

He turned on the heel of his hiking boot and stomped angrily back into the forest. Spock gazed after him with a quizzical expression.

Jim wasn't all that sure he knew the answer to McCoy's question.

J'Onn was slightly breathless by the time he reached the top of the sand dune. He had crossed the desert during the most intense heat of the day, and the journey had been a long one. But J'Onn was not at all tired: he felt exhilarated and very young.

The desert was as grim and lifeless as ever, but today he saw only its stark beauty and its promise. For the first time in his life he had a purpose other than maintaining a meager existence. He smiled gratefully up at his benefactor.

The Vulcan had said his name was Sybok. Other than that, he would answer no questions about himself, about whether he had come here as a homesteader, about why he had chosen—if it was true that he was not an accused criminal—to come to Nimbus III.

Whatever the reason, J'Onn was glad the Vulcan had come. For if ever a place was in dire need of a messiah, it was Nimbus III, and if ever there was a messiah with the strength to save such a miserable planet, it was this Vulcan, Sybok.

Others, too, had recognized Sybok's power and followed; as he had said, "There are more of us than you know." J'Onn had not climbed the dune alone. Beside him, behind him, marched at least a hundred homesteaders—like him, poor, ruined by the drought. The group comprised every possible alien race, all of them united by a common cause: their gratitude to Sybok.

The Vulcan reined in his steed; the two poised majestically at the crest of the highest dune. Behind him, the small ragged army of homesteaders kicked up dust. J'Onn stopped and gazed up expectantly at his master.

Sybok smiled down at him, then raised a powerful arm and pointed straight ahead into the distance. J'Onn squinted and saw nothing but black waves of heat rising from the yellow sand.

"My friends," Sybok cried, his voice clear and ringing. "Behold Paradise!"

And then J'Onn saw: the high, worn walls of a ramshackle village, a single outpost rising up in the heart of the desert. For no reason he clearly understood, the sight brought him unutterable joy.

Sybok spurred his horse onward, and his army followed.

Chapter Three

THE WOMAN PAUSED at the entrance of the Paradise Saloon to gather herself. The front doors were oddly constructed—they came only as high as her collarbone and as low as her knees, so that her view of the saloon's interior was unobstructed. And what she saw of it was daunting indeed.

The patrons were hostile-looking homesteaders, unwashed, dressed in rags, and conspicuously displaying illegal homemade weaponry. At least, the woman told herself, the composition of the crowd was laudably heterogeneous: Romulans, Klingons, humans, Andorians, Tellarites, and representatives of a dozen more races, all under one roof.

But they were scarcely achieving any minor victories for intragalactic peace. The different groups kept to themselves except when involved in arguments or fistfights. She watched amazed as an Andorian—obviously chemically befuddled—leaned over to address a table of surly Klingons. Their response to the Andorian was a fist in the face. He staggered backwards several meters before falling unconscious across a table of disinterested humans, who promptly nudged him off onto the rough sand-covered floor.

Through it all could be heard a noise that she supposed was music, but it was harsh, strident, offensive to her delicately pointed ears.

Remember, Caithlin, you volunteered. . . .

The air inside the bar was filmy. Perhaps it was full of dust, like the air outside. Once she was sure that all hostilities within the bar had temporarily come to a halt, the woman stepped inside. The double doors slid open before her, then snapped shut behind her with a fatalistic click. She drew in a breath through her breathing filter, then grimaced; the smell was pungent, decidedly unpleasant. The air wasn't full of dust at all, but of some noxious substance, probably smoke from some illegal substance such as tobacco. . . .

Or perhaps the vapor was generated by the homesteaders themselves.

Now is not the time for illusions of superiority. You volunteered. . . .

It took Caithlin a moment to realize that all conversation had stopped the moment she stepped inside. The entire population of the saloon had turned its attention on her; she straightened, drew herself up as tall as possible, and walked with fearless dignity through the very center of the crowd. As she came close to a low platform around which many patrons sat drinking, a barely clad felinoid female, who up to that point had been entertaining the crowd with a seductive dance, growled low in her throat at the interruption and switched her long striped tail in the air. That growl was the only sound in the bar; no one, Caithlin knew, would dare try to stop her—unless they wished to incur the wrath of her entire government.

She was Romulan, though her given name was due to the unfortunate fact that her grandfather, Liam James O'Malley, was human. Caithlin had thus far spent her entire life trying to make amends for her ancestry. As soon as she was old enough, she had applied for the diplomatic service, making it immediately clear to the admissions board that she knew herself to be an exceptionally qualified candidate and that if she was turned down, she would not hesitate to take legal action.

In the end, she was accepted. Regardless of her family background, she was too bright, too skilled, too eager to succeed for them to turn her away. But she had known that, because of her heritage, she was unlikely to receive a good assignment; in fact, she was liable to be given the worst of them. And so she had asked for Nimbus III.

She knew what she was doing; she knew that Nimbus was considered a lost cause, a boondoggle, a joke, a failed experiment that nothing shy of a miracle would save. Which was precisely why she had applied for the job.

Caithlin paused momentarily in the dim, hazy bar; she did not see the two men she was searching for. The bartender, a grizzly Tellarite who could barely see over the top of the bar, took pity on her and jerked an appendage in a specific direction. Deciding to follow his advice, she headed for the far corner of the saloon. In a dark recess, a narrow entryway opened onto an L-shaped foyer, so that Caithlin could not see inside. Even so, she stepped boldly into the foyer without knocking—given her current situation, an air of confidence was imperative—and walked into the room.

It was a dark, dingy storage area full of extra tables and damaged chairs. On one wall hung a large mirror with a huge diagonal crack. The floor was covered with the omnipresent gritty yellow sand. At one of the tables, in the only two chairs that were whole, the Nimbus representative of the United Federation of Planets sat conversing with the consul from the Imperial Klingon Empire.

Both of them were too drunk to notice Caithlin's entrance. If she could have raised her breathing device without seeming too rude, she would have done so: for some reason, the stench was stronger here in the back room. Caithlin lowered her breathing filter and waited silently while the men drank—the human from a large tankard of what looked, ironically, like Romulan ale, and the Klingon directly from a dust-covered flagon.

After a moment, while they remained oblivious to her presence, Caithlin said, in a voice that would have wakened the unconscious from an intoxicated slumber, "Gentlemen. I am Caithlin Dar."

"Well, well." The human, a malnourished light-haired male, rose languidly from his chair. The act seemed to tire him a good deal. *He's ill,* Caithlin thought at first, until she saw that his tankard of ale was almost empty. Any human who could finish off that much Romulan ale and retain enough motor coordination to get out of his chair had to be an alcoholic. She had heard of the phenomenon, and on rare occasions, actually seen an individual who suffered from it.

The human ran his hand through his limp, disheveled hair and smiled wanly as he extended a bony hand. Recalling the custom, Caithlin reached out and grasped it firmly. His grip was weak, the grip of a coward.

"Well, well," he repeated. "So our new Romulan representative has come at last."

Most Romulans would not have noticed anything odd about the man's accent, but Caithlin noticed immediately that it was British; Liam O'Malley would not have cared for this man, either.

"Welcome to Paradise City, capital of the so-called Planet of Galactic Peace, Miss Dar," the Englishman continued. "I'm St. John Talbot, the Federation representative here on Nimbus. I must say, I have never met a Romulan by the name of Caithlin before."

"Nor I a living saint." She held the thin, frozen smile in place as she turned to exchange hostile glances with the Klingon. Technically, the Klingon and Romulan empires were allied, a result of economic necessity rather than mutual admiration.

"Ah, yes." Talbot recovered from her retort. "My ever so charming companion, the Klingon consul, Korrd."

Talbot was capable of irony, at least. Korrd, old and

immensely obese, kept his seat. His narrow eyes glittered as a result of alcohol. They flicked over her quickly, and then he turned away abruptly, as if bored, and took a substantial swig from the dust-covered flagon in his huge paw. As if to punctuate his disdain, he emitted an earthshaking belch.

Caithlin maintained her composure. "I expect that's Klingon for 'hello.'"

Talbot reached out to touch her hand with an obsequiousness that repelled her. "I realize there's no love lost between your peoples, Miss Dar, but you must forgive him. He's not exactly trained in Romulan social customs—or human ones, for that matter. He doesn't even speak English, I'm afraid."

Caithlin lifted an eyebrow. It was typical of the Klingon government to send a delegate who was unprepared to converse in a common tongue with the other diplomats. Fluency in English was not a necessity, but it was a courtesy. "I suppose we can resort to using a universal translator. But that does tend to slow down negotiations."

Talbot made a gesture that conveyed helpless embarrassment. "I'm afraid . . . well, I'm afraid that we don't have one."

"Don't have one!" Caithlin exclaimed.

"I'm afraid our governments aren't willing to invest any more than is necessary—perhaps even less than that—in Nimbus Three. Surely you've noticed."

Caithlin narrowed her eyes at Korrd. The Klingon's tunic, though decorated with dozens of medals, was stained and covered with wrinkles . . . and it was too small to cover Korrd's expanding bulk. From where

Caithlin stood, she could see Korrd's bronze-colored stomach bulging out under the hem of his tunic and over the waistband of his trousers. She averted her eyes in disgust; the old Klingon warrior continued to drink with gusto, oblivious to her scrutiny. "I don't speak Klingon, Mr. Talbot."

"I'm afraid I do." He motioned with a smooth white hand at his own chair. "Please sit, Miss Dar."

Caithlin settled into the filthy chair while Talbot located one that was not too seriously broken and dragged it up to the table. He brushed the seat vigorously and coughed at the clouds of dust generated.

"May I get you a drink, Miss Dar?"

"No," she replied emphatically. She'd been as polite as possible; now it was time to speak her mind. "Quite frankly, Mr. Talbot," she said as he took his seat, "I'm shocked at what I've seen here. Nimbus supposedly represents the best our three governments can offer, and yet hunger and poverty are rampant here, law enforcement nonexistent."

Talbot took a very long pull from his tankard before turning his bloodshot gaze on her. "It's the bureaucracy, Miss Dar. Our three governments have generated a complex maze of laws, and now they're arguing about how to enforce them. You must have known all about this before you came here."

"And you must have known about it, too, Mr. Talbot. So why are the two of you sitting here getting drunk in the middle of the day?"

Talbot said nothing to defend himself, but his expression saddened so suddenly that Caithlin felt an inkling of pity for him. With oddly appropriate timing, Korrd let loose with a guttural barrage of Klingon that sounded suspiciously hostile, as if he had understood all too well what Caithlin had just said.

Caithlin frowned at him. "What did he say?" she demanded of Talbot.

Talbot's sallow complexion suddenly turned pink. "He says he hopes you'll enjoy your tour of duty here. We are drinking, Miss Dar, because our once-illustrious careers have culminated in an assignment to Nimbus Three. Perhaps they didn't bother to tell you that your predecessor died of shame and sheer boredom. Might I ask what horrible thing you did to get yourself banished to this armpit of the galaxy?"

"I volunteered," Caithlin said evenly. It occurred to her that the Englishman might have assumed she was sent here because of her human blood . . . and perhaps he wouldn't be far from wrong. Still, the thought disturbed her.

Talbot had just taken a mouthful of ale; at Caithlin's answer, he spewed it in Korrd's direction and started choking. The Klingon pounded enthusiastically on the Terran's scrawny back.

"Vol . . . un . . . *teered?*" Talbot wheezed finally. He turned to translate the word for Korrd; the Klingon threw back his head and laughed scornfully.

Caithlin had anticipated that the other diplomats on Nimbus III would be angry, frustrated, or at the very worst, indifferent. She had been prepared for all of those attitudes, but she was not prepared to find trained diplomats engaging in utter debauchery. She leaned forward, trying to keep the defensiveness she felt from her tone. "Nimbus Three is a great experiment. Twenty years ago, when our three governments agreed to develop this planet together, a new age was born."

Talbot smirked at first, but the smug expression faded quickly as he seemed to realize she was quite serious. "Unfortunately, Miss Dar, things that sound perfect in theory generally don't work. Your new age died a quick death. The Great Drought put an end to it. And the settlers we conned into coming here—forgive me, but all of our governments did it—were the dregs of the galaxy. Convicted criminals, most of them. They immediately took to fighting among themselves. You can see what good the laws against weapons did: They made their own."

Perhaps, Caithlin decided, there was an intelligence lurking behind Talbot's drunken facade; about Korrd she was not so sure. If she could just convince the human . . . "Maybe I've arrived just in time, then. Mr. Talbot, hasn't it occurred to you that the policies the three of us agree on could have very far-reaching—"

"My dear," the human interrupted, "we're not here to agree. You're very young and very idealistic, and believe me, I applaud that. But you must realize that governments rarely do things for the reasons given the public. We were sent here to disagree. My comrade here"—he nodded at Korrd—"tried to make a difference, and look where it landed him. This 'great experiment,' as you call it, was instigated merely to satisfy a bunch of bleeding hearts whining for galactic peace. It was intended from the beginning to fail."

Caithlin felt her expression harden at Talbot's words, but she forced herself not to give up. "I'm afraid I don't share that view. We could *make* it succeed, regardless of anyone's original intention."

But Talbot shrugged her words off. "There, you see?" He smiled as if pleased. "We're disagreeing already."

She persisted. "I'm here to open discussions for a solution to these problems. Mr. Talbot, why don't—"

Korrd suddenly came to life; he spat out a disgusting mouthful of Klingon, then leaned back in his chair, which seemed on the verge of splintering under his weight, and roared with laughter at his own wittiness. Whatever he said caused Talbot to wince noticeably.

It did not take a translation for Caithlin to understand that she had just been insulted. "What did he say?" She glared at Talbot in a way calculated to make the human realize that she would no longer tolerate any deception, no matter how polite or well intended. "I want his *exact* words. No lies this time."

Talbot seemed to shrink in his chair; his expression became miserable. "He said"—his voice was so faint she had to lean very close to hear—"he said that the only thing he'd like you to open is your blouse. He's heard Romulan women are different." He looked away, too embarrassed to meet her eyes.

Caithlin stood up so abruptly that her chair very nearly tipped over backwards. A rush of blood warmed her face. So the old bastard spoke English after all. There was no way he could have understood her last comment; Talbot had not been translating.

Caithlin had told the truth when she said she spoke no Klingon. Except for one particular epithet. She hurled it at Korrd with venom and hoped her accent was correct.

It was. Korrd hoisted his ponderous girth out of the chair and hurled the flask aside. It shattered on the gritty floor, spraying glass and evil-smelling liquor everywhere.

"Screw *you*, too!" he snarled—in near-perfect English.

Talbot gasped in what appeared to be genuine surprise; apparently Caithlin hadn't been the only one the Klingon had deceived. "Korrd, you sly old bugger! All this time—"

"So." Caithlin smiled triumphantly. "You *do* speak English. I'm glad to hear it . . . It will make our work that much easier."

The old Klingon was on the verge of replying when, outside in the distance, a warning siren began to wail. Korrd and Talbot froze.

Shouts came from the street, followed by the sounds of customers making a hasty exit from the saloon. Caithlin frowned in confusion. "What is it? What's happening?"

"The city," Talbot said, listening, his eyes wide. "Someone's trying to invade the city . . . though God knows why anyone would want to."

Korrd snorted at the idea, but he strode from the back room out into the now-emptied bar and through the double doors into the dirt street outside. Caithlin and Talbot followed.

A ragtag army of grim-faced homesteaders, all of them armed with pipe guns, was making its way down the street. In its midst, a lone white-cloaked figure rode regally on horseback.

The soldiers were very clearly headed this way.

"What the devil . . . ?" Talbot breathed next to Caithlin's ear.

The town's dwellers were already in hiding. Caithlin thought of the phaser and the long knife with the delicately carved nacre handle, both of which she had left behind on her home planet, and swore under her breath at the intruders. By Romulan standards, their weapons were laughably crude, but she had no means now of protecting herself from them.

She turned to ask Talbot if he knew who the soldiers were—and saw that he and Korrd had fled back into the saloon. She went inside and found the Klingon behind the bar, pouring the contents of an upended bottle down his throat.

Talbot had gone to a far corner of the bar and yanked a dusty cover from a communications terminal. He bent over it now in a desperate attempt to get it working. Caithlin joined him to see if she could help, but the terminal was ancient; she had never seen one with similar controls. Clearly it was as old as the city of Paradise, and it had probably not been used since the outpost was first constructed.

Talbot jabbed furiously at the controls again, then waited for a response, eyes focused on the viewscreen, long trembling fingers poised over the keys.

The screen remained dark.

"I don't understand," Caithlin said next to him. "I wasn't briefed about any group that wanted to seize control of the city. Who are they? What do they want?"

Again Talbot stabbed at the controls in vain. "I don't know," he said unsteadily. When the terminal again failed to respond, he straightened and looked at Caithlin with uncertainty and fear in his eyes.

"I don't know," Talbot repeated, and then he visibly took control of himself. His tone lightened. "My dear, you know as much as I. What do *you* think on seeing an armed group of hostile homesteaders marching this way?"

Caithlin heard a steadily growing rumble in the background—the sound of soldiers approaching on foot.

"They clearly mean to seize control of whatever government exists here," Caithlin answered. "Which means that our lives could be in danger. I think we should do what the townspeople have already done— flee. After all, they have weapons, and we have none."

"Korrd has a pistol," Talbot offered weakly.

She shook her head. "Hardly enough to do us any good. We should leave."

Talbot raised his pale eyebrows in feigned surprise. "And you a Romulan! I thought you never surrendered."

"Even a Romulan finds no disgrace in avoiding conflict when the opponents are unevenly matched."

"Then go." Talbot sighed. "You're young: you have a future—that is, if you can get past the stigma of having Nimbus on your résumé. But there's no reason Korrd and I should go with you."

"They might kill you!"

"They might." Talbot smiled thinly. "That would probably be one of the nicer things to happen to either

44

of us in a very long time. But if the group outside has gone to all this trouble to find the government . . . well, I think it would be rather rude for no one to be here to greet them. Someone's got to listen to their demands." When Caithlin remained, frowning at him, he said gently, "Go, my dear. Korrd and I will handle them. After all, someone has to notify our governments."

The rumble grew threateningly loud; the crowd was almost outside the saloon.

"No," Caithlin said. She was no longer quite so sure that she disliked St. John Talbot. "I'll stay. As a representative of the Romulan government, I need to find out what these people want. Maybe they're peaceable. After all, we haven't heard any shots fired."

"Yet," Talbot said. "Look, if you go now, you can get out through the back room." He bent over the dark terminal screen and listlessly pressed a few keys. "You see, it simply isn't going to work."

The saloon doors crashed open and several homesteaders swarmed into the bar, all of them bearing handmade weapons. One of them pointed a pipe gun at Talbot and Caithlin.

"Get away from that screen!" he shouted, aiming his weapon at it as if he meant to destroy the terminal. He was pitifully stooped and scrawny, physically even less imposing than Talbot, and yet there was a fire-bright fanaticism in his eyes that made him appear dangerous. Caithlin did not doubt that if either she or Talbot disobeyed, the homesteader would use his pathetic weapon to kill them both. She hesitated, then slowly backed from the screen.

Talbot did likewise and half raised his hands in the human gesture of surrender. "There's no point in shooting it," he remarked casually, with a nod at the terminal. "It's been dead quite some time."

As abruptly as it had begun, the alarm stopped wailing, leaving behind an eerie silence. Soldiers continued to enter the saloon. Before a full minute had elapsed, they filled the bar and herded Caithlin, Talbot, and Korrd, who reeked of ethanol, into the room's center.

A man entered, wearing a white cloak with the hood drawn up. He was the one who had ridden on horseback, the one Caithlin had recognized instantly, from his bearing and the reactions of the others, as the leader. Of all of them, he alone carried no weapon. His followers parted to let him through to the place where the three diplomats waited. He strode up and stood before them, tall and regal, and threw back the hood.

He was a Vulcan. Caithlin nearly gasped aloud at the revelation, but contained herself; renegade Vulcans were extremely rare, but they did exist. More than one of them had abandoned the Federation for the Romulan Empire. This one, neither young nor yet middle-aged, seemed scarcely better off than his followers. His cloak was worn and frayed, of questionable cleanliness. Its wearer was bearded, unkempt, unwashed, the same as any homesteader, but something in his demeanor—his authority, his confidence, the frightening intelligence in his eyes—set him apart from them.

He stopped before his captives and turned to address his followers. "Well done, my friends. You have taken Paradise without a shot."

Sounds of satisfaction rippled through the crowd. The Vulcan turned to face the three diplomats, taking time to scrutinize them slowly, one by one. Against her will, Caithlin found herself flushing under his intense gaze.

"Romulan. Human. Klingon," the Vulcan said to each of them in turn. "Consider yourselves my prisoners."

Talbot snickered softly. "Prisoners? That's rich. We're *already* prisoners on this worthless ball of rock. Of what possible value could we be to you?"

The Vulcan smiled faintly. "Nimbus Three may be a worthless ball of rock, but it does have one unique treasure."

Caithlin almost shuddered; somehow, she knew the Vulcan's exact words before he said them.

"It's the only place in the entire galaxy that has the three of you."

Korrd let loose a roar and reached for the pistol at his hip. But the instant before his thick bronze fingers touched it, four of the Vulcan's soldiers cocked their guns and pointed the barrels squarely at the center of the Klingon's massive chest. For a tense moment, the old warrior seemed to consider trying to take some of the soldiers with him—but he was clearly outgunned. With a gurgle of impotent rage, Korrd let his own weapon clatter to the floor.

Caithlin addressed the Vulcan with a boldness she did not feel. "Who are you?"

"A friend."

She frowned, frustrated by the cryptic response. The Vulcan merely smiled, apparently amused at her irritation. He was toying with her, and if there was one thing Caithlin despised, it was an individual who refused to take her seriously.

"You're the leader of these homesteaders. What is your purpose?" she demanded. "What do you want?"

"To find the purpose of existence," he replied. At first she thought he was being sarcastic, and she started to respond angrily, but as he continued, she saw he was quite sincere. "To understand creation. And we want"—he hesitated and caught her eye—"you."

Her skin prickled at the way he said the word "you." As he spoke, his dark eyes seemed to grow huge, dominating her dismal surroundings until Caithlin could see nothing else. Suddenly she became dizzy, terrified for reasons she did not understand. She closed her eyes briefly and fought for control.

When she opened them again, the fear and the strange effect had gone: the room was as it had been before.

"As hostages," she managed to say. "As you said, we're your prisoners; that's clear enough." She paused, searching her imagination for a common cause that would link this oddly charismatic Vulcan to the group of poverty-stricken settlers . . . and could find none. "The question is *why?* What are your demands?"

The Vulcan's expression was enigmatic. "That will become clear with time."

"All right," she said, "so you won't tell us who you are or what you want, but I can tell you this: our governments will stop at nothing to ensure our safety."

"That's exactly what I'm counting on," the Vulcan said. And, seeing her confused expression, he gave a smile that was wide and absolutely beatific.

A smile, Caithlin thought, reserved exclusively for saints . . . and madmen.

Chapter Four

Uhura tucked the food pack inconspicuously under one arm and stepped from the lift onto the new *Enterprise*'s bridge. The scene was pure chaos: dismantled consoles and monitors were strewn everywhere in an ungodly hodgepodge while a skeleton repair crew examined each component for flaws and then lazily pieced them all back together.

Uhura sighed as she cautiously navigated over exposed cables. The sight was more than a little depressing; except for Chief Engineer Montgomery Scott, *nothing* on the new ship worked. Well, almost nothing. Yesterday, with Scott's help, she had finally gotten her communications board up and running. Maybe, Uhura considered, the gods were getting even with them for scoffing at *Excelsior*'s unspaceworthiness.

She gingerly made her way over to Scott, who was reclining on the floor, his weight resting on one elbow, and scowling up at a panel of bared circuitry beneath the navigation console.

"Scotty." She did her best to sound cheerful.

At first he seemed too absorbed in his task to register her presence. She was about to speak again when, without taking his gaze from the panel, Scott muttered darkly, "'Let's see what she's got,' the captain said. Well, we found out, didn't we?"

"I'm sure you'll whip her into shape, Scotty," Uhura reassured him, or at least tried to. But the mess on the bridge made feigning confidence difficult. "You always do."

Scott turned his head just far enough to narrow his eyes at her. "The old *Enterprise* was easy to whip into shape. This new ship . . ." He faced the circuit panel again and shook his head. "I don't know. I just don't know. If they wanted to replace the *Enterprise,* they should have taken their time and not given us such a piece of—"

"Don't say it, Scotty," Uhura pleaded sadly.

"Rubbish," Scott finished bitterly. "Fell apart the minute she left spacedock. She'll never replace the old *Enterprise.*"

It was what the entire bridge crew felt, and what none of them dared voice. Emotionally, Uhura agreed with Scott, but she also knew that no good could come of such an attitude, and so she had been consciously trying to develop a positive feeling about the new ship. Strange, the way each vessel took on a personality all its own. The original *Enterprise* had been nothing more than an inanimate object, a lifeless collection of metal and circuits, and yet here they all were, still acting as if a family member had died, and resenting this interloper who had tried to take her place.

"No ship can ever replace the *Enterprise*," Uhura told Scott softly. "But we've got to give this one a chance. She's all we've got."

Scott grunted, clearly unconvinced. Uhura watched him work in silence for a while. And then, abruptly, an expression of confusion crossed Scott's face. He stopped working, turned around, and sat up, facing her. "Uhura, why aren't you on leave?"

She had to smile. Scott might complain about the new ship, yet he was so concerned about getting her to one hundred percent efficiency that he had entirely forgotten the promise he'd made. "I thought we were going together," Uhura answered. She affected a rather pathetic Scottish burr. " 'There's nae fairer than the Highlands this time o' year.' Does that bring back memories?"

She had planned her first trip to Scotland for this shore leave and had mentioned it to Scott, but upon learning that she had signed up for a package tour, the engineer had been outraged. He would take her himself, he insisted, and show her far lovelier sights than the tourists would ever see. And there would be no paying for hotels, either. She would stay with his sister's family and that was that. It would be no imposition at all.

Scott groaned and brought the heel of his palm to his forehead. "Uhura, forgive me. I completely forgot. At the time I made the promise, I dinna know the extent of the ship's"—he paused; obviously, "damage" wasn't quite the right word—"affliction. But I'll notify my family you're—"

"You'll do no such thing," Uhura replied firmly. "I won't impose on them. I'll take the tour, just as I planned." That was a lie—she'd missed the deadline —but there was no point in making Scott feel any guiltier. She would remain on the ship and help out as best she could, and when she couldn't help, she would head for the recreation deck. *Who needs shore leave, anyway?* Uhura asked herself, and barely managed to cut the thought off before the honest part of her mind answered, *I do*.

"I'm sorry. Someday I'll make it up to you." Scott gestured helplessly at the panel behind him. "But I canna leave the ship when she needs me the most."

"I had a feeling you'd say something like that." She grinned and produced the food pack from under her arm. "So . . . since you seem to have skipped so many meals lately, I brought you some dinner."

Scott took the pack from her and finally managed a smile of his own. "Lass," he said, with genuine warmth, "you're the most understanding woman I know."

You're probably right, Uhura was going to agree, when an earsplitting siren interrupted. The bridge alert light began to flash.

"Red alert," said the computer at the communications console—the one she *thought* had been working. "Red alert."

Both she and Scott moaned.

"I just fixed that damn thing," Scott half shouted over the siren's wail. "Turn it off, will you?"

Uhura rushed over to her console, almost tripping over loose cable on her way, and switched the alert off. The siren died with an unhealthy gurgling sound. "Gremlins on board," Uhura muttered. She was just about to turn away when she saw the light flashing on the communications board. Someone was attempting to contact the ship.

She pressed a button. "This is *Enterprise*. Please identify yourself."

A stern masculine voice responded. *"Enterprise, this is Starfleet Command. We have a Priority Seven situation in the Neutral Zone."*

"Stand by, Starfleet." Disbelieving, she put the signal on hold and gestured at Scott. "Scotty, this is for real."

"I heard." Aghast, Scott shook his head. "They canna be serious. The ship's in pieces and we've less than a skeleton crew on board."

Uhura pressed another button. "Starfleet, are you aware of our current status?" It was a polite way of asking, *Are you kidding?*

The voice remained cold and unapologetic. *"Current status understood. Stand by to copy operational orders and recall key personnel."*

"Standing by." So much for shore leave, period. Uhura sighed and glanced over at Scott, whose expression was one of irate indignation.

"The Neutral Zone! This ship already proved she can't make her way out of spacedock without falling apart!"

"I know," Uhura said. "But if anyone can pull it off, Scotty, you can."

It sounded lame even to her own ears. Scott gave a snort of disgust and went back to his work.

Commander Hikaru Sulu tipped his head back to catch a glimpse of sky beyond the tops of the tall pines. The sun was no longer visible overhead, but had slipped toward the horizon. The air was already beginning to cool. They had an hour, Sulu figured, an hour and a half at most, before dark. The brilliant blue sky was already starting to fade to gray.

"Admit it," Chekov's weary voice said behind him. "We're lost."

Sulu smiled and slowed his pace through the dense woods to allow Pavel to catch up to him. The Russian was beginning to sag under the weight of his backpack; they'd been hiking since midmorning. It was true: Sulu was quite lost. Foolish of him not to bring a compass—but that would have taken all of the adventure out of it. He felt as tired as Chekov, yet the sensation was enjoyable, pleasant, and he could not get upset about being lost in this primeval wilderness. Its beauty was too heady, too exhilarating, to permit anything to mar it. Sulu drew in a lungful of cool air scented with evergreen and felt refreshed.

For a moment, it was easy to imagine that he was a kid again in Ganjitsu's tall forests . . .

But that image brought unpleasant memories with it, memories of another time when he had been unable to find his way. He pushed the memories back and turned to face Chekov.

"All right," he admitted cheerfully. "We're lost. But at least we're making good time."

Chekov was not amused; he groaned and came to a full halt. "Very funny. I suppose *you* have no blisters."

"Blisters?" Sulu cast a concerned glance at Pavel's obviously new boots. "Didn't you remember to synthesize a half-size larger and then wear—"

A shrill beep from the communicator on his right hip made him stop in midsentence. Both he and Chekov stared at it in amazement.

"I don't believe this." Sulu pulled the communicator from his belt and flipped it open. "Even Scotty couldn't have put the ship together this fast." He raised the device and spoke into the grid. "Commander Sulu here."

It felt odd using the old rank, now that he'd finally gotten used to being addressed as "captain"—almost as odd as it felt to refer to James Kirk as "captain" again instead of "admiral." Not an altogether comfortable feeling, and yet, Sulu reminded himself, he had not actually been demoted, as Kirk had. At his request, he had been temporarily reduced to the rank of commander so that he could serve aboard the new *Enterprise.*

The alternative had been to take a ship of his own, a prospect he'd found tempting. And yet, Sulu reasoned, the *Enterprise* was as much his ship as Kirk's. The admiral—that is, the captain—might give the orders, but it was Sulu who safely guided her through the stars.

Then there was the question of loyalty. After all he had endured with the captain and the others, there was no question that he would ask to serve with Kirk again—and gladly take the reduction in rank in order to do so.

Kirk had been furious when he'd heard. He gave Sulu hell for not looking after his own career. And then he'd thanked him.

"Commander Sulu, this is *Enterprise*," Uhura's voice said. The tense formality in her tone indicated that she was about to say something she knew Sulu did not want to hear. "Bad news, gentlemen. Shore leave's been canceled."

Sulu frowned, disappointed. *"Slava Bogu,"* Chekov breathed thankfully. "Rescued at last."

Uhura continued. "Return to the prearranged coordinates for pickup."

Sulu and Chekov exchanged amused glances.

"Don't tell her we're lost," Pavel whispered. "She'll never let us live it down—a helmsman and a navigator who can't find their way out of the forest!"

A pause. Uhura asked, "Is there a problem, gentlemen?"

Sulu grinned and hoped it didn't show in his voice. "Er . . . as a matter of fact, there is. We've been caught in a blizzard."

Chekov rolled his eyes; Sulu spread his arms in a gesture that said, *Well, then, you try to think of something better.*

To his credit, Chekov played along with it. "We can't see a thing!" he shouted at the communicator. "Request you direct us to the coordinates." He pursed his lips and affected the sound of a furiously howling wind. It was, Sulu thought, rather convincing.

Another pause. "Sulu . . ." Uhura's tone was one of thinly veiled amusement. "I'm so sorry to hear about your weather. Funny, but my visual says you're enjoying sunny skies and seventy degrees."

"Your console's probably malfunctioning," Sulu suggested helpfully, "just like everything else on the bridge."

"Sorry. Fixed it myself."

Not to be discouraged, Chekov cried, "Sulu! Look! The sun's come out! It's a miracle!"

Uhura gave up and laughed aloud. "So the navigator and the helmsman don't want to admit they're lost, huh? Don't worry, fellas. Your secret's safe with me."

Sulu's smile became sheepish. "Uhura, we owe you one."

"I'll chalk it up with the other ones. Transporters are still out, as you've probably guessed. I'll be sending down the shuttlecraft to pick you up." She hesitated a beat. "I sure hope they can find you in all that snow."

Sulu was too shocked to respond humorously. "They're sending the ship on a mission before the transporters are fixed?"

"You heard right. And the transporters are the least of our worries, according to Mr. Scott. Figure that one out if you can. *Enterprise* out."

Chekov sank wearily onto a nearby boulder and shook his head as he struggled to pull off a hiking boot. "On a mission before the ship's repaired. The captain won't be pleased."

"That's for sure," Sulu agreed. He sat next to Pavel and was suddenly aware of the extent of his exhaustion. "I could have gone to Yosemite with the captain; I've never been there before."

"And miss walking around lost for hours with me?"

Chekov asked, indignant. "Besides, if you've seen one national park, you've seen them all."

Sulu glanced absently over his shoulder at the wilderness they were leaving behind. In the distance, a great mountain thrust into the sky, five faces carved into the stone. All of those honored here were political figures who had died centuries before Sulu was born, including the most recent addition to the momument, Sarah Susan Eckert, the first black Northam president.

Sulu did not answer Chekov's question. He was thinking again about how shoddily the new ship had been constructed. Until now he had not permitted himself to think about all of the problems or to compare the new ship with the old *Enterprise*. Mr. Scott would fix the ship, would make her an even finer vessel than the old *Enterprise* had been . . . or so Sulu had convinced himself. But to take her out in her current condition . . .

He began to wonder if his loyalty had led him to make a very big mistake.

"Come and get it!" McCoy yelled as he banged a metal spoon against a frying pan. Dinner simmered in a covered dutch oven perched atop white-hot coals raked neatly to one side of a blazing campfire.

Seated less than a meter away, Jim Kirk put his hands over his ears. "Knock it off, Bones. We're right here and we're starving." He did not say it kindly. After this morning's climb and near-disastrous fall, Jim was tired and sore—but too proud to ask the doctor for something to ease his aching muscles. And painfully hungry. Dinner smelled wonderful, but McCoy had insisted on cooking it the old-fashioned way, and Jim and Spock had sat waiting for the last three hours.

At least the act of fixing dinner seemed to have improved the doctor's foul mood. That, and the considerable amount of bourbon he'd consumed; at this point, McCoy was beginning to be a little unsteady on his feet. Still, Jim suspected he had not heard the last of the El Capitan incident.

McCoy gave a lopsided grin and crouched beside the covered pot, evidently relishing his audience's undivided attention. "My friends, you are in for an unequaled culinary treat! Ta-daa!" And with a flourish, he whisked the top off the pot to reveal a steaming mass inside.

Spock stared at it with faint suspicion. "Bipodal seeds, Doctor?"

"Beans, Spock," McCoy corrected him with pride. "But these are no ordinary beans. These are from an old southern recipe handed down to me by my father, which he got from *his* father, and so on. And if you dare turn your Vulcan nose up at them, you're not just insulting me, you're insulting countless generations of McCoys."

Spock weighed the potential consequences gravely. "I see. In that case, Doctor, I have little choice but to sample your . . . *beans."*

McCoy ladled his concoction into bowls and passed them out.

Jim was starving and tore into his. Happily, the beans tasted as good as they smelled. He glanced up as he was chewing to see McCoy watching them both expectantly.

"How are they?" the doctor asked.

"They're great, Bones," Jim mumbled through a mouthful of beans. There was a faintly familiar flavor component that Jim couldn't quite identify. He took another huge mouthful and tried to figure it out.

"Of course they are," McCoy smiled, pleased. He served himself and was about to take a bite when he paused to watch Spock.

Jim looked over at the Vulcan. Spock raised a forkful to his nose, smelled it, then very gingerly tasted *one* bean.

"Well?" McCoy demanded. It was impossible to tell from Spock's expression what his reaction was.

Spock swallowed deliberately. "Surprisingly good," he admitted. "However, it contains a flavoring with which I am unfamiliar."

McCoy smiled diabolically. "That's the secret ingredient."

Spock lifted a brow at that, but seemed to decide against pressing the issue. He began to eat with enthusiasm. McCoy continued to watch with the same self-satisfied little grin. All of a sudden, Jim fit the puzzle together: that distinctive flavor, the drunken flush on McCoy's cheeks, the obvious amusement with which he watched Spock . . .

He snickered and looked over at McCoy. "Got any more of that secret ingredient, Bones?" Come to think of it, he could ease his aching muscles without having to admit to the doctor that he was sore from his recent adventures.

McCoy's expression lit up. "You bet your buns." He reached into a backpack near the campfire, pulled out a half-empty bottle of bourbon, and passed it over to Kirk. Jim filled his cup and handed the bottle back.

Spock stopped in mid-chew. He looked down at his plate, then over at McCoy and the bottle. Jim had to bite his lip to keep from smiling.

"Am I to understand," the Vulcan inquired solemnly, "that your secret ingredient is . . . alcohol?"

"Bourbon, Spock," McCoy replied, and giggled suddenly. *"Kentucky* bourbon. Care for a snort?" He proffered the bottle to Spock.

"Snort?" Spock frowned. "I was unaware that ethanol was consumed in that manner."

"Figure of speech, Spock. He means a drink." Kirk could no longer keep from grinning. He looked over at McCoy and jerked his head in the Vulcan's direction. "Bourbon and beans. A pretty explosive combination. Do you think Spock can handle it?"

"I don't *think* I put that much booze in there," McCoy said gleefully. "'Course, I don't really remember. And as far as the beans go, they couldn't possibly affect his Vulcan metabolism."

"Do these particular legumes have some sort of physical effect—other than intoxication?" Spock asked, missing the point entirely. McCoy winked impishly at Jim.

"You don't want to know," Kirk told him.

Spock persisted. "Perhaps I, too, will be affected. As you are so fond of pointing out, Doctor, I *am* half human."

McCoy's smile faded somewhat. "I know. It certainly doesn't show."

"Thank you," Spock replied.

The doctor shook his head. "This guy never changes. I insult him and he takes it as a compliment." He reached down and refilled his cup from the bottle, then screwed the cap back on it and set it aside. When Jim looked questioningly at the amount of liquor in the cup, McCoy's mood darkened suddenly; obviously McCoy had enjoyed a lot more bourbon than Kirk and Spock had realized. He scowled at Jim. "You know, the two of you could drive a man to drink."

Kirk's eyebrows flew up. "Me? What did *I* do?"

McCoy spoke with such startling vehemence that even Spock glanced up from his dinner. "You really piss me off, Jim. You're acting like nothing at all happened today, nothing at all." He jabbed a fork savagely in Jim's direction. "Human life is far too precious to risk on crazy stunts like the ones you've been pulling lately. Maybe it hasn't crossed that macho mind of yours, but when you fell off that mountain today, you should have been killed. If Spock hadn't been there—"

"It crossed my mind," Jim answered shortly, cutting him off. He didn't want to talk about the fall. For some reason, that subject made him angry and defensive—which meant that McCoy had struck a nerve.

"And?" McCoy persisted.

Kirk took a sip of bourbon and forced the hostility back, forced himself to answer honestly. "It was very strange. There was a flash of fear the instant I realized I was going to fall, but then"—he let out his breath and stared down at his plate of beans—"I wasn't afraid at all. It was funny, but even as I was falling, I knew I wouldn't die."

McCoy gestured with his cup at Spock. "I thought *he* was the only one who's immortal. That's a very dangerous notion to entertain, Jim, particularly when white-water kayaking or climbing mountains."

Kirk gently shook his head. "It's not that I think I'm immortal, Bones—I haven't fallen prey to megalomania in my old age. It's hard to explain . . ." He paused, trying to sort out the reason; even as he said it, it was a revelation to him. "I knew I wouldn't die because the two of you were with me."

McCoy set down his fork and cup and stared. His pale blue eyes were very wide. "Excuse me?"

Even Spock stopped eating long enough to gaze at Kirk with intense curiosity. "Captain, I do not understand."

Jim stared into the bright orange heat of the campfire. The statement surprised him as well . . . and yet he knew with heavy certainty that it was true. His friends no doubt thought he'd gone off the deep end. *And maybe they'd be right.* "I've always . . . I've always known I'll die alone." The words brought with them a chill of fear far more terrifying than this morning's free-fall.

"Oh, now we're psychic, are we?" McCoy snapped cynically, but there was a hint of good humor beneath the sarcasm; no doubt he, too, was disturbed by what Jim had said, and was trying to lighten the tone of the conversation. "In that case, I'll just call Valhalla and reserve you a room."

Jim managed to smile faintly at him.

Spock was frowning. "Captain . . ."

"Jim."

"Jim. I fail to understand how you can claim to know such a thing . . . unless you are precognitive, and true precognitives are extremely rare."

"I don't know, Spock." He sighed, unable to understand it himself. There was no logic to it, certainly, and yet he was as utterly convinced of it as he was of Spock and McCoy's friendship. "I just *do,* that's all."

The doctor's expression became melancholic—the bourbon, Jim wondered, or the topic of conversation? —as he gazed into the fire. His tone was thoughtful. "You know, it's a mystery what draws the three of us together."

Spock appeared puzzled by the turn the discussion had taken. "Are you suggesting, Doctor, that we came along to Yosemite because we sensed the captain— Jim—might be in danger? Again, you are assuming precognitive—"

"Spock, I'd call you soulless if I didn't know better from personal experience! Think about it. We found you, saved you, brought you back from the dead, all on a hunch, if you want to call it that. At the risk of sounding maudlin"—McCoy took a sip from his cup as if to brace himself for what he was about to say—"there seems to be some sort of . . . I don't know, call it a psychic bond between the three of us. All that time in space, getting on each other's nerves . . . and what do we do when shore leave comes along? Spend it together. Most people have *families.*"

"Other people, Bones," Jim said wistfully, thinking of David and Carol Marcus. A gray blanket of depression began to settle over him. "Not us."

"Untrue," Spock countered, unmoved by the sharp

looks directed at him. "The captain has a nephew with whom he could stay. You, Doctor, have a daughter—and a granddaughter, if I am not mistaken —with whom you could live. And I have a family on Vulcan. No, the three of us *choose* to serve together rather than live with our families."

Jim's lips twisted wryly. "Thank you, Mr. Spock, for rescuing me from the throes of self-pity."

"Just for that," McCoy said lightly, "when we get back up to the ship, I'm gonna force both of you to look at four dozen holos of that granddaughter of mine. Still, I'm disappointed in you, Spock." He took a final mouthful of beans and put his plate down.

"I do not understand."

McCoy hadn't quite finished chewing when he said, "For not making fun of my psychic bond idea."

Spock set down his own empty plate, then picked up a stick and examined the end with a finger. "Actually, I quite agree with your theory. After all, you and I had some difficulty *dissolving* our link after *fal tor pan.* And the captain has managed to contact me telepathically before. As to whether you and the captain are linked together . . ." He broke off to retrieve a bag from his knapsack, then reached into it and pulled out a soft, pristine white marshmallow.

Kirk grinned, delighted. "What are you doing, Spock?"

"I am," Spock replied gravely, as he attached the marshmallow to the pointed end of the stick, "preparing to toast a marsh melon."

"A marsh *what?*" Jim blurted, but McCoy silenced him with an elbow in the ribs. Clearly, the doctor was enjoying a little practical joke at the Vulcan's expense.

"Well, I'll be damned," McCoy remarked pleasantly and perfectly straight-faced, while Jim did his best to hide a smile. "Toasting marsh melons. Where did you learn that, Spock? Did your mother teach you?"

Spock held the marshmallow over the fire with great seriousness. "No. Before leaving the ship, I consulted the library computer in order to familiarize myself with the custom of camping out. The evening meal is traditionally followed by the toasting of marsh melons." With his free hand, he offered sticks and marshmallows to the doctor and Kirk, who hurried to finish off his beans. "Though I must admit to a certain degree of puzzlement: I do not see any physical resemblance between these small confections and any melon with which I am familiar."

Jim improvised. "It resembles a certain type of melon grown in a—"

"A southern swamp," McCoy finished helpfully. "Hence the name, *marsh* melons. My grandfather used to grow whole fields of them. Quite a thing to see right before harvest time."

"Indeed." Spock nodded with interest.

Now it was McCoy's turn to fight a grin. "Tell me something, Spock," he said, with a shade too much solicitousness, "what do we do *after* we toast the marsh . . . er, melons?"

Spock's marshmallow was puffing up and turning a glorious golden brown. "We consume them."

"I *know* we consume them. I meant *after* we eat them."

"Ah." Spock removed his marshmallow from the fire, slipped it from the stick, and popped it into his mouth with surprisingly little mess. He grimaced slightly at the taste. "I believe we are required to engage in a ritual known as the sing-along."

Jim grinned, his moment of depression forgotten. "I haven't sung around a campfire since I was a boy in Iowa. What should we sing, Bones?"

McCoy puckered his brow as he searched his memory. "How about 'Camptown Races'?"

"'Pack Up Your Troubles,'" Jim countered. He twirled his stick so that the marshmallow's sides were evenly exposed to the flame.

Spock turned to him. "Are we leaving, Captain?"

McCoy was clearly enjoying himself. "It's a song title, for God's sake, Spock! Don't *you* have any song titles you'd like to suggest?" He leered expectantly.

"Ah," Spock said, then thought. "No."

McCoy seemed taken aback. "The computer didn't list any?"

Spock shook his head. McCoy deflated in obvious disappointment and confusion.

"How about 'Moon Over Rigel Seven'?" Jim suggested.

"Naw," McCoy said. "Too mushy. Hey, I've got it: 'Row, Row, Row Your Boat.'"

Jim smiled. "Excellent. You know that one, don't you, Spock?"

"I did not encounter it in my research."

"You'll learn it in a matter of seconds. The lyrics are simple: 'Row, row, row your boat, gently down the stream . . . Merrily, merrily, merrily, merrily, life is but a dream.'"

Spock arched a brow. "They are also quite redundant."

"Songs aren't meant to be logical, Spock. Bones and

I will start it off, and when we give you the signal, join in. Doctor, if you please . . ."

McCoy took another swig of bourbon, gargled with it, then swallowed. He smacked his lips. "All right . . . but don't say I didn't warn you."

He began to sing in a voice that was not particularly pleasant, but adequately on key. "Row, row, row your boat, gently down the stream . . ."

When he reached the first "merrily," Jim joined in. Maybe it was the bourbon, but it seemed that the two of them sounded pretty good. At the appropriate moment, he signaled for Spock to jump in . . . but the Vulcan merely regarded him with a perplexed expression.

"What is it?" Kirk asked, mildly exasperated. "Why didn't you join in?"

"I was trying to comprehend the meaning of the words," Spock replied. "I must admit, I am unable—"

McCoy lost patience. "It's a *song*, you green-blooded son of a Vulcan! You just *sing* it. The words aren't important; what's important is that you have a good time singing it."

Spock digested this in silence, then said, with utmost sincerity, "I apologize, Dr. McCoy. Were we having a good time?"

McCoy rolled his eyes toward the starry sky. "I give up. I think I liked him better before he died."

"I think we've fulfilled sing-along requirements. Why don't we call it a night and get some sleep?" Jim suggested. The small amount of liquor he'd drunk had made him sleepy in his already exhausted condition. "I'm anxious to have another go at El Cap in the morning." He had thought it but had not meant to say it aloud; he knew the instant the words were out that it was a mistake.

McCoy, who had abandoned his burnt marshmallow and was already rolling out his sleeping bag, snorted. "Over my dead body, Jim."

"Drop it, Bones. At least until morning."

They went to bed.

Twenty minutes later, Kirk lay exhausted in his sleeping bag, listening to McCoy's insistent snoring. He was on the verge of drifting off when he heard someone speaking to him.

"Captain?" Spock had no doubt guessed he was awake; the Vulcan's voice sounded unusually troubled.

"We're on leave, Spock. Call me Jim."

"Jim."

"What is it, Spock?"

There was a dramatic pause before Spock, in all seriousness replied: "Life is *not* a dream."

"Go to sleep, Spock."

In the back room of the Paradise Saloon, Talbot sat at the round table with Caithlin Dar and Korrd. Dar sat stiffly, her spine not touching the back of the chair. Korrd lay slumped across the table, still passed out as a result of the incredible amount of liquor he'd imbibed in anticipation of his capture. The exit was barred by an armed sentry—a shabby homesteader with a handmade pipegun.

So they sat, waiting . . . for God knew what.

Talbot ran a trembling hand over his forehead; his palm came away shining, damp with perspiration.

More than at any other time in his life, Talbot craved a drink. The recent excitement had sobered him up quickly, resoundingly, so that his mind was entirely clear, so that he could think.

That was worst thing of all, being able to *think*.

Not that he was afraid of thinking about what the homesteaders and their maniacal leader—whom Dar insisted was Vulcan, not Romulan; Talbot believed *that* about as much as he believed the leader's reassurance that they would not be harmed—would do to him. No, in a way, he welcomed the thought of dying. He had long ago given up wanting to live.

He preferred to stay in a pleasantly dull alcoholic haze, because when he thought, he *remembered*.

Seven years before, St. John Talbot had been one of the most, if not *the* most, respected diplomats in the Federation service. At the time, he had been rather impressed with himself and his talents. After all, he had negotiated a truce between Capella and Xenar, avoiding an interstellar war, and as a result, had received the Surakian Peace Prize and been awarded a coveted assignment to Andor.

Up to that time, Talbot had led a charmed life. Born to wealthy parents, sent to all the best schools. He was a precocious boy; it had always been easy for him. So easy, so very, very easy.

The Federation Diplomatic Service was a goal that only the very best strived to attain. Talbot was admitted without a hitch; he never worried for a moment that his application would be rejected. After all, he was rich, he was brilliant, he was talented, he was handsome . . . and there was nothing in the universe to stop him.

But now the memory of his arrogance filled him with pain. Oh, he had boasted then of his diplomatic conquests. "Not a drop of blood shed," that was Talbot's motto. St. John Talbot, bringer of peace, miracle worker.

He'd become too cocky, too sure of himself. On Andor, his overconfidence got the better of him.

The capital city had a large population of disaffected immigrants, most of them miners from the neighboring system of Charulh. The Andorians were not generally hospitable to outworlders, even if the outworlders had lived and worked on Andor and benefited the Andorian economy for the past seven generations. A small group of Charulhans, in a desperate demand for a voice in the Andorian government, had kidnapped a number of influential citizens, including the adolescent son of the city's female Andorian governor, with whom Talbot had worked closely.

A hostage situation. Talbot had successfully handled a half-dozen of them during the twenty-year course of his career. He felt more than competent to handle the situation—alone, at his insistence. After all, he was at the top of his form. The great St. John needed no native cultural advisers to help him clean up the mess.

He had acted on his own, sending the kidnappers a message intended to defuse the situation, but inadvertently, thanks to Talbot's spotty knowledge of Charulhan culture, the message had insulted the lot.

The response was almost immediate.

Talbot slowly squeezed his eyes shut in a futile

attempt to blot out the image formed by his sobered brain . . .

The street outside his office in the capital. The body of the governor's son. Only a child, really. The Charulhans were honorable even when committing violence; they had broken the boy's neck, so that his head veered from his body at an entirely unnatural angle. The attached note assured the reader that the child had died easily.

So very, very easily.

Talbot was first to find him; Talbot was the one obliged to inform the child's mother. It was Talbot's first real brush with crushing failure, with shame, with defeat.

His career went downhill overnight. He sank into alcoholism and despair—again, ever so easily.

He preferred to drink bootleg liquor, when he could get it. Romulan ale appealed to him because it was stronger, and it was untreated, so that it would damage his liver, kill his brain cells, and give him horrendous hangovers. Talbot had concluded that he deserved to suffer.

More accurately, he had concluded that he deserved to suffer and *die*, except that he was too much of a coward to kill himself outright. And so he was content to kill himself slowly.

After all, the ale did a most marvelous job of fogging his memory.

Talbot stared at the bored guard standing in front of the exit and thought that this situation might be the answer to his prayers. Perhaps the Vulcan-Romulan leader of the rebels would interrogate them and then kill them. Talbot's mind emphatically refused to contemplate the possibility of torture.

A poetically just way to end the career, Talbot reflected, for him to be taken hostage. He could not feel sorry for himself or for Korrd. The two of them were spent, washed up, waiting to die. The best part of their lives was years past.

But for Dar he felt great pity. Her death would be a horrid waste. He looked over at her, as she sat beside him, staring at nothing in the far distance. He could feel a subtle emanation of warmth from her, no doubt due to her higher body temperature. She was young, strikingly beautiful, clearly brilliant, full of an intense determination Talbot found more alluring than any physical attribute.

If I were twenty years younger, Talbot told himself wistfully, and stopped. Age had little to do with it. *More aptly, if I were not a wretched, wasted, sottish excuse for a human being . . .*

He ceased all thought as a second soldier—dirty-faced, dressed in rags rather than a uniform, but possessed, like the guard, of an expression of such fanatical devotion that outward signs of his allegiance were unnecessary—entered the room and pointed the barrel of his rifle at Dar's smooth, unlined forehead.

"Let her alone. I'll go first," Talbot said quietly. He rose.

Caithlin began to protest, but the soldier interrupted. "Suit yourself," he said to Talbot, and gestured with the rifle for Talbot to go ahead of him through the exit. The other guard silenced Dar with a wave of his gun.

Talbot studied the guard's face. He considered

bolting, pretending to make an escape attempt, to get it over with quickly, but again, cowardice won out. He could contemplate death as long as it lurked somewhere in the future, but he could not face it at that precise moment, staring down into the black void of a dirty pipe-gun barrel.

Besides, if his current run of luck held, a blast from the gun would probably only wound him, which would be even worse.

He paused in the doorway to turn and smile tremulously at Dar. "Farewell, my dear. Just in case . . . I'm quite sorry it turned out this way, sorry that your career was cut short. I should have enjoyed working with you. If I don't come back, would you tell Korrd when he wakes up that I said good-bye?"

"The leader is a Vulcan," Dar said matter-of-factly, but her eyes were troubled. "You'll come back. He won't kill you."

A Vulcan who smiles, Talbot thought, *may very well be a Vulcan who kills.* Dar knew that, of course, but for Caithlin's sake, he did not say it aloud.

"That would be a shame," Talbot said cavalierly, as the soldier prodded him in the back with the rifle. He stepped forward into the darkness.

Chapter Five

THE ANCIENT PROBE hurtled aimlessly through the blackness of uninhabited space. Its designers were long dead, its purpose forgotten; it was now no more than a piece of flotsam, like the millions of bits of celestial debris that had collided with it, scarring its once-smooth surface. Still visible on one side of the probe, etched into the metal, were images: two naked adult humans, a male and a female, hands raised in a gesture of greeting. Beside them were various mathematical and scientific symbols. The probe had obviously been launched by humans who hoped to contact intelligent extraterrestrial life forms.

Ironic, thought First Officer Vixis, that it should encounter them here, centuries later, in the Klingon empire. From the bridge viewscreen of the Bird of Prey *Okrona*, she watched the probe's movement with interest, occasionally calling out an order to the helmsman, Tarag, to ensure that the Bird kept pace with the device. Vixis smiled thinly at the screen. She had notified her captain, Klaa, of the probe's existence; she could tell as his voice filtered through the intercom that the captain had been greatly pleased by the news. He was on his way to the bridge even now.

The humans, of course, would have venerated the object; judging from its wounds, it predated the Federation, possibly even the development of warp drive. Should the Klingons extend the Federation the courtesy of informing them of its existence in Empire space, the humans would be willing to pay a dear price for it and, upon receipt, would enshrine it in a museum.

But since it was Klaa's ship, the *Okrona,* that had found it, the Federation would never be given such a chance—if, indeed, *any* Klingon ship would have bothered. Vixis was a shrewd officer; she notified Klaa the instant the probe was spotted and saw to it that the ship remained well within range. She had not served under Klaa long, but already she knew him well; he would be most anxious to deal with the device personally, and he would never have forgiven her if she had left its disposal to the gunner.

The doors to the bridge parted. Vixis swiveled in her chair and watched as Klaa entered. He was broad-shouldered, stocky, muscular; he emanated power and strength. Of all the captains who had graced *Okrona'*s bridge, Klaa was the most respected —and the most envied. He had received her as a reward for heroic action on the Romulan border during a skirmish in which he, a gunner, was solely responsible for the destruction of three Orion vessels and the salvation of his own ship. Even before the incident, Klaa had been widely hailed as the best gunner in the Empire. Now, he was its youngest captain.

At the sight of him, Vixis rose from her station. She no longer smiled; too much simpering could be interpreted as a sign of weakness. Yet she doubted that Klaa failed to notice the attraction she felt for him. If he did, he did not show it, and that perplexed her, for she knew without false modesty that she was beautiful, and that Klaa was an unattached male.

"Captain Klaa," Vixis said. Her voice rose with excitement. "We have a target in sight. An Earth probe of ancient origin."

Eyes focused intently on the viewscreen, Klaa crossed to his command chair and rested a hand on its back. "Difficult to hit?"

"Most difficult," Vixis assured him.

"Good." Klaa glanced meaningfully at her as he said it, an indication that he was pleased with her performance. She nodded, then turned quickly back to her station and sat down, before her expression betrayed her.

Klaa sat in his chair and began to strap himself in. *Okrona* had been outfitted especially for its new captain, with an elaborate gunner's rig at the command console so that the phasers mounted on the ship's wings could be individually controlled from the captain's station.

"All weapons to my control," Klaa ordered.

The gunner, Morek, complied immediately, though Vixis sensed the surge of hostility emanating from him. Morek had been gunner long before Klaa's meteoric ascent to command; no doubt he felt he would continue in that position well after Klaa's departure. But with Klaa aboard, Morek's responsibilities were severely curtailed, limited to the most menial duties. Still, even he had fallen somewhat under the spell of Klaa's forceful charisma; with the rest of the crew, he turned from his station to watch the young captain with anticipation.

Klaa drew the target scanner, a custom-designed device that lowered from the ceiling like a periscope, to him and leaned forward to peer into its sights. "Aah," he whispered. His large hands hovered over the controls, then pulsed in an incredibly quick movement, and were still again.

Vixis swiveled her head. On the main screen, a flare of light struck the probe, severing a flange, which flew off to follow its own separate heading. The probe reeled, buffeted from its aimless course.

The crew shouted its approval. Inspired, Klaa flexed his hands, then let them fly over the gun controls again . . . and again. The second blast obliterated a fin on the rear of the craft; a third destroyed the antenna. Klaa was clearly taking his time, enjoying his prey.

The bridge reverberated with the crew's cheers. Vixis turned from the viewer to give her captain an admiring glance. But Klaa sat frowning at the screen, his expression one of utter dissatisfaction.

He shook his head, disgusted. "Shooting space garbage is no test of a warrior's mettle. I need a target that fights back." He watched without further comment as the battered remnants of the probe soared past on the screen. The gunner and helmsman glanced at each other in perplexed silence.

But Vixis was filled with admiration. Klaa was right; a true warrior would scarcely be satisfied with an unthinking opponent. But where in the Empire would they find an antagonist who could match Klaa's skill, Klaa's cunning?

She did not have time to contemplate her question. The communication signal on the first officer's console flashed. Vixis responded, and heard a computerized voice instructing the *Okrona* to prepare for a priority message.

"Captain," she said, interrupting Klaa's silence. "We are receiving a priority message from Operations Command."

Klaa unstrapped himself from his gunner's rig and moved quickly to Vixis's station; the message was already coming through. Vixis switched it over to her monitor so that Klaa could watch. He stood behind her and leaned forward, placing a hand on her shoulder. Vixis flushed, but pretended not to be aware.

General Krell appeared on the screen. "A critical situation has developed on Nimbus Three," Krell thundered in his bass voice.

"Nimbus Three?" Klaa scoffed over the sound of the general's words. "Since when does the Empire worry about what happens on Nimbus?" But his voice held a tremor of anticipation. Nimbus was in the Neutral Zone, and the Neutral Zone offered many opportunities for combat.

Krell's message was taped, leaving no opportunity to respond, or to question orders. He continued droning away. "The three diplomats there have been taken hostage by a rebel group." Krell's stern visage disappeared and was replaced by the image of Nimbus itself, an unimpressive sand-colored planet, and then the image of the outpost there, a grim-looking frontier town bearing the unlikely appellation of Paradise.

"You are hereby ordered to proceed to Nimbus Three," Krell said, "and take whatever action is necessary to free them. Details follow."

Klingon script scrolled across Vixis's screen. Klaa turned away and began pacing while she read. "One of the hostages is a Klingon—General Korrd." She frowned slightly, puzzled that the Empire should suddenly be concerned about Korrd, whose career had culminated in disgrace—and the assignment to Nimbus. And then she remembered a certain fact about Korrd's sister. She smiled to herself, eyes still watching the screen. "Korrd is, of course, Krell's brother-in-law," she murmured.

"And the others?" Klaa demanded.

"A human and a Romulan." Vixis's smile broadened as she grasped the implications of that combination of races. She half swiveled in her chair to look up at Klaa.

He, too, smiled. "That means the Federation will be sending a rescue ship of its own. Helmsman!" Klaa barked, turning. "Plot course for Nimbus Three."

He strode back to his chair, still grinning. "My whole life, I have prayed for this . . . the chance to engage a Federation ship."

He settled into the rig, peered into his sights, and with one swift, deft motion, fired.

Vixis watched the screen as the probe burst into a thousand spinning bits of shrapnel.

Caithlin awoke with a start as the doors to the back room opened with a gentle *whoosh*. She'd been drowsing, arms folded on the hard surface of the table, forehead pressed against her arms. She, Talbot, and Korrd had been escorted by a surly guard to their table in the back room while the Vulcan and his recruits worked outside in the bar to get the communications terminal operating. Apparently the Vulcan honestly did not mean to harm them . . . or so Caithlin had thought until a second guard came for Talbot.

As she watched the human go, white-faced with terror but with a semblance of dignity, Caithlin did not permit herself the luxury of fear; at least, she refused to acknowledge such a weakness in herself. Their captor was a Vulcan, after all, and surely a Vulcan would not condone torture, or murder.

Though neither of them had dared say it aloud, she had seen her own thoughts reflected in Talbot's face: this Vulcan was a renegade. This Vulcan smiled.

Even so, Caithlin refused to be afraid for herself, though she felt concern for Talbot. The human was not as strong, mentally or physically, as she or Korrd; she did not doubt that Talbot would succumb quickly to the mere threat of pain. No doubt that was why they had chosen to question him first.

Next to her, Korrd sat with his face pressed flat against the table, sleeping off the effects of liquor consumed shortly before his capture. Caithlin strained to filter out the sound of his snoring, to hear what was happening in the next room.

She could hear a voice, deep and well modulated, pleasing—clearly the Vulcan's, but she could not distinguish the words. The voice continued for some time, then stopped.

For a time, Caithlin heard nothing at all. And then came a sharp, strangled cry of pain, almost a sob. Talbot. So they were torturing him after all. Perhaps they had just killed him. After that one brief cry, Caithlin heard nothing at all, save Korrd's stertorous breathing beside her.

The tension of waiting was exhausting. The sun was just setting when Caithlin buried her face in her folded arms and dozed. It was dark by the time St. John Talbot reentered the room.

She jerked up her head, immediately awake. "Talbot?" She was honestly relieved to see him alive.

Talbot's eyes were more red-rimmed than usual, as if he'd been weeping, but he did not appear harmed— far from it. His entire demeanor had changed from one of weakness to one of confident strength; his sallow face was incandescent with joy. He reached down and clasped Caithlin's hand firmly.

"Caithlin." He smiled and squeezed her hand almost painfully. "My dear Miss Dar."

Caithlin frowned at him. "What the hell is going on?"

Talbot ignored her and glanced down at the slumbering Klingon with a look that was pure pity. "Poor Korrd. Do you know his history, Miss Dar?" He did not allow her a chance to reply. "Korrd was quite a famous warrior until one day he became sick to death of killing. Lost his two youngest—a son and a daughter—in one of those useless battles the Klingons love to stir up. Korrd had risen to the High Command when he finally spoke out publicly in favor of Nimbus, of trying to get along better with the Federation. After all, they had a treaty with the Romulans.

"Oh, the rest of the Command went along with it. After all, Korrd is related to the number two man in the HC. They couldn't exactly shut him up by assassinating him—so they managed to make him an ambassador and a laughingstock at the same time. To the Klingons, Nimbus is a joke. I'm afraid the shame of this assignment was too much for him."

"Talbot!" Dar pulled her hand free; it was quite a struggle, as Talbot's grip had become amazingly strong. She pulled herself up straight in her chair and narrowed her eyes suspiciously at the human. "Talbot, what's wrong with you? Did they torture you? Use a mind-sifter?"

He laughed, a light, airy sound. "Nothing's wrong with me, dear Caithlin. Quite the contrary. For the first time in my life, everything is *right.*" He rested his palms on the table and leaned toward her, grinning.

For the first time, Caithlin realized that no soldier had accompanied him, and the lone guard sat some distance away by the door, watching with only the vaguest interest, as if he trusted Talbot completely.

She drew back. "You didn't answer my other questions. What did they *do* to you?"

Talbot's eyes blazed suddenly with a look that was familiar: Caithlin had seen that look before, that light of fanaticism, in the Vulcan's eyes.

"You mustn't be afraid of him, Caithlin." Talbot's voice dropped to a confidential whisper. "Sybok is our friend. He's here to help us, to give our lives meaning again. Trust him, and it will be easier."

"Trust him!" she said. The look on Talbot's face chilled her; she rubbed her upper arms to warm them. "You've been brainwashed, Consul. What did he use on you? Drugs? A sifter?" Whatever it was, death would be preferable."

Talbot chuckled sadly. "Ah, my dear, I can see you don't believe me. "No matter . . . You'll understand soon enough. I've been sent to take you to him."

It was Caithlin's turn to scoff. "I suppose you think if you ask politely, I'll go with you."

"Not at all," Talbot answered pleasantly. He produced a small pistol and aimed it squarely at Caithlin's forehead. "Rise and accompany me, Miss Dar, or I shall certainly scatter your brains all over this table . . . and Korrd wouldn't appreciate having his nap interrupted, would he?"

"Get that damn light out of my face!" McCoy mumbled, swatting at it as if it were a fly. He was nestled comfortably in the soft recesses of his sleeping bag with the top cover pulled up to the tip of his nose. After dinner—and several more shots of bourbon— he had fallen into a deep, blissful sleep . . . only to be awakened by the horrifying vision of Jim Kirk diving head first down the side of El Capitan while the doctor stood by helplessly and cursed Jim for his suicidal recklessness.

It had taken time for the panic of the dream to subside, for McCoy to get his heartbeat back to normal and settle into sleep again—at least an hour, probably more, while he lay awake and listened to the cries of wild nocturnal creatures, and the sounds of Jim's snoring and Spock's steady, rhythmical breathing.

He was therefore more than a little irritable when someone had the nerve to shine a flashlight right in his eyes. *"Dammit!"* McCoy swore again, when the light did not abate. Surrendering finally to consciousness, he struggled to a sitting position and opened his eyes.

He immediately squinted and put a hand up to shield them. The sight was eerie. . . . It wasn't a flashlight at all, but a giant beam of light, as large as a man, and from its center, a dark figure in silhouette emerged.

McCoy sucked in a breath. For a minute, he hoped he was having another nightmare, and then he recognized the figure as it stepped forward out of the glare.

"Sorry, sirs," Uhura said. She was in uniform— not, McCoy realized even in his stupor, a good omen. The light behind her came from the shuttlecraft. "Mr. Scott apologizes for having to send the shuttlecraft, but the transporter beam is still nonoperational. Captain, we've received important orders from Starfleet."

Both Jim and Spock were sitting up in their sleeping bags. The Vulcan was perfectly groomed—*How the hell does he do it?* McCoy wondered—as if he hadn't slept a wink. Jim, on the other hand, looked as disheveled and disoriented as the doctor felt. As Uhura spoke, Kirk frowned and ran a hand through his tousled hair.

"Then why didn't you beep my communicator, Commander?" he asked.

The corner of her mouth twitched wryly as she answered, "Sir, you forgot to take it with you." She bent down, out of the glow of the shuttlecraft lights, to hand it to him.

"Ah." Kirk grinned sheepishly at her; he hadn't, the doctor knew, forgotten it at all, though Uhura was too tactful to suggest otherwise. "Wonder why I did that?" He turned to Spock and McCoy, his tone abruptly official. "Well, gentlemen, it appears shore leave's been canceled. Pack out your trash."

"Hallelujah," McCoy sighed, and ignored Jim's puzzled glare. The doctor was sorry to leave Yosemite's breathtaking wilderness—it renewed a part of him, made it far less painful for him to return to the narrow confines of the ship—but at least this way, he wouldn't have to watch Jim fall off the side of a cliff in the morning. This way, at least, they could all return to the *Enterprise,* and be safe.

Chapter Six

As the shuttlecraft *Galileo 5* neared its destination, Uhura snapped on the main viewscreen for the benefit of the three passengers. It was a spectacular view.

Kirk drew in a slow breath at the sight: *Enterprise,* suspended in space, sleek and radiant against the backdrop of a full moon. For a moment, Jim allowed himself to forget that she was only a replacement, and an ill-prepared one at that. He felt moved to poetry.

"'And all I ask is a tall ship and a star to steer her by.'"

McCoy, seated on Kirk's right, gave him a quizzical look as if to say, *Have you already forgotten our little conversation? That's not* Enterprise, *that's an impostor.* But the sight of her hull, glistening with moonlight, seemed to silence all complaints for the moment. The doctor merely said, "Melville, isn't it?"

Jim was hard-pressed to remember.

"John Masefield," Spock corrected. The Vulcan sat on Jim's left, leaving Jim between the two opponents. Jim opted to stay out of the discussion, and said nothing. Spock was probably right, as usual, but McCoy leaned forward to challenge him.

"You sure about that?" The doctor eyed Spock suspiciously.

"'I must down to the seas again,'" the Vulcan quoted, "'to the lonely sea and the sky, and all I ask is a tall ship and a star to steer her by.' John Masefield, 'Sea Fever,' 1902, Old Earth Date. I am well versed in the classics, Doctor."

"Oh, yeah? Then how come you don't know 'Row Your Boat'?"

It was a question for which Spock did not have an answer.

Jim smiled faintly but kept his gaze directed ahead at the viewscreen. Outwardly, at least, the vessel appeared to be the *Enterprise;* certainly the sight had moved him as if she were. Perhaps he had been immature to resent the new ship. . . .

"Ready for landing maneuver," Uhura said at the pilot's console. *"Enterprise,* you have control."

"And God help us all," McCoy muttered under his breath.

Sulu's voice replied. "Roger, *Galileo Five.* Open bay door. Transfer power to the tractor beam."

Both Sulu and Chekov had taken a temporary reduction in rank to serve under Kirk, and Jim felt more than a few pangs of guilt about that. Sulu had deserved a ship of his own for a long time, but as he had pointed out to Kirk, he did precisely what he wanted to, and if Kirk did not want to make use of his services, he had only to turn down Sulu's request.

Jim couldn't bring himself to do it. Sulu was one of the best helmsmen in the Fleet if not *the* best, Chekov one of the best navigators. Refusing them would only serve to engender ill will . . . or at least, so Jim convinced himself. Yet he couldn't quite shake the lingering guilt.

Enterprise loomed larger on the viewscreen as the tractor beam took control and eased *Galileo 5* toward the landing bay entrance. The great doors parted; the shuttlecraft was pulled smoothly inside the larger vessel. Within seconds, the craft glided to an uneventful landing.

Next to Jim, McCoy let out a shaky breath.

Uhura opened the hatch and led the rest of them out of the craft. Jim's illusion that he was returning home to the old *Enterprise* abruptly dissolved. The large bay was cluttered with debris and virtually deserted, save for a couple of repair workers scurrying across the deck.

Engineer Scott appeared, out of breath, exhausted, clad in grimy coveralls. Dark circles showed under his bloodshot eyes; he looked as if he hadn't slept in days.

"Captain!" he said, with unexpected energy. "Sirs! I'm afraid no one was available to greet you." He made a sweeping gesture at his attire. "Sorry, this isna exactly an honor guard uniform, though I suspect it's the uniform of the day."

"It's all right, Engineer." Kirk dismissed it with a wave, impatient to ask the question that had been bothering him. "So the transporters are still out. How about the rest of her? Is she spaceworthy?"

Scott tilted his head and rolled his eyes. "All I can say, sir, is that they don't make 'em like they used to."

Kirk did not smile. "Mr. Scott, you told me you could have the ship operational in two weeks. I gave you three. What happened?"

Scott's enthusiasm disappeared. He pondered the captain's question seriously for a minute, then answered, "In all honesty, I think you gave me too much time, Captain."

Too much time, Kirk almost repeated, until he realized he was being had. He repressed a smile. "Very well, Mr. Scott. Carry on."

"Aye, sir," Scott sighed, but there was a hint of satisfaction in his voice. "No rest for the weary." He headed off. Jim and the others made their way for the turbolift.

"I thought it was no rest for the *wicked*," McCoy remarked.

"I doubt Scotty would appreciate the implication." Jim glanced over at the engineer, who was waving an instrument at an unfortunate crewman bent over a console at the other side of the bay.

"How many times do I have to tell you?" Scott scolded him in the most paternal of tones. "The right tool for the right job!"

Jim stepped into the lift, where Uhura and the others were already waiting.

McCoy nodded in Scott's direction. "You know, I don't think I've ever seen him happier."

"You could be right," Jim said. "He can't complain that he doesn't have the challenge of his life."

"Level, please," the computer slurred drunkenly.

Kirk exchanged uncertain looks with Uhura and

the doctor. Even Spock seemed mildly perturbed. "Bridge. I hope."

The lift doors closed with a distinctly unreassuring grinding sound. Jim braced himself.

Fortunately, the lift rose smoothly upward.

He sighed and stretched his stiff muscles, which still ached after his fall from El Capitan. "I could sure use a hot shower."

"Yes," Spock agreed behind him. McCoy snorted.

They made it in one piece to the bridge, but only the left door slid open. The right stayed put—and McCoy walked into it full-force. He bounced off and gingerly rubbed his nose. "For God's sake . . ."

"Doesn't *any*thing work on this ship?" Kirk asked in disgust, as he stepped onto the bridge.

No one answered. The bridge was a pathetic mess. With the exception of two coverall-clad repair workers, Hikaru Sulu was the only crewman present.

Uhura and Spock moved to their stations without comment, but McCoy was indignant. "Starfleet's got some nerve sending us out in this condition. Why, this ship's a virtual ghost town."

Sulu was scrunched down beneath the helm, frowning up at a couple of exposed circuits. At the sight of Kirk and the others, he got to his feet and snapped to attention. "Sirs! Welcome back."

"Thank you, Commander." Kirk nodded at the helm. "Don't tell me that isn't working, either, or we'll never get out of here."

Sulu answered with a cheerfulness that sounded forced. "Oh, it's working, Captain, or she'd never have gotten out of spacedock. It's working." He paused a beat, then added as an afterthought, "Pretty much."

"Pretty much," Kirk repeated skeptically. He walked over to the conn.

"Captain." Uhura, already seated at the communications board, swiveled to give him a glance. "Ready for Starfleet transmission."

As if on cue, one of the workers began drilling to remove more access panels. Jim raised his voice over the high-pitched whine. "Could we have a little quiet, please?" The embarrassed worker stopped the noise at once.

"Thank you." Kirk turned to Uhura. "On the main screen, Commander."

Uhura complied. An image began to coalesce—the face and shoulders of a Starfleet admiral—but before it formed completely, it blurred and began breaking up.

"Am I on?" the image asked uncertainly, and leaned forward. The sound, at least, was clear. Jim was sure that the voice was that of Bob Caflisch, an admiral with whom he'd served at Starfleet Command. Ironically, Kirk had been a grade above Caflisch in rank at the time; now the situation was reversed, and Caflisch was Kirk's superior.

"Bob?" Jim took a step closer to the screen.

Bob seemed not to hear; at any rate, he did not respond. *"Enterprise, this is Starfleet Operations."* The image suddenly cleared. Caflisch had bristly salt-and-pepper hair, a narrow, olive-skinned face, and a mysterious tendency to squint despite his 20/20 vision. He did so now as he peered at the screen. "Jim, is that you?" He smiled crookedly. "You're dressing rather informally these days, I see."

Jim glanced down at himself and remembered he was still wearing the overripe camping jacket. He shrugged. "You know how it is, Bob. You caught me on the way to the shower."

"Look, I'm sorry to interrupt your shore leave, but we've got a very dangerous situation brewing on Nimbus Three."

"You mean the Planet of Galactic Peace?"

"The very same." Caflisch's thin lips twisted at the irony. "From what we can make out, a terrorist force has captured the only settlement and taken the Klingon, Romulan, and Federation consuls hostage." He paused. "Now, I realize *Enterprise* isn't completely up to specs—"

"That's quite an understatement, Bob. With all respect, *Enterprise* is a disaster. There must be other ships in this quadrant—"

"Other ships, but no experienced commanders. For this, Captain, we need Jim Kirk and his crew."

Kirk sighed. "Bob, God knows I appreciate the compliment, but we're at a grave disadvantage here. To begin with, we don't even have a full crew complement."

Caflisch's tone cooled. "That's the way it is, Captain."

Starfleet had apparently made up its mind. Kirk yielded, but not graciously. "Very well, Admiral. Go ahead."

"Your orders are to proceed to Nimbus Three, assess the situation, and avoid confrontation if at all possible. Above all, you've got to get those hostages out safely."

An unpleasant realization struck Jim. "What about the Klingons . . . and the Romulans?"

"The Romulans don't seem to give a damn about their consul. Their official line is that they will not get involved or negotiate with terrorists, period . . . and their representative can always be replaced." Caflisch shook his head. "Unbelievable."

"And the Klingons? Have they reacted?"

"No, but you can bet they will."

"Klingons don't negotiate," Jim said. "They annihilate. They're liable to blow up the hostages just for the chance to revenge themselves on the kidnappers."

Caflisch's smile thinned to a grim line. "I know. That's why you've got to get there first, Jim."

"Bob, I'm not even sure if the warp drive's up to snuff yet."

"At least you've got a head start on them. Positionally, the *Enterprise* is closer than any of their vessels. Do what you can. And good luck, Jim."

"Understood. Kirk out."

Caflisch's image dissolved in a loud burst of static.

Kirk turned to address his expectant crew. "I'm afraid the ship's problems will have to be solved en route. Since we're understaffed, I'm counting on each of you to give your best. End of speech." He went back to the conn and sat. "Let's get to work. Mr. Sulu, plot a course for Nimbus Three."

"Course already plotted, Captain."

The doctor sidled over to the conn and began, out of the side of his mouth, "If you ask me, Jim—"

"I didn't." Jim cut McCoy off with a matter-of-fact wave of his hand. The anger he had felt during McCoy's earlier tirade at Yosemite was gone; this time he knew exactly what Bones was getting at, and this time, he had to agree.

McCoy scowled at him, undissuaded. "Go ahead, call me a Cassandra. But you have to admit, this is a terrible idea. We're bound to bump into the Klingons, and they don't exactly like you."

"The feeling's mutual, Doctor." Jim glanced over at him. "Now all you have to do is convince Starfleet of the fact. Believe it or not, I have no suicidal urges to go chasing after Klingons. I'm no more pleased about this mission than you are." He punched a button on the arm of the console. "Engineering."

A voice filtered up through the intercom grid. "Scott here."

"We'll need all the power you can muster, Mr. Scott, if we're going to make it to Nimbus before the Klingons get there."

"Don't you worry, Captain," Scott reassured him. "We'll beat those Klingon devils if I have to get out and push."

Kirk raised his brows and glanced at McCoy as if to say, *There. Happy?* "I'll keep your offer in mind," he said to Scott. "It may come to that." He closed the channel and addressed the helm. "Best speed, Mr. Sulu."

"Aye, sir."

Jim squirmed in his seat in an effort to get comfortable.

"What's wrong, Jim?" McCoy asked.

Jim looked up at him sharply. "I miss my *old* chair."

The *Okrona* sped toward the Neutral Zone.

Klaa paced the cramped confines of the bridge, ignoring the occasional curious glances of his crew. Since Nimbus III lay closer to Federation than to Klingon territory, the starship would no doubt arrive there first. *Okrona* had merely to cloak herself before arrival, then quietly steal up on her waiting prey.

Simple, very simple . . . and yet the young captain could not control his nervous pacing. Part of his restlessness was the result of sheer anticipation of the fight. Klaa had not tasted battle in the month since he had become captain of the *Okrona*.

Another part of it was the realization that he had become captain through a single heroic act and that some, such as his thick-skulled gunner, Morek, resented Klaa's meteoric success and were praying for a chance to bring him down, to see the invincible young captain fail.

None disputed that Klaa was the Empire's best gunner, but many suggested a ship of his own was too great a reward. He had heard the gossip: the most jealous of them called him an idiot savant—a genius behind the gunner's rig, an imbecile when it came to command. What Klaa needed now was yet another incredible victory, to cement his reputation as captain. And he could do that himself, without the moronic Morek's help, without anyone's help.

He walked past the helm and glanced at the back of Morek's thick, balding head. *You'd like me to fail at this, wouldn't you, Morek? Well, it's not my days aboard* Okrona *that are numbered . . . but yours.*

Klaa turned to pace in the opposite direction—and nearly collided with his first officer, Vixis. His initial reaction was to smile, but he frowned instead. It was more in keeping with his portrayal of the intense, restless young captain, eager for battle.

"Captain Klaa," she said, smiling. Her eyes shone; her golden complexion was flushed. Her expression was much the same as it had been when she first told him of the diversion to Nimbus, and so Klaa knew the message she brought would be a welcome one. "We've just intercepted an encoded message on the Federation frequency. The starship *Enterprise* has been dispatched to Nimbus Three."

"Enterprise," Klaa whispered. "Kirk's ship . . ."

He had expected good news; he had never dared dream it would be this good. He felt like throwing back his head and roaring with joy at the second gift the gods had just dropped in his lap—but he restrained himself in front of the crew.

Kirk, the criminal who had killed almost an entire crew of Klingons, stolen their vessel, developed the Genesis device with the intention of committing genocide against the Empire . . . To destroy James Kirk and his ship would be the achievement of a lifetime, of a thousand lifetimes. Kill Kirk, and Klaa would no longer be concerned about his status as captain of *Okrona*. The Empire would reward him with an entire fleet of vessels! Klaa folded his arms tightly across his chest and permitted a low laugh to escape.

Vixis's smile was dazzling. " 'There will be no peace

as long as Kirk lives,'" she said, quoting Ambassador Kamarg's deathless words to the Federation Council. "Our Empire's highest bounty has been placed on his head."

Klaa paused to study his first officer. She was statuesque, of elegant beauty and bloodline, and he had noticed that she watched him. He trusted no one, a trait that had served him well thus far.

You would like to see me destroy the Enterprise, *wouldn't you, Vixis? For then you would be the first officer—and possibly, someday, the consort—of the Empire's greatest hero.*

He did not know her well enough yet to trust her, though in truth, Klaa found the prospect altogether appealing.

"James T. Kirk," he said slowly. He stroked his chin as he stared at Vixis. "I've followed his career since I was a boy." His own career gave promise of paralleling Kirk's. "A man I admire . . . and hate. If I could defeat Kirk—"

"You would be the greatest warrior in the galaxy," Vixis breathed.

Klaa turned like a whip to face Tarag, the helmsman. Morek, seated next to him, wore a sour expression that evaporated instantly. "Maximum speed!" Klaa roared.

"Yes, my captain," Tarag replied. Morek's expression was now one of subservient respect.

"Success!" Klaa cried. He turned to Vixis and saluted her with a fist struck against his heart. If all went well, perhaps he would offer her the chance to be his paramour as well as his first officer. Perhaps, if she remained loyal and kept his interest . . .

She returned the gesture with passionate grace. "Success . . . my captain. Death to James Kirk and the crew of the *Enterprise.*"

"Captain's Log, Stardate Eighty-four—"

The log recorder gave a muffled groan. Jim Kirk did likewise, and put a hand to his forehead, as if to forestall the onset of a headache. "Replay."

The recorder played back a stretch of static that sounded to Jim like bacon frying.

He drew in a deep breath. He was not about to be outdone by a machine. "Try again," he said, in what he considered an admirably patient tone. To his delight, the computer log complied; the recording light on the console came on.

"Captain's Log," Jim began confidently, "Stardate Eighty-four—"

The recorder groaned again, then made a new noise that sounded suspiciously like a death rattle.

"Forget it. Just forget it," Jim said. The recording light went out as he rubbed his temples.

"Getting a bit of a headache?" McCoy asked cheerfully, in a voice that struck Jim as just a bit too smug. Since he wasn't needed in sickbay, the doctor remained on the bridge and seemed to be relishing the mechanical chaos that ensued the instant the *Enterprise* warped out.

"I know you're not a big fan of technology, Bones. You've run a personal vendetta against transporters ever since I've known you, but"—Jim squeezed his eyes shut and massaged the bridge of his nose—"you don't have to rub it in."

"Who's rubbing it in?" McCoy's eyes widened innocently. "I just asked you if you had a headache."

"You know what I mean." Jim opened his eyes and sighed. "Dammit, Bones, they issued us a lemon with the name *Enterprise* painted on it."

"Down south we have a more colorful expression for it." McCoy's smile became mysterious.

Jim lifted his eyebrows questioningly and waited.

The doctor leaned closer and lowered his voice so that only the captain could hear. "Piece of sh—"

"Don't say it," Jim warned, with a sudden ferocity that surprised them both. "That's not funny, Doctor."

McCoy drew back defensively and shrugged. "Hey, *you're* the one who called her a lemon, and now you're defending her as if she were the *real Enterprise.* Make up your mind."

Jim opened his mouth, ready to retort hotly; fortunately, Uhura interrupted.

"Captain, we're receiving the hostage information you requested."

Jim swiveled to face the main viewer, his anger forgotten. "On screen, Commander."

Spock left his station to stand beside the conn.

An image—Kirk got the briefest impression of a woman's face, very young and very attractive— fizzled onto the screen, out of focus, then broke up and faded to black. Uhura worked furiously at her station, muttering something under her breath that Kirk was afraid to guess at, and then the young woman's face flashed again onto the screen.

This time Kirk had time to notice that she was a Romulan. Biographical data, very scanty, threaded

101

across the bottom of the screen. It gave her name, rank, age . . . and no further information whatsoever. The Starfleet compiler of the data let it be known that the Romulans had refused to release any more background on their consul, Caithlin Dar.

At the name, even Spock reacted by raising a brow.

"Caithlin?" McCoy wondered aloud. "Correct me if I'm wrong, but isn't that an *Irish* name?"

Kirk didn't answer; the visual had changed to an image of someone he recognized, though the Klingon seemed older and heavier than he remembered. "Not *General* Korrd," he remarked absently.

"The same," Spock replied. "He has apparently fallen out of favor with the Klingon High Command. His appointment to Nimbus appears to be a form of banishment."

"A damn shame," Kirk said, with a surge of fondness. "Korrd was one hell of a soldier. His military strategies were required learning when I was cadet at the Academy. When they put me out to pasture, I hope I fare better than Korrd."

The visual changed again, so that the screen displayed a holo of the Federation consul, a fair-haired, middle-aged human male. His name, St. John Talbot, was one that Kirk vaguely recognized as well.

"Not even dead, and already they've canonized him," McCoy said dryly.

Talbot's picture faded; a tape of uneven quality began. It was a static scene of the three diplomats standing together, flanked by a grim army of impoverished settlers. Many of them clutched crude guns made of metal pipe. The diplomats seemed dazed.

Perhaps they had been drugged, Jim thought, but no, their eyes were too wide, too clear.

"This must be the hostage tape," McCoy said.

Spock studied the scene with intense interest. "Their weapons appear to be extremely primitive—" he began, but lapsed into silence when the Romulan hostage, Dar, began to speak.

She had clearly been designated spokesperson for the hostages. She delivered her talk precisely, without hesitation; Jim suspected she had rehearsed it many times. "At fourteen hundred hours," Dar said, "we willingly surrendered ourselves to the forces of the Galactic Army of Light."

"Interesting," Spock murmured. "A religious crusade?"

Dar continued. "At this moment, we are in their protective custody. Their leader assures us that we will be treated humanely as long as you cooperate with his demands. I believe his sincerity."

McCoy shook his head. "Hostage mentality if I ever saw it. Poor things have been brainwashed."

Kirk raised a hand to silence him as Dar concluded her speech. "He requests that you send a Federation starship to parlay for our release. Be assured that we are in good health and would appreciate your immediate response."

Her image and those of her companions were blocked as someone strode in front of them.

There was a swirl of white, and then a new face came into focus—that of a male, evidently a Nimbus settler. He exuded the power and charisma of a natural leader.

And he was a Vulcan.

A renegade Vulcan. Jim shook himself and glanced over at Spock and McCoy; both of them were staring transfixed at the screen.

Spock's expression was one of stunned recognition.

"I deeply regret this desperate act, but these are desperate times." The Vulcan's voice was soothing; as he spoke, Jim found himself wanting to believe what he said.

"I have no desire to harm these innocents," the leader continued, "but do not put me to the test. I implore you to respond within twenty-four standard hours."

The transmission ceased abruptly.

With peculiar urgency, Spock strode over to Uhura's console, where he reversed the tape and froze it on the image of the leader's face.

"What is it, Spock?" Kirk rose from his chair and stepped behind his first officer, who stared, mesmerized by the image on Uhura's console screen. "You look like you've just seen a ghost."

Spock was as distracted as Jim had ever seen him.

The Vulcan straightened and faced Kirk.

"Captain"—for a moment, Spock seemed as dazed as the hostages—"perhaps I have. Permission to leave the bridge."

"Granted," Kirk said. "But what—"

The Vulcan turned and was gone.

McCoy watched him in wonder. "What the devil is wrong with him?"

Chapter Seven

ON THE FORWARD observation deck, Spock stood next to the antique ship's wheel and looked out at the stars. The deck was deserted, silent, dimly lit; it offered Spock the privacy he required to untangle and examine the chaotic jumble of memories.

The image on the viewscreen had been most unclear. *I am mistaken,* Spock told himself. *It has been too many years . . . and after death and the ritual of* fal tor pan, *my memory of the past is faulty, unreliable.*

He ran his hand absently over the surface of the wooden wheel. After its years at sea and the subsequent passage of five centuries, its surface was scarred and pitted beneath layers of protective sealant.

Yet Spock seemed to have no difficulty now in remembering. That part of his past had been so deeply impressed upon his mind and spirit that even death could not blot it out. The images swept over him like a tide and would not cease, images that had lain undisturbed and forgotten up to the moment Spock saw the terrorist leader's face.

The leader's face wavered, changed; in its stead Spock saw a much younger face, one much like his own.

I will find Sha Ka Ree, the young one said. An indistinct, half-formed picture: the young one turning away to go forever. Spock closed his eyes, astonished at the depth of sorrow he still felt at the memory.

But more than thirty years had intervened; how could he possibly recognize that face, that voice, after the passage of so much time?

Another part of him had no doubt.

Spock stiffened instinctively at the sound of the lounge doors parting behind him; he let go of the ship's wheel and clasped his hands firmly behind his back. He was beginning to learn, after his prolonged experience of sharing consciousness with Leonard McCoy, how to relax among humans, how to mentally achieve what McCoy referred to as "not taking himself so seriously." Spock was even beginning to understand their humor. But he did not want his friends to see him in pain.

Footsteps neared, then stopped behind him. He did not have to turn around to know that it was Jim Kirk and Leonard McCoy.

"Spock," Jim asked quietly. "What is it? Do you know this Vulcan?"

Yes, Spock almost replied, until doubt assailed him

106

again. "I cannot be sure. The transmission was most unclear."

"But he *does* seem familiar?" Jim persisted.

Spock gave a small sigh of surrender. He suspected that before the Nimbus mission was over, he would have to reveal his past in far more detail than he wished.

But for now, he revealed only what was necessary to satisfy Kirk. "He reminds me of someone I . . . knew in my youth."

"Why, Spock," McCoy teased, "I didn't know you had one."

"I do not often think of the past," Spock replied simply. He knew the doctor well enough to understand his sarcasm; it was a defense against intense unpleasant emotion. McCoy had evidently sensed Spock's distress and was uncomfortable. As a result, he used humor in an attempt to draw attention away from it. Perhaps an effective weapon; perhaps Spock would test it in the future.

The captain would not be distracted. "Spock, exactly *who* is it he reminds you of?"

Someone who was once closer to me than either of you, Spock might have said. *Someone whom, for the past thirty years, I have been constrained to think of as dead. Among my family, among my people, I am forbidden even to speak his name.*

Instead, he told them, "There was a young student, exceptionally gifted, possessing great intelligence. It was assumed that one day he would take his place among the great scholars of Vulcan. But he was"— Spock searched for the appropriate term, did not find it, and substituted one that could not quite convey all that he meant—"a revolutionary."

"I don't understand," Jim said. "How could a Vulcan become a revolutionary?"

Spock hesitated. His memory was crystallizing as he spoke. These were things of which he was forbidden to speak to outsiders—even to uninitiated Vulcans.

Cautiously, he said, "The knowledge and experience he sought were forbidden by Vulcan belief." He half turned to face Kirk.

The captain was frowning. "Forbidden? I thought the Vulcans were a tolerant race." He clearly was not going to stop until he had a satisfactory explanation.

Spock returned his attention to the stars and did his best to answer without telling an outright lie—or giving the details of the truth. "He rejected his logical upbringing and embraced the animal passions of our ancestors."

"Why?"

"He believed that the key to self-knowledge was emotion, not logic." Spock knew without looking that the doctor smiled.

"Imagine that," McCoy said. "A passionate Vulcan. I might actually learn to like the guy."

Spock continued without reacting. "When he began to encourage others to follow him, he was banished from Vulcan, never to return." He stopped and hoped that Jim would deem the explanation sufficient . . . and would not ask a question Spock could not answer.

"Fascinating," Jim said. No one spoke for a moment. And then Jim's voice again, determined to have an answer, yet faintly apologetic for the invasion of privacy: "This Vulcan, Spock . . . how well did you know him?"

It was the question Spock had feared. He was saved by the intercom whistle, followed by Uhura's shipwide page. "Captain to the bridge."

Kirk went over to the bulkhead and pressed the button. "On my way." He and McCoy headed for the exit, but Spock, still contemplating the stars and the void, vaguely heard him pause expectantly at the threshold.

"Spock . . .?"

Spock forced himself to travel the thirty years back to the present. "Coming, Captain."

But he carried the memory of the young Vulcan with him.

J'Onn found Sybok sitting alone in the outer room of the saloon, which was dark save for the bluish glow from the aged communication terminal. The Vulcan had been so lost in thought that he had not heard his second-in-command enter.

J'Onn took a moment to study his leader's face. It was strong and lined, and radiated determination. Yet J'Onn fancied he saw a trace of sorrow there, a sorrow that Sybok kept carefully hidden while in the presence of others.

J'Onn had come here out of gratitude, to thank Sybok again . . . and also, in all honesty, because he had from time to time seen sadness in the Vulcan's eyes; this troubled J'Onn greatly. It did not seem fair that the one who had helped them all should himself suffer. J'Onn moved forward until he stood beside the Vulcan.

Sybok turned his head quickly to look up at him, but he did not seem at all startled. It was almost as if he had expected someone to approach. Now the sadness was gone from his expression.

Perhaps, J'Onn thought, *I simply imagined it.*

"Hello, J'Onn," Sybok said quietly. He did not smile; J'Onn noticed the fact because he smiled so easily and often.

"I came because I wished to tell you how grateful we all feel for the freedom you have given us." J'Onn paused, searching for the courage to say what he truly meant. "You have helped all of us deal with our private sorrows—me, the other soldiers, even the diplomats. I have spoken with them all. Yet you speak to no one about yourself . . . about your own sorrow."

Sybok sat silently, focused on some vision perceived by his eyes alone. J'Onn waited until, at last, the Vulcan answered without looking at him.

"I have been given the grace to bear my own sorrow. I understand death and loss very well . . . well enough to be of some use to those who need me."

"I want to help you, as you have helped me and the others."

Sybok smiled unhappily. "You cannot do that. But you will help us to procure a starship. That is more than enough."

J'Onn crouched beside his chair and hesitantly placed a hand on his leader's forearm. It was like touching carved stone.

"Share your pain with me," J'Onn said.

The present fell away.

A face emerged from the darkness. J'Onn recognized the eyes instantly: arresting, magical, framed by dark hair, but the features were as decidedly feminine as Sybok's were masculine.

A woman. T'Rea, Sybok's mother. A child clutching her and sobbing.

I swear to you by the Masters, I will take you away, to Sha Ka Ree. . . .

As quickly as the image appeared, it melted into darkness. Then another vision materialized: Sybok as a youth, standing before a massive stone door.

J'Onn's self-awareness faded; he merged into the memory, seeing through Sybok's eyes. . . .

It was the night when Sybok committed the crime for which he was banished from Vulcan forever. He stood in the dark cavernous depths of Gol with the Watcher, Storel, guarding the black stone entryway to the Hall of Ancient Thought.

Inside, in the eternal gloom of the great Hall, his mother's spirit waited.

For Vulcan's past two peaceful millennia, the post of Watcher had been an unnecessary bow to tradition. The secret wisdom of the ancients was, in these more placid times, safe. But there was a time in Vulcan history when such knowledge was recognized for the dangerous treasure it was, and there were those who were willing to risk everything—banishment, even death—in order to gain access to the great Hall.

As Sybok was willing that night. He was young, scarcely an adult by Vulcan legal standards, and yet at this moment he felt very, very old and bitter unto death.

He was here on the occasion of the first anniversary of his mother's death and the entombment of her undying spirit in the Hall of Ancient Thought. In the same manner as all the High Masters before her, T'Rea's *katra*—her unique essence, containing all knowledge she had gleaned from this life—had been placed in a specially prepared receptacle where it would remain for all eternity, so that other adepts could consult her and gain from her wisdom.

Sybok opened his mind, and J'Onn understood all in the Vulcan's life that had passed thus far: T'Rea's disgrace, the maniacal devotion she and her son felt toward each other, the promise the boy had made his mother, to take her to the Source, to Sha Ka Ree—a legend known to the Romulans as Vorta Vor.

With a sense of wonder, J'Onn caught his first glimpse of Vulcan mysticism. He marveled at the concept of High Master, of the possibility of enshrining a Master's knowledge for all eternity.

Of all High Masters, T'Rea had been the least honored. The separation of her katra from her dying flesh had been done hastily, in secret, without the ceremony that normally accompanied the passing of a Master. Her heresy had cost her the revered position and—so Sybok believed—hastened her death.

After his mother's collapse, he had been kept from her, and so had not been allowed to keep his promise to her. Nor was he, like most family members, allowed into the Hall during the transference.

Only time, and the fact of Sybok's parentage, which was revealed to him after his mother's death, softened the kolinahru so that they permitted him to honor his mother on the anniversary of her passage into the Hall. It was a hallowed tradition observed by all adepts, as a sign of respect and honor for the deceased High Master who had trained them.

Even then, Sybok was not allowed to serve as Watcher alone.

He stood in the dim belly of the mountain with Storel and waited until the hour was late, until all of the kolinahru had retired to their separate cells. There was no need to gather courage; Sybok had more than enough anger left in him to fuel his actions.

What he was about to do would require him to leave Vulcan forever. He felt no regret about that. There was nothing to hold him here now that T'Rea was dead. He would sacrifice himself and meld his consciousness to hers, and begin their quest.

Before dying, T'Rea had confessed to him that the Ancients had revealed to her the actual location of Sha Ka Ree—but that secret had gone with her into death. Sybok desired nothing more than to learn the secret location, and take his mother there.

True, melding one's mind with a disembodied katra was considered dangerous, reserved only for the gravest emergencies, as it could lead to madness.

But Sybok was willing to risk it. After all, his mental control was superior to that of the average adept; he doubted he would go mad.

And if he did, at least T'Rea would be with him.

Sybok eyed the Vulcan next to him. Storel was frail-looking, with hair as snow white as his robe, but in physical strength, he was almost a match for the youth.

Sybok wished the contest could be a purely physical one, but circumstances required that he pit himself against a more formidable opponent: Storel's mind. The Watcher was a highly skilled adept in the mind rules, second only to the High Master.

There was no other way. Storel possessed knowledge Sybok sorely needed: the precise location of his mother's vrekatra, the orb that housed her intangible remains. The Hall of Ancients was a vast, dark maze of passages filled with thousands of such orbs. If Sybok was to make an escape, he would need time, time that could not be wasted wandering in the Hall, searching for T'Rea's vrekatra.

They had stood together for hours without speaking; now Sybok broke the silence.

"Storel," he said.

The older Vulcan faced him. Sybok waited to speak until he focused his hypnotic gaze intently on Storel's gentle, numinous eyes.

Share your pain with me, Sybok said, without speaking aloud.

No. Storel pulled away as if instinctively sensing the danger of Sybok's gaze. The aged Watcher began to send out a mental cry to the adepts for help.

Sybok reached out and clutched Storel's head in his hands. He entered Storel's mind, forcing his way through the old Vulcan's mental shields, blotting out all cries for assistance.

It was a brutal act. There would be permanent damage to Storel's mind.

But in the midst of regret, Sybok felt a surge of victory. His mental powers were far beyond those of the Watcher. Sybok was a highly trained adept—so skillful that he discovered he could take whatever information he pleased from Storel's mind with only a little struggle.

The sense of power was utterly intoxicating.

He drew what he needed from the Watcher's brain: a perfect, clear vision of the great Hall, the interior of which Sybok had never seen and, within, T'Rea's shining vrekatra.

Sybok let go of Storel's head and caught the old Vulcan as he fell; he lowered the Watcher to the floor. There was no time to feel remorse for what he had just done. The damage to Storel's mind was unavoidable, and Sybok's desperate loyalty to his mother outweighed all other considerations.

Sybok went to the massive door and pushed with the whole of his strength. The door slid open with the faint grinding sound of stone against stone.

The sight within filled Sybok with reverent awe. Before him, a high, vast cavern lined with glowing vrekatras, full of the knowledge of the centuries, stretched into apparent infinity. The chamber was sufficiently lit by the luminous force fields surrounding the receptacles.

Sybok ran lightly through the chamber, past a thousand spheres of living light until he reached the one so clearly envisioned in the Watcher's mind.

He stopped. Before him, chest-high and nestled against the polished black stone of the mountain's interior, his mother's vrekatra rested upon a stand of ebony trihr wood. Beneath the receptacle a name had been simply carved in old Vulcan script: T'Rea. The legend was drenched in the radiance cast by the retaining field, whose light reflected off flecks of diamondlike crystal embedded in the onyx wall.

Sybok knelt before the receptacle and reached up. His hands sought out the orb's vibrating surface and rested there. The tips of his fingers prickled and tingled with the field's energy . . . or was it the restless energy of T'Rea's mind?

He directed a single thought into the globe.

Mother . . .

Her response was so immediate, so powerful and joyous that Sybok gasped aloud and struggled to keep from falling backwards.

Shiav . . .

He clutched the globe and wept without sound, without tears. *I have come to keep my promise to you, Mother. Tell me where Sha Ka Ree is and I will take you there with me.*

She responded, not with thoughts or images, but with wordless, grateful love. For a moment, he basked in it.

And again T'Rea shared with him the vision from the One, the Other, the Source. But it was not the gentle vision she had bestowed upon her young child. This time, T'Rea withheld nothing from him . . . and the experience was almost too terrifying for Sybok to bear.

At first he shrank from it in fear. The vision was one of darkness—complete and hideous blackness, evoking within him mindless fear. It swirled about him, engulfing him within its center.

When he thought he could stand no more, that his

heart would cease beating from sheer terror, the darkness parted, and gave way to light.

The sight was one of unutterable glory. In the cold clarity of space, a lone planet circled a single white star.

The planet loomed toward him; Sybok sank down, into its atmosphere.

Its surface teemed with life, with beauty—lush vegetation, dense forests, rivers, oceans, lakes, streams—more precious water than Sybok, born to a desert world, had ever seen.

And the mountains! Higher, more majestic than Mount Seleya herself. The tallest of them formed themselves into a perfect circle, a ring. And at its center . . .

Intrigued, Sybok strained to see, but his sight failed him.

Herein lies the One, a voice said.

It was not T'Rea's voice but, Sybok realized with ecstasy, the voice of the One Itself.

He swooned, lost to himself.

How long he remained unconscious was unclear. When he awoke, he found himself still within the great Hall, on the floor beside T'Rea's vrekatra.

Beside him stood the High Master and three attendants.

He pushed himself to a sitting position and stared up at them in total confusion—until he remembered Storel. Sybok's crime had been discovered.

Worse, T'Rea's consciousness was no longer with him . . . but he could not remember intentionally severing the link. Panicked, he glanced up at the receptacle.

It was dark.

"My mother!" He jumped to his feet and glared at T'Sai. Whatever fear or respect he might have had for the position of High Master fled him in that awful moment. "What have you done with her?"

In his desperation, he was prepared to engage in physical and mental battle with them all—T'Sai and her three most powerful adepts—to find the vanished T'Rea. His rational mind understood he would most likely destroy himself in the attempt, but he was too distraught to care.

T'Sai remained implacable in the face of his dismay. "We found both of you thus." She gestured at the floor. "T'Rea refused to reenter the vrekatra. It was her choice to embrace annihilation instead."

Sybok closed his eyes. T'Sai was still speaking, meaningless words: *You have committed a grave offense, for which there can be no forgiveness.*

He heard without understanding as his heart descended into darkness. . . .

Sybok sat, head bowed, in the blue glow of the monitor.

J'Onn, still crouched beside him, was filled with sadness for him. "How do you bear it?" he whispered. "How do you bear it, and all our sorrows as well?"

Sybok raised his head. "The vision sustains me."

"Sha Ka Ree?"

Sybok nodded. J'Onn could hear the strength return in the Vulcan's voice. "I am bound to go there; it is the only way T'Rea's death can be given meaning. I *will* find it." He looked at J'Onn with eyes that burned like a prophet's.

J'Onn's home planet was ruled by Romulans. He spoke their language and knew of their legends. The name T'Rea came from Reah, the ancient goddess of the underworld, of death and bereavement.

J'Onn also remembered that Sybok's mother had called him by a special name. It was a very ancient word, almost as ancient as the root from which the name T'Rea had sprung, a word that J'Onn recognized as having a cognate in the Romulan tongue. He understood its meaning and the legend behind it very well.

J'Onn stood and laid a hand upon the Vulcan's shoulder.

"Shiav," he said.

Chapter Eight

"I DON'T LIKE THIS," McCoy muttered, shaking his head. "I don't like this at all." They were on their way to the bridge—for once, the lift was functioning smoothly—and for Spock's sake, Jim and McCoy had changed the subject to the *Enterprise*'s space-worthiness. The doctor was less than pleased about the fact that the ship had just entered the Neutral Zone—without benefit of a cloaking device.

Jim didn't much care for the idea himself, but he did what he could to reassure McCoy. Spock, lost in reverie, seemed quite oblivious to the conversation. "We're sticking carefully to the Nimbus corridor," Jim said. "It's off limits. No one can attack us here."

"You mean no one's *supposed* to," McCoy contradicted him darkly. "You think when the Klingons see NCC-1701-A emblazoned across our hull, they're just going to say 'Drat! We're in the Nimbus corridor. I guess we'll just have to wait to blast them to kingdom come'?"

Jim thought for a moment. "Chekov's scanning for them. We'll know the instant they approach. You have to admit, Klingons don't hang around Nimbus very much; there's nothing for them to steal, no one looking for a fight. We aren't going to run into any Klingon vessels until—"

"Until the one that's probably gunning for us arrives." McCoy's expression was glum.

"Well . . . yes," Jim admitted. Behind them, Spock maintained his mysterious silence. "But look at it this way, Bones: we seem to have beaten them there."

"Joy of joys," McCoy said, with something less than enthusiasm.

The lift eased to a smooth stop. "Bridge," the computer announced brightly, in a pleasant feminine voice.

"Well, I'll be." The doctor smiled and took a step forward as the lift doors began to part. "Something on this ship finally *works.*"

Spock caught him by the shoulder just in time to keep him from colliding with the unopened left door. Jim forced it open and let them pass.

"It could have been worse," he told the scowling McCoy. "At least the right door worked."

Together they stepped onto the bridge.

"Approaching Nimbus Three," Sulu said.

The main viewscreen showed a pale ochre planet with only a few microscopic dots of blue.

"Hailing frequencies open," Uhura told the captain. She glanced at the three as they crossed to their customary places: Kirk at the conn, Spock replacing Chekov at the scanner, McCoy as always at the captain's left.

Kirk took his seat. "Standard orbit, Mr. Sulu." He looked over at Spock, who was already bent over his scanners. As distracted as Spock had been at the sight of the terrorist leader, he was now—ostensibly at least—composed and perfectly focused on the task at hand.

"Captain." Uhura's voice struck a note of urgency. "We're receiving a transmission from Paradise City. They demand to know our intentions."

"Give us some time, Commander. Respond with static. Let them think we're having difficulties." The corner of Kirk's mouth twisted wryly. "It wouldn't be that far from the truth."

Uhura leaned toward her speaker. "Paradise City, can you boost your power? We're barely receiving your transmission."

"Spock," Jim said. "Any sign of Klingon vessels?"

"Negative, regarding the immediate vicinity." The Vulcan kept his eyes on his screen. "Commencing long-range scanning."

Kirk allowed himself a very small sigh of relief, then pressed the intercom. "Transporter room. Status."

"Scott here, Captain. The transporter is still inoperative. Even if we could manage to locate and lock on to the hostages, we couldna beam them up."

"How much time do you need, Scotty?"

"I canna say exactly, sir, but several hours, minimum."

Kirk's lips thinned. "Without a cloaking device, I

can't sit around waiting for Kruge's relatives to find me." He paused. "Do what you can, Mr. Scott. I suppose we'll have to get the hostages out the old-fashioned way."

Spock turned from his viewer to catch the captain's eye. "Klingon Bird of Prey now entering this quadrant. Estimating one-point-nine hours until her weapons come to bear."

"Damn," Jim said softly. They had less than two hours to find the hostages and get them back up to the ship without a transporter . . . and then attempt to outrun the Klingons. He rose. "Let's move."

Sybok sat alone through most of the night in the darkened saloon and stared at the bright, blank communications screen. His plan had thus far met with success: Dar, Talbot, even the stubbornly resistant Korrd were his to command.

Now he merely watched and waited. He could afford to be patient. It had taken him the greater part of his life to get this close to his goal; he could wait a few hours more.

Soon one of two events would occur. Either the Klingons would arrive and blast Paradise City cleanly from the planet's surface . . . or a Federation starship would come. Only a starship bore the weaponry impressive enough to strike fear in the hearts of desperate terrorists; only a starship possessed the capabilities Sybok required to complete his quest.

Sybok believed in fate. If the Klingons arrived first and killed him, the homesteaders, and the hostages, then it meant Sybok had been misguided, that his mission was a self-created idle fantasy. But if a starship came first . . . If a starship came, it would show that he, Sybok, was in fact divinely guided, divinely protected. It would prove him to be the *shiav* of legend, and it would quell his private doubts that he had been indulging himself in egotistic fantasy.

The last few hours, despite his self-imposed calm, had not been easy. The painful recollection of the loss of T'Rea had stirred up the past. Old memories returned to trouble him, from a time and a life so far removed from the present that Sybok had believed them forgotten—resolved and buried long ago.

But here they were. Memories of Spock, and the old pain. *Why do I think of Spock?* Sybok wondered. *Why now? Does he think of me? Could that be the source of these thoughts? Spock, wherever you are—on Vulcan, no doubt, or perhaps on Earth—are you thinking of me now, through all this time, this space?*

He should have quashed the memories immediately; they only served to distract him from his goal. Still, the thoughts of Spock reawakened an old fondness that was pleasant.

Sybok placed a hand atop the terminal and gently laid his forehead against it. At times such as these, when weariness overtook him, he found himself assailed by doubt and strange thoughts. No matter; he would rest, and these emotions would pass.

He jerked his head up suddenly as the screen flickered. A human face, female, dark and lovely, appeared before him.

"Paradise City," she said. Her voice was as pleasing as her countenance, but it was her words that moved

Sybok to tears of joy. "This is the Federation starship *Enterprise*. Please respond."

"A Federation starship," Sybok whispered. He squeezed his eyelids tightly shut and regained control of himself. It was a sign, an omen from the Source, that he had acted according to the Light. This vessel was a gift, given so that Sybok might reach his goal and uncover the ultimate mystery. He trembled as the screen flashed again, and the image changed to that of the starship's interior.

A human male, dark-haired and authoritative, frowned at the screen. It was all Sybok could do not to laugh aloud with ecstasy, with amusement at the absolute absurdity of it all.

"This is Captain Pavel Chekov speaking," the human said. Sybok smiled at him, but the smile had no effect; the captain's expression remained oppressively serious. "You are in violation of Neutral Zone treaty. I advise you to release your hostages at once, or suffer the consequences."

How we struggle against our true destiny, Sybok mused, *caught up in our petty lives with their petty concerns and regulations! Is that what gives your life meaning, Captain Pavel Chekov? To warp around the galaxy enforcing the silly rules of the overgrown bureaucracy that calls itself the Federation?*

"I would appreciate it if you would stop smiling and respond," Chekov said.

"Forgive me," Sybok replied. He had not been aware that he was still smiling. "But your threat amuses me. Exactly what consequences did you have in mind, Captain Chekov?"

And at the human's confused expression, Sybok threw back his head and laughed.

The lights were dimmed inside the shuttlecraft *Galileo 5* as it streaked downward through Nimbus's stratosphere. Kirk took the phaser and hand-held force shield Uhura offered him; she turned away and continued dispensing equipment to the seven-person security team accompanying them.

Kirk returned his attention to Spock, who sat huddled over a graphics screen. "Their scanning systems are primitive and of greatly limited range, but efficient," the Vulcan stated. He pointed to a spot on the grid. "I recommend we land here, at coordinate eight-five-six-three."

Jim frowned as he studied the blinking screen. "That puts us pretty far away from Paradise City, Spock, and time is a major concern."

Spock looked up, his expression implacable. "To land any closer would be to risk detection."

The statement was impossible to argue with. They'd simply have to find a *fast* way to get to the city undetected. Jim sighed unhappily. "Did you get those coordinates, Mr. Sulu?"

Sulu half turned from the pilot's seat to nod at him. "Aye, sir. Programming coordinates in now. All hands, prepare for landing."

"Joy of joys. I can't wait," McCoy muttered sarcastically, fastening his restraints. He sat directly behind Jim.

Kirk turned to give him a sharp look. "It's a little early to be complaining already, Doctor. Besides, you were the one who insisted on coming along. I tried to talk you out of it, remember?"

McCoy sighed. "Don't remind me. But you know as well as I do that the hostages might need medical help. Besides, I've gotta keep an eye on you these days, Jim."

"What's to worry about? As long as you and Spock are with me—"

"As long as we're with you, we won't let you pull any more ridiculous stunts, and that's the extent of it. Don't let yourself get superstitious. Next thing you know, you'll be taking us with you to go to the head."

Jim grimaced and turned back to fasten his restraints and settled back in his chair. McCoy wasn't all that far off the mark. Jim *had* felt relieved when the doctor volunteered for the landing party. He glanced at Spock, seated beside him. The Vulcan had once again withdrawn into the privacy of his thoughts.

"Spock," Jim admonished, and leaned over to fasten the Vulcan's restraints.

Spock did not react. Concerned, Jim peered at him. Clearly, Spock was hiding some bit of information about the Vulcan terrorist from them—something that was troubling him greatly—but Kirk knew his old friend well enough to know that it was futile to pressure Spock to reveal anything. He would explain things if and when it became necessary, and not a moment before. Feeling helpless, Jim asked, "Spock, are you okay?"

Spock stiffened as if startled by the question, but recovered immediately. "I am fine, Captain." And, when Kirk appeared unconvinced, he added, *"Damn fine."*

Jim smiled faintly. "We're not in the twentieth century, Spock. You don't have to swear to persuade me."

Spock acknowledged this with a brief nod, then withdrew into himself again as *Galileo* began her descent.

"Even as we speak," Captain Pavel Chekov said, "a Klingon warship is on its way to Nimbus. We estimate arrival within the hour."

Sybok nodded. He no longer feared death at the Klingons' hands. His mission would succeed; his confirmation of that fact was this very starship. He and this vessel, the *Enterprise,* were divinely protected, and no Klingon Bird of Prey, no dark force in the galaxy, would be able to harm them. "I imagine the Klingons will be quite angry."

The human bristled. "You are a master of understatement. They are likely to destroy the planet! You and your hostages will be killed!"

Sybok responded with good humor. "Then it's fortunate I have you and your starship to protect me. In the meantime, Captain, I instruct that you and your first officer beam down to my coordinates."

The young captain eyed him cagily. "We will be happy to beam down, but first we must have certain . . . assurances."

With a twinge of frustration, Sybok realized the human was stalling for time. This could not be allowed. Oppressed by a sudden overwhelming weariness, he ran a hand over his hot forehead. He was physically and emotionally drained from the events of the past few days, and he had expected no obstacles, not even a minor one such as this. Not now; not after the moment of confirmation.

Perhaps his belief had been unrealistic, or perhaps this was a test.

Sybok drew upon his deepest reserves of strength and straightened to face Captain Chekov with a face devoid of emotion, a trick he'd acquired during his early days on his native planet.

"Name them," he told Chekov.

With impressive finesse, Sulu navigated the *Galileo 5* to a soft landing in the sand, where it nestled, hidden from a view of the city by an imposing dune. They had descended in radio silence at night, without benefit of landing lights, but Jim was still concerned. He made his way out of the craft, then struggled to the crest of the dune to get a better view of their destination.

Undimmed by the glow of civilization, the stars and twin moons shone fiercely on the desert landscape, almost obliterating the feeble spark of the town ahead. Jim lifted infrared binoculars to his eyes to get a better view.

"At foot speed, I estimate the journey to Paradise City at one-point-two hours," Spock said.

"We don't *have* one-point-two hours, Mr. Spock."

"Agreed," Spock admitted. "However, I am at a loss to suggest alternate means of travel."

Kirk scowled as he stared through the binoculars. There was nothing between the *Galileo* and Paradise City but a flat, unbroken expanse of sand. Jim scanned the area for obstacles, or the Vulcan leader's scouts, until he caught sight of something bright orange and flickering and, next to it, something hulking and dark. "Wait a minute . . ."

It was a fire, and the dark hulks were tsemus, beasts of burden the human settlers on Nimbus indiscriminately referred to as horses. Less than a kilometer away from the dune was a small oasis, a pathetic spring where a group of six armed soldiers had gathered to warm themselves by a campfire and let their tsemus drink. If they had seen or heard signs of the *Galileo*'s arrival, they seemed unconcerned by it.

Jim was on the verge of muttering a curse. Trying to get past these six, obviously part of the Galactic Army of Light, would cost time. Attacking them directly would cost time as well.

He grinned suddenly. How could he have missed something so obvious? Here was the solution to their time problem standing right before them, tethered to a few scraggly desert trees.

"Captain?" Spock asked softly, puzzled by the abrupt change in Jim's expression.

"Mr. Spock, have you ever ridden a tsemu?"

"Indeed not, Captain."

"Well, you're about to have your first lesson."

A Rigellian homesteader named Arreed sat on his haunches in the sand and watched the fire with the others while his horse drank from the little spring. A mere five years ago, Arreed had come to Nimbus on the advice of his defense attorney. The plan had been to save Arreed from serving fifteen to twenty years of rehab for his small role in a plot to smuggle outlawed weaponry into the Federation—for collectors, of course, Arreed had assured the judge. At the time, Nimbus had sounded like a good idea; now Arreed promised himself that if he ever made it home, a certain Rigellian public defender would suffer. Nimbus made the rehab colonies, which many of Arreed's peers had frequented, sound luxurious in comparison.

No one had told him about the drought. It was impossible to make a living as a farmer here, even more ridiculous as a miner. The planet was as barren as its two moons, and just as devoid of anything valuable. Even his former skill, smuggling, was useless here: there was nothing worth smuggling, and no trader ships came near the planet, anyway. There was, quite simply, no escape.

Arreed was still young, and yet here he was on Nimbus, wasting away on a dry, worthless rock. Had there been the slightest chance of leaving—of stowing away on a vessel, perhaps—Arreed would have happily risked his life in the attempt. In the interim, he survived by virtue of his association with a band of thieves. There was no wealth to be had, but most times they were able to steal supplies: food, perhaps a freshly slaughtered tsemu, or property that could be bartered with the city dwellers for rations. Arreed had grown thin and bitter on such fare.

But recently something strange had happened to Jesha, the leader of the group. He spoke of a Vulcan called Sybok, who could free the others from the pain of existence. The others, one by one, had gone with Jesha to see this Vulcan, this Sybok, whom Jesha called a prophet. Soon the others refused to ply their trade against the homesteaders; Sybok had shown them the truth, they said, and they no longer had the desire to harm their co-worlders. Jesha said that Sybok would gladly do the same for Arreed, free the young Rigellian from his pain.

"Pain!" Arreed scoffed. The radical shift in philosophy mattered not to him, so long as he was well fed . . . and in truth, since the Vulcan had arrived, the group had not wanted for supplies. But he would not be forced into madness; his friends had turned into wild-eyed religious fools. This Sybok was nothing more than a hypnotist, and Arreed would be damned before he'd let a hypnotist control *him*. "All this ridiculous talk of pain! The only pain *I* feel is that of an empty stomach—from starving to death in the middle of this damnable desert!"

Then they told him about the starship.

He still refused to see the hypnotist, as he called the Vulcan, but he ceased his protests and did everything this Sybok ordered. When the starship came, Arreed promised himself, he would find a way to board her.

At the present moment, Arreed sat patiently with his friends and felt the warmth from the campfire in an effort to offset the night's growing chill. He could afford patience: it would not be long before he tasted freedom. Word had spread through Sybok's army that the Federation starship had arrived. Before long, Sybok would release it from the grasp of its crew as easily as one might steal money from a corpse. Arreed and his cohorts were one of three groups charged with the responsibility of guarding the outskirts of Paradise.

And, like the other groups, Arreed and his friends were caught up in the spirit of celebration at the news of the starship's arrival. Jesha had surreptitiously removed three bottles of fine liquor from the Paradise saloon and passed them around the circle of six. It had been some time since any of them had tasted hard liquor—a weak native wine was somewhat less rare, but in such demand that Arreed had not had any in the past month—and it was not long before all of them reached a festive level of intoxication. Arreed drank until he noticed that the campfire seemed to be slowly revolving.

Loud talk and much laughter followed. They were thus engaged when the shuttlecraft passed overhead, and none of them paid it any notice. Some moments later, however, something much subtler, much softer, caught Arreed's attention and held it.

A sound. Arreed reached out and grabbed the arm of a gesticulating companion, then raised a finger to his lips. The sound came again: Arreed strained this time to hear. The sound emanated from a point above and behind him: it was a woman singing, low and sweet.

Arreed turned. The sudden movement made his head spin, and he held the pose until the vertigo passed. There, on the crest of a gray-white dune, a female form swayed gracefully, silhouetted against the brightness of low-hanging twin moons. In the stillness, her song traveled easily to the oasis below; it spoke of seduction, of deep mystery.

For a heartbeat, no one moved, so startled were they by a sound of such ethereal loveliness in the desert. In one swift, simultaneous motion, the homesteaders scrambled to their feet. Women either rode with the gangs for protection or stayed within the questionable safety of the outpost walls. A woman alone in the desert was a remarkable rarity.

Too much so for Arreed and his companions to resist. He staggered toward the moonlit vision; he would have dismissed her as an apparition caused by the alcohol, but the others saw her, too. And so Arreed stumbled with difficulty through the yielding sand.

His mind was a swirl of bizarre and drunken thoughts, but he managed to seize upon one of them. His knowledge of human religious lore and custom was almost nonexistent, but he vaguely remembered human myths of a moon goddess. Perhaps this beauteous apparition was some sort of goddess of the moon—correction: *moons,* at least here on Nimbus—and she had appeared to them as a sign of . . . Here Arreed's questionable train of reasoning faltered. A sign of approval, perhaps, of what Sybok and his followers were doing, a sign that the starship was now theirs to command.

Arreed hiccuped and laughed aloud at the absurdity of such a thought as he lurched unevenly toward his goal. He prayed with his entire being that this was no goddess at all, but a real flesh and blood female. He had little use for goddesses, but a *woman . . .* the thought was altogether more divine. He reached the foot of the dune and began to climb on his hands and knees in the still-warm sand.

The climb took a great deal more effort than Arreed had anticipated; the dune was unusually tall and steep, and Arreed, who had been first, fell behind. He was gasping by the time he stopped three arm-lengths behind Jesha, who was by now near the summit. The woman was very nearly in their grasp. She stood only a few meters from them now, and in the moonglow, Arreed could see that she was as comely as her song: large-eyed, dark-skinned, slender. Clearly, she saw her pursuers, but instead of reacting with fear, she continued to sing, as if to welcome them.

I am having a dream, Arreed told himself, *the most wonderful dream imaginable.* He renewed his efforts, anxious to reach the dream's denouement.

Jesha cocked his head, then abruptly ended his pursuit—so abruptly that Arreed's face slammed into the heel of Jesha's boot—and turned his head to shout. Arreed cursed him, then turned to follow Jesha's gaze.

At the same time, he realized that a few seconds before, he had heard, but not entirely registered, a sound—a frightened neighing from the oasis far below.

Three dark figures had reached the campfire, and were stealing their horses.

Arreed roared with anger at the deceitful songstress. He reached for the knife on his belt; like fools, they had left the rifles back at the camp. Above him, Jesha fumbled for a weapon as well; the horses were lost, but at least they would have the pleasure of shredding the dark temptress to ribbons.

The music ceased. Startled by the absence of sound, Arreed glanced up at the summit; far from showing fear, the moon goddess was smiling. Each delicate hand held a phaser—one directed at Jesha's head, the other at Arreed's. On either side of her, uniformed Federation soldiers appeared, all of them similarly armed.

"I've always wanted to play to a 'captive' audience," the woman said.

Chapter Nine

KIRK DREW THE COWL of his stolen cape over his face to avoid breathing in the sand kicked up by the tsemus' hooves. The barrel-chested animals kept up an admirable pace: the stark night landscape hurtled past as Kirk and five of his crew—Spock, Sulu, McCoy, and two from the security team—drew closer to the glittering lights of Paradise. All six wore clothing surrendered by the captured members of the Galactic Army of Light; the long cloaks caught the chill breeze and whipped in the air.

Even in the darkness, Jim caught an eerie sight: moonlight glinting off the great bleached rib cage of an unfortunate tsemu. Jim's own mount was gasping and lathered from her effort. She was stockier and shaggier than any Earth horse, and the species had not had time to adjust to the abrupt changes in Nimbus's weather following the Great Drought. Still, she responded well enough to Jim's signals.

Spock rode close to captain. At first, Jim almost shouted for the Vulcan to allow more room between the animals, to avoid an accidental collision—until he looked over to see Spock, bouncing stiffly in the saddle, one hand on the reins, the other clutching the saddle horn for dear life. Jim grinned faintly, remembering his own unfortunate first experience on horseback, painful at the time, amusing only in retrospect. If this kept up, the Vulcan would be too sore to be of much help.

"Mr. Spock." Jim shouted to be heard over the thunder of the beasts' hooves.

"Yes, Captain?"

"You've never even ridden a *horse* horse, have you?"

The Vulcan's face was hidden in the shadows of his hood, but the dryness in his tone was quite evident. "Obviously."

Jim fought hard to repress a grin. "Look, Spock . . . the way you're bouncing up and down in the saddle—well, you could injure yourself. In a very vulnerable area, if you know what I mean."

A pause. "I'm afraid I'm well aware of that, Captain. Damage has already been done."

It was a good thing he couldn't see the Vulcan's face; if he had, he would probably have laughed aloud. As it was, he could no longer hold back a smile. "Loosen up your hips, Spock. You've got to sway. And the most important advice . . ." Kirk paused dramatically, unable to resist his chance for revenge.

Spock waited, still slapping miserably against the saddle.

"Be one with the horse."

Again, the faint rumble of thunder on the desert.

J'Onn stood on the high rampart of the city wall and squinted out at the darkness. This time, the sound reminded him not of rain, but of something ominous: the sound of approaching battle.

Fear brushed against him, but he refused to embrace it. Fear was no longer a part of him, or of what he and the rest of Sybok's army were about to do; yet, despite J'Onn's resolve, as the rhythmic thuds of hoofbeats increased, so did his uneasiness. He had joined the soldiers on the rampart not out of necessity, but out of restlessness . . . perhaps, in all honesty, out of impatience to see their commmon dream fulfilled: to capture a starship and escape from Nimbus, to at last be free after all these years.

He refused to even consider the possibility that one so deserving as Sybok might fail to see his destiny fulfilled.

One of the sentries directed a spotlight onto the desert, revealing a small band of riders. With a slight jolt of alarm, J'Onn recognized them; their unexpected, hasty arrival meant that something had gone wrong, seriously wrong. J'Onn shouted an order to the soldiers below.

"It's our lookout party! Open the gates!"

He turned back to gaze intently at the dark, shadowy figures on horseback as they approached the massive gate.

* * *

With the tsemus' help Kirk and the others arrived in a short time at the gates of the city. Stealing the soldiers' clothing had paid off; as the six approached the walls, the massive gate swung open to permit them entry.

The tsemus galloped in at full speed. Jim played his role to the hilt; cowl in place to hide his features, he shouted frantically at the sentries who stood high atop the wall at their lookout posts.

"Federation soldiers—about a kilometer behind us! Close the gate!"

Homesteaders scurried to draw the huge metal gate shut. Jim reined his mount to a halt; Spock and the others followed suit. Crowds of men and women swept past, ignoring them. One settler, however—an emaciated, balding male from Regulus—headed right for Kirk. His manner clearly indicated that he was in charge . . . and the way he was frowning made Jim distinctly nervous. Kirk tipped his head back and shouted at the sentries: "There's more than a hundred of them! Fortify the walls!"

It worked. The Regulan hesitated, then grabbed the shoulder of a passing homesteader and began barking orders as he pointed a bony finger at a high rampart.

Jim released his breath silently, then glanced at Spock beside him. The Vulcan gave a slight, almost imperceptible nod: the coordinates lay directly down the unpaved dirt street. As nonchalantly as possible, Jim coaxed his horse in the direction Spock had indicated. The group rode slowly down the street; no point in attracting any more attention than they already had.

On the rooftops of the run-down, dingy buildings

huddled more members of the Army of Light, each of them armed with crude—but probably very deadly, Jim reminded himself—rifles. If they were to become suspicious of the six riders on the street below . . .

Fortunately, the soldiers' attention was consumed by the commotion as reinforcements scaled the walls. Several soldiers struggled to place a gigantic metal bolt across the gate. One by one, so as to not arouse suspicion, Sulu and the two from security stole away from the group to lay down cover for the upcoming escape.

"Spock," Kirk whispered, when he was certain they were not being watched.

"Hold your horse, Captain," Spock replied quietly. "I am scanning." The Vulcan had effectively concealed a tricorder beneath his black robes; now he held it uncovered, but too low for anyone but those beside him to notice. Jim detected a faint hum as the device did its work. Spock glanced furtively at the readout, then inclined his head toward an area a few dozen meters away. "The hostages are in the structure just ahead."

Jim looked. It was an unappealing two-story box of a building with old-fashioned swinging doors, a rickety porch, and, facing the street, a single large window so dust-covered that peering inside was impossible. Flashing across its filthy surface in illuminated letters was the legend:

PARADISE SALOON

Kirk shielded his communicator with his hand and cautiously raised it to his lips. *"Galileo,* this is Strike Team. Start your run."

"Aye, sir," Uhura's voice replied. "On my way."

Timing was now critical. If the strike team failed to free the hostages by the time the shuttlecraft arrived at the city, the mission would have to be aborted . . . and the time necessary to regroup would give the Klingons a chance to arrive and blow the planet—not to mention the *Enterprise*—off the charts. Jim refused to think about what might happen if the shuttlecraft failed to show.

He replaced his communicator and nudged his tsemu toward the saloon.

While the others on the ramparts directed their attention to the desert, J'Onn alone turned to see where the recently arrived lookout party had gone. The sense of foreboding he'd experienced since he first heard the sound of hootbeats pounding across the desert increased steadily. There was something not quite right about the group, something indefinably *wrong* . . .

J'Onn peered down the dim, unpaved street and saw the dark figures, still on horseback. "Where are *they* going?" he asked no one in particular. They were not, as they should have been, hurrying to fortify the walls.

Instead, they were cautiously making their way toward the saloon, toward Sybok and the diplomats.

In a flash of understanding and rage, J'Onn dashed to the nearest spotlight and swung it so that its brilliant beam flooded down onto the intruders.

Kirk was immediately blinded by a painfully brilliant beam of light. The masquerade was over. He shielded his eyes with his left hand and squinted; someone high on a rampart was shining a spotlight on them. His left hand dove for the phaser hidden beneath his cloak. "Phasers on stun! Get rid of the mounts! Sulu, take out that light!"

Graceful as a centaur, Sulu spurred his steed. Together they charged the spotlight, ignoring the blasts of pebbles that whizzed by them. As they neared the giant light, Sulu half rose in his saddle and took aim. A beam of pure force streamed from his phaser into the center of the spotlight, shattering it.

The street darkened instantly, lit now only by the flare of weapons and the faint illumination coming from inside the saloon. The soldiers on the rooftops opened fire.

At the sound of gunfire, Sybok turned away from the communications screen, where he had been engaged in a pointless and frustrating dialogue with the starship captain. He had been on the verge of threatening violence—a lie, of course, but how was the Federation to know?—against his captives when the sounds of battle floated into the room.

He was seized by sudden irrational fury. How dare the Federation try to trick him! If they would only try to understand what he was trying to do . . . but people were never willing to change, to listen to reason. All they understood was force.

"What's going on?" Sybok demanded of the image on the screen. His voice shook with ill-contained rage.

The starship captain did not flinch at the display of temper. "I instruct you to surrender at once," Chekov said. His voice was as cold and hard as flint. "You are under attack by superior Federation forces. There is no way for you to win, and no way to escape."

"You *fool!*" Sybok exploded. He brought a fist down hard beside the terminal, denting the metal surface of the desk. The outmoded keyboard rattled. "Do you realize what you've done? Now there will be killing! It wasn't bloodshed I was after!" Robes furling, the Vulcan turned to leave.

"Wait—" Chekov protested. But it was too late.

Grieved and angered by the sounds of violence, Sybok strode from the room.

Spock was first to make it through the gunfire and stampeding tsemus to the saloon. He dismounted with silent thanks to the creature for its assistance. The direct physical contact with it had allowed for a small degree of mental contact as well. The tsemus were benevolent beings, of limited intelligence but nonetheless highly adaptable, as their survival despite Nimbus's severe climactic changes proved. Spock had found the mental experience most pleasant; and, in time, the physical experience had grown less painful, for the more he concentrated on his mount's thoughts (or, more accurately, its sensations) the easier it became to attune his body to the animal's movements.

The creature snorted as if in response to his expression of gratitude. Spock left it untethered so that its chances of making it to safety would be improved. He hoped he would have no further need of its help.

Spock had scarcely turned his back on the tsemu to dash into the saloon when an odd combination of sounds—the dull slap of clothed flesh against leather, followed by the tsemu's nervous whinny—made him look back. A homesteader had leapt from the saloon's balcony onto the creature's back—and landed directly in the saddle. Spock felt faint admiration for the skill necessary to accomplish such a feat—but the emotion was short-lived. The soldier brandished a sword and urged the animal forward; it was quite clear that his intent was for the tsemu to trample Spock to death.

In a matter of a few seconds, Spock found himself pressed against the side of the building with no obvious means of escape. The soldier tugged hard at the reins, forcing the frightened, reluctant animal to rear up on its hind legs; the tsemu's hard, keratinous hooves grazed Spock's chest.

He reached for the phaser hidden beneath his cloak, intending to stun the soldier, but before he could take aim, the tsemu reared again, knocking the weapon from Spock's hand.

He was left with no alternative. Spock relaxed and caught the animal's eye. Although he was a touch telepath, perhaps at this perilously close distance, he would be able to communicate his intent to the tsemu.

He concentrated. The creature, as if in response to the message, loomed even closer. Spock sidled toward it, and this time with a silent word of apology, reached out with his right hand. It rested upon a massive, bunched muscle in the tsemu's shoulder.

Spock squeezed.

The tsemu's dark green eyes rolled back until nothing but blue-veined whites showed. It gave a shrill little cry, then, with a rumble, toppled onto its flank.

The rider barely managed to scramble out of the huge creature's way in time. He paused, stunned, and gaped at Spock in disbelief for a few seconds—then dropped the sword and ran away.

Meanwhile, Kirk thundered up the saloon steps on horseback. As he swung down from the saddle, his peripheral vision caught a dark blur—an approaching soldier. Instinctively, he fired his already-drawn phaser. The soldier fell backward, unconscious.

Cautiously, Kirk stepped through the swinging double doors, The room was dark and empty, and for an instant Kirk felt a twinge of disappointment; it seemed Spock's renegade friend had taken the hostages and gone. And then, as his eyes grew accustomed to the dimness, he saw a doorway at the far end of the room. Hopefully, he began to make his way toward it.

He was halfway there when he heard a shrill yowl behind him and felt the stab of claws ripping deep into the flesh of his back.

Spock found that retrieving the phaser was impossible: the heavy beast had fallen on it, and lifting its bulk was too great a challenge even for a Vulcan. Spock left the weapon behind and made his way through the old-fashioned swinging doors into the dimly lit saloon.

The only light was furnished by the blue glow of a terminal screen. The army's leader must have stood here only moments before, talking to Chekov. . . .

"Spock," Jim said. He stepped forward out of the shadows, gasping and rearranging his cloak. At the same instant Spock noticed an unconscious felinoid floating face up in a shallow gaming pool. Water had sloshed onto the dusty floor and the front of Jim's cloak, leaving a dark stain. The water in the pool was still rippling; something had happened only seconds before Spock stepped through the entrance.

Questions were unnecessary. Spock directed his attention to possible routes of escape from the barroom and came to the same conclusion as Jim. Without a word, the two made their way to a closed door in the rear of the saloon. Jim tested it; the door was locked. The captain drew his phaser and focused a small beam directly on the lock.

The door slid open a half-meter; Spock pushed it the rest of the way while Kirk kept his phaser trained on whoever was inside.

"Thank God," Jim breathed. Spock sensed the captain relax next to him.

He looked up. He had expected to encounter the Vulcan, but the leader had apparently fled. Indeed, there were no soldiers inside—only three distinctly well-fed, well-dressed individuals seated at a round table. Spock recognized them from the images he'd seen aboard the *Enterprise:* the wan, dissolute image of St. John Talbot; the aging, jowly features of the Klingon general, Korrd; and the severe, somber features of the curiously named Romulan female, Caithlin Dar.

The three looked up, startled, as Spock and Kirk entered. Spock caught sight of the captain's face: Jim was regarding Korrd with a mixture of admiration and pity.

Jim lowered his phaser and strode quickly to the

table. "Captain James Kirk of the Federation starship *Enterprise*. Gentlemen, madam . . . if you will come with us, please. I'm afraid there isn't much time."

"There's quite enough time, Captain." Dar rose gracefully from her chair and, keeping her arm stiff and straight, aimed a handmade pistol at Jim's forehead.

"What the hell—" Jim started to reach for his phaser, but stopped when Dar cocked the weapon with an ominous click. Flanking her, Talbot and Korrd rose, brandishing pistols of their own. Korrd pointed the barrel of his weapon squarely at Spock's chest. Resistance seemed unwise. Spock raised his hands to show that he was unarmed.

"Please cooperate," Dar said, with an earnestness that was compelling.

The expression of muted euphoria in her eyes told Spock what he most dreaded: that he had correctly recognized her messiah . . . and would soon face him again, after many years.

"I do not wish to kill you," Dar said, "but I will, if necessary."

With eminent sobriety, Talbot came forward and extended a hand toward Kirk and Spock. "Would you mind handing over those weapons, gentlemen?"

"It appears," Spock said to his frowning captain, "that the hostages have taken *us* hostage."

Dar and the others led them out onto the dusty street, where swarms of homesteaders, some of them bearing torches, gathered around the captured shuttlecraft. A disheveled Dr. McCoy scowled at the captor who prodded him along with a rifle.

"This is a fine pickle, Jim," McCoy said acidly, as he joined them.

Perhaps, Spock reflected, the doctor was employing a Standard metaphor. The Vulcan had actually sampled a pickle on what turned out to be a less than pleasant occasion. Indeed, his reaction at that time was, figuratively speaking, quite similar to his (private) reaction to the current situation.

Jim's expression remained grim. "I thought I told you not to come."

"I suppose you did," McCoy admitted grudgingly. He fell silent as the shuttlecraft hatch opened.

Uhura and two security personnel were herded out by soldiers with stolen phasers. In a moment, they, too, joined Kirk and the others. "I'm sorry, sir," Uhura said softly as she stepped up next to Kirk.

His reply went unheard over the deafening shouts from the crowd. Spock glanced up to see a white-robed figure emerging from the shuttle. The soldiers began to chant his name: "Sybok! Sybok! Sybok!"

"Well done, my friends," Sybok cried over the noise. "Well done." He lifted his hands for silence; the gesture only encouraged another round of cheers. The Vulcan lowered his hood, revealing his profile, set against a frame of indigo hair. His face was strong and square.

Spock drew in a sudden breath . . . then regained control of himself and released it slowly. He had known who it was, of course, the instant he heard the name. But the sight of him brought a deluge of bitter memories. Spock found himself struggling to suppress the sense of betrayal that came with them.

He took a cautious step forward. In the periphery of his vision, he saw Dar tighten her grip on the pistol. He waited another moment, then took a second tentative step.

"Sybok." Spock struggled to be heard over the shouting; his voice blended with those of the homesteaders. Frustrated, he cried: *"Qual se tu, Sybok?"*

He asked the question in Vulcan. He asked without reflecting on his choice of words, scarcely realizing until after the words were out of his mouth that he had used the intimate pronoun—the one reserved for one's *t'hyla,* one's closest friend or dearest relative. At one time, Sybok had been both. Still later, he realized that he had phrased the question exactly as he had at their parting.

Qual se tu? "Is it thou?"

The question echoed across the span of thirty years. Spock recalled himself at thirteen, asking the same question with such anguish . . . and turning away bitterly upon hearing the answer.

He was aware of Jim and McCoy's quizzical glances, and of the sounds of pistols cocking, including Dar's, and he knew that almost every weapon on the street was aimed at him. Yet he could not stop now. He took another step forward.

At the sound of Spock's voice, Sybok stiffened and tilted his head to one side; his expression of triumph faded, replaced by one of haunted recognition. He did not turn to face his questioner; Spock got a brief mental impression that Sybok was afraid to do so.

At Sybok's reaction, the crowd fell silent. Boldly, Spock demanded again: *"Qual se tu?"*

In the glow from a nearby torch, Spock saw Sybok's

lips move silently. He read the response they formed —the same answer he had given thirty years before.

"I am he. . . ."

Sybok pivoted and faced Spock from a distance of several meters. At the sight of the other Vulcan's unmistakable face, posture, expression—even half shadowed as they were in the flickering torchlight— Spock wondered why he had ever doubted Sybok's identity at all.

"Spock," Sybok breathed, his voice choked with emotion.

Spock forced himself not to turn away in distaste; but a much younger part of him experienced a tug of love and pain. He remained carefully composed, aware of a hundred awed gazes directed at him. Even Dar saw, and lowered her weapon somewhat.

"Spock!"

The shout was one of pure joy. The crowd parted before Sybok as he rushed to embrace his fellow Vulcan.

Spock stopped him with a gesture.

Sybok came to a halt an arm's length away. Spock read the hurt and confusion on his face . . . No, perhaps he was not being honest with himself. He *felt* Sybok's hurt and confusion. Intentionally, Spock reinforced his mental and emotional shields against unwanted intrusion. His link to Sybok belonged to the dead past.

Sybok's expression traveled through many emotions: love, hate, bitterness, anger, love again. Spock thought it was rather like watching a constantly shifting pattern of clouds on a windy day. At last, Sybok's features resolved themselves into a look of wary amusement. He smiled wryly and, to Spock's utter dismay, switched to Standard. Their communication would now be public—Sybok's retaliation, perhaps, for the slight.

"Still tight-assed," Sybok said, nodding. Despite his wounded feelings, there was genuine fondness in his tone. "Still believing everything your elders told you. You haven't changed a bit since you were thirteen, Spock. I was hoping you'd grown a little since then."

Clearly, Sybok was trying to elicit an emotional reaction. Stone-faced, Spock stared at him.

Sybok made a desperate sweeping gesture, palms outward. "Spock, it's *me*. It's Sybok. More than thirty years, and you've finally caught up with me. Isn't there anything that you want to *say?*"

"Yes," Spock admitted.

Sybok waited a beat, then, exasperated, asked, *"Well?"*

"You are under arrest for violating seventeen counts of the Neutral Zone treaty."

It did not have the effect Spock anticipated. Sybok's black eyes widened. "Spock, there must be a hundred guns pointed at your heart!"

"Sixty-three by my count," Spock replied levelly, without a trace of humor.

Sybok's face underwent another series of amazing transformations, from incredulity to skepticism to amusement. He took a step back, put a hand on his stomach, and laughed.

He continued laughing, eventually clutching his midsection with both arms, until tears glittered in his eyes. His soldiers joined in. Soon the entire crowd, with the exception of the *Enterprise* crew, was howling with laughter. Spock saw nothing amusing whatsoever about the situation.

"Why, Spock," Sybok gasped finally, "you've developed a sense of humor after all. Good for you. Now, if you could just master contractions . . ."

"It was not my intention to amuse you," Spock replied coldly. "These are serious charges. If you surrender now—"

Sybok shook his head and waved Spock's words away with a sweep of his hand. "I'm sorry, Spock, but I can't surrender now. I'm not through violating the Neutral Zone treaty. In fact, I'm just getting started. And for my next violation, I intend to steal something. Something very *big.*"

Spock stared at him. He suspected what Sybok was hinting at, but found himself quite unable to believe it.

"I must have your starship." Sybok was no longer smiling.

Indignant, angry, Kirk took a step forward. "You staged this to get your hands on my ship!"

Sybok swiveled his head to give him an annoyed glance. "Who are you?"

"James T. Kirk, captain of the *Enterprise.*"

Sybok's eyebrows lifted. "But I thought Chekov . . ." He broke off and smiled again briefly. "I see. Very clever, Captain." He turned back to Spock. "Spock, it would appear that you've been given a second chance to join me. What do you say?"

Spock's placid expression belied the inward surge of emotion, for which he berated himself. There was no question of his loyalty to his captain, to the *Enterprise,* to her crew . . . and it was absurd that after all this time, his response to Sybok should be tinged with regret, even sorrow.

"I am a Starfleet officer," he said. "I shall do everything in my power to stop you."

The briefest flicker of pain crossed Sybok's face and was gone, replaced by an expression as cold as Spock's own.

"Very well," Sybok responded, with serene confidence. "Then I'll take the ship without your help."

He turned his back on them.

"That's telling him, Spock," McCoy hissed. "Chekov and Scotty'll never let him aboard unless we cooperate with him."

"Doctor," Spock replied slowly, "I know for a fact that Sybok is extremely intelligent and resourceful. If he says he will take the ship without my help, he will most certainly do so."

"Shuttle en route," Scott said.

Chekov caught himself nervously drumming his fingers on the arm of the command console and forced himself to stop. Things were not going at all the way they were supposed to. The leader of the terrorist army had severed all communications, and none of the landing party responded to signals. By this time, the *Galileo 5* should have been requesting permission to enter the hangar deck, but no one aboard the shuttlecraft answered Chekov's signals on any frequency.

"Position Bird of Prey?" Chekov asked.

Scott's expression was grave. "Closing."

Something had obviously gone wrong. Chekov

hoped he was wrong, of course, but instinct told him he was not. *Galileo* and all aboard her were in serious trouble—perhaps captured, perhaps killed.

Still, reason demanded that he wait until the last possible moment to hear from the captain. And that moment was fast approaching, along with a Klingon vessel.

Okrona closed in on Nimbus III and her quarry, *Enterprise.*

Klaa hovered over his first officer as Vixis sat at her station, her attention glued to the scanner readout. Both of them started as *Enterprise* appeared with a loud blip on the screen.

Klaa composed himself. After exchanging a triumphant glance with Vixis, he drew a hand briefly along her strong, graceful shoulder before moving to his gunner's rig.

Vixis squinted at the data filling her screen. "Estimating attack range in . . . eight thousand kellicams."

Klaa fastened himself into the rig and lowered his targeting sight. His fingers trembled slightly in anticipation of the glory to come. "Stealth approach," he snapped at Tarag. "Slow to one-quarter impulse power. Prepare to cloak."

The siren howled; the bridge pulsed with red light. Klaa felt his heart beat faster. "Engage cloaking device," he said, and congratulated himself silently on his ability to keep the excitement from his tone.

Okrona would cloak, steal unobserved into firing range, and with one or two well-placed hits, destroy the *Enterprise* and all aboard her, and James Kirk would never know who had killed him.

In a way, it was a pity. But Klaa's ultimate dream was now within his grasp, and he would not jeopardize it by announcing *Okrona*'s arrival.

There was nothing anyone could do now to stop him.

Scott, who had been huddled over Spock's viewer, finally raised his head and peered grimly at Chekov. "Mr. Chekov, I've lost the Bird of Prey. She must have cloaked."

Chekov nodded; he understood what such a tactic meant. The Klingons would remain invisible until they appeared without warning and fired on the *Enterprise*.

The best Chekov could do was to second-guess them . . . but the risk of doing so was too great.

"Raise shields," he ordered reluctantly. With shields in place the ship was protected from attack . . . but the *Galileo,* wherever she was, would be unable to dock while those shields were up.

Scott began to protest. "But the shuttle—"

"*Do* it," Chekov said.

Scott sighed and programmed the command into the computer, then squinted at the brightly colored graphic that winked onto his terminal screen. It showed *Enterprise,* surrounded by a glowing force field and thus off-limits to both Klingon phaser blasts . . .

And those aboard *Galileo V.*

Chapter Ten

GALILEO MADE HER WAY HOMEWARD. Sulu and Uhura piloted her under the supervision of armed guards, while Kirk sat between Spock and McCoy and stared glumly down the rifle barrel pointed at his face. Across the aisle, Sybok conferred earnestly with the diplomats. The leader sat backwards in his passenger's chair so as to address Caithlin, Korrd, and Talbot, all of whom sat in the row behind him. Sybok spoke in tones too soft for Kirk to make out; Jim suspected they were discussing the takeover of the *Enterprise.* Perhaps Spock, with his keen hearing, could pick up what they were saying.

Jim glanced over at the Vulcan sitting next to him. Spock appeared to have mentally detached himself from his surroundings; he sat, mute and stone-faced, his eyes focused straight ahead at nothing. Jim got the impression that he was ashamed of whatever connection he had to the leader of the Galactic Army of Light.

As for himself, Jim had experienced an undeniable revelation: He was reacting exactly as he would have had someone tried to steal the old *Enterprise*. Spaceworthy or not, the new *Enterprise* was *his* ship and he'd be damned before he let a lunatic Vulcan and his fanatical army of zealots have her.

"Hey," Jim said suddenly in a loud, irritable voice. He addressed Sybok and his group. "What do you intend to do with my ship?"

Sybok paused to frown over at him, then nodded at Talbot, who rose from his seat and walked over to Kirk. Sybok went back to speaking in the same hushed, unintelligible drone.

As Talbot made his way over, McCoy whispered in Jim's left ear, "They sure don't appear to have been tortured, do they?"

"Drugs?" Jim asked softly, conscious of the rifle aimed at him, but the guard did not seem to mind if he conversed with the doctor.

"This long-lasting? Haven't seen any hypos yet." McCoy lifted his shoulders in a skeptical shrug.

Talbot arrived and smiled amiably at them. As the doctor had pointed out, the man appeared perfectly normal, not at all like someone who had undergone the agony of a mind-sifter; Jim had seen a few of those victims, and there had been nothing left of them but physical shells. Talbot, however, appeared quite cheerful—perhaps *too* cheerful, considering the circumstances. There was a joyous animation in his features that had been entirely lacking in his Starfleet file holo.

"Captain Kirk," Talbot intoned, with such dignity and warmth that Kirk could understand why the diplomatic service had chosen him. "What can I do for you—besides setting you free, that is?"

Talbot's charm did not dampen any of the anger Jim felt. "I want to know what the hell you intend to do with my ship!"

The diplomat chuckled politely. "Hell has very little to do with it, actually. Very little, indeed." At Jim's furious glare, he hastened to add, "Once we've taken control of the *Enterprise*, we'll bring up the rest of our followers."

Sulu interrupted with a terse announcement. "Approaching *Enterprise*, Captain." He switched on the shuttle's main viewer; the starship filled the small screen.

Kirk opened his mouth to respond, but Sybok responded faster. "Tell them," the Vulcan said, "that we wish to land."

Uhura looked askance at the captain; when Kirk nodded, she swiveled in her chair to face the control panel. "*Enterprise*, this is *Galileo Five*. Request permission to begin landing procedure."

Kirk turned back to Talbot. "You'll bring up the rest of your followers. And then . . . ?"

"Sybok will fill you in on the details. Later. After he deals with your . . . attitude." Talbot's smile took on a faintly ominous tinge.

"Look," Jim said, his volume rising with his frustration, "Our transporter's out, and the Klingons are out there. Why don't you ask General Korrd what their reaction is likely to be? We'll be lucky to get back to the ship ourselves. With a Klingon vessel in the area, my people will—"

He broke off as Chekov's voice filtered over the shuttle's radio. *"Galileo,* this is *Enterprise.* Condition red alert. Bird of Prey approaching. She is cloaked. Raising shields. Recommend *Galileo* find safe harbor until situation secure. Acknowledge."

Awaiting instruction, Uhura and Sulu both turned from the control panel and fastened their attention on Kirk. He was about to reply—until his guard nudged him with the rifle barrel. Sybok looked up from his conference with Caithlin and Korrd.

"No reply," Sybok said with maddening calm. "Remain on course."

Kirk forced himself not to explode angrily—to do so meant he risked having his head blown off with stone pellets, an unattractive prospect. He took a slow breath, then said, with the same degree of serenity as the Vulcan leader, "Sybok, listen to me. For this craft to enter the landing bay, *Enterprise* must lower shields and activate the tractor beam. To bring us aboard and then raise the shields again will take—" He hesitated, groping for an approximate figure.

For the first time since leaving Nimbus, Spock spoke up. "Exactly fifteen-point-five seconds." He did not look at either Jim or Sybok.

Kirk nodded vigorously. "An eternity, during which time we'll be vulnerable to a Klingon attack." In desperation, he addressed the Klingon diplomat. "General Korrd, tell him."

Korrd shifted his girth in his chair to face Kirk and Sybok. After a moment's consideration, he said, in a

160

deep bass voice, "Kirk speaks the truth. If my people are cloaked, they intend to strike." He began to say more, stopped himself, then decided to continue. "One more thing you should know, Sybok. My people have a quarrel with Kirk. There is a bounty on his head. I have no doubt they intend to destroy the *Enterprise,* and they will certainly destroy this shuttle if they discover he is aboard. Your plan is in grave jeopardy."

Still unruffled, Sybok spread his hands in a gesture of helplessness. "What can we do? We are in destiny's hands now. We cannot turn back."

Kirk sat forward in his chair, causing the soldier who guarded him to tighten his grip on the rifle. "Then let me do something," Jim urged.

Sybok regarded him suspiciously. With deliberate movements, he rose and walked over to where Spock sat next to Kirk. The first officer did not acknowledge his acquaintance's presence with so much as a glance.

"What say you, Spock?" Sybok asked. It was evident that Spock was the only one whose counsel Sybok valued.

Spock drew a breath and finally met his adversary's gaze. Kirk thought he saw rebuke in Spock's eyes.

"You must allow us to act," Spock said. "The alternative is to see your 'plan' fail." He looked away again.

But Sybok appeared satisfied. "Very well." He nodded at Kirk. "Do what you must, but no more. Trickery will be punished."

Sybok handed Kirk his communicator. Jim flipped the grid open; he was not quite sure what he was going to say until he actually said it.

"Enterprise, this is Kirk aboard *Galileo.* We understand the situation, but are unable to return to the planet. Stand by to execute"—he faltered, then pulled a name out of the air—"Emergency Landing Plan B."

Confused silence over the airwaves. Then Chekov said, *"Galileo,* we did not copy that last message. Can you repeat?"

Kirk thought grimly, *Translation: We know you're in trouble, but what the hell is Emergency Landing Plan B?*

"Execute Emergency Landing Plan B," he repeated, then added, as inspiration struck him, "That's *B* as in 'barricade.'" *Come on, Chekov, read my mind.*

"Aye, sir," Chekov replied uncertainly. "Executing."

Kirk turned back to Sybok, whose expression was distrustful. Jim offered an explanation. "In order to lower and raise shields as quickly as possible, we're going to forgo the tractor beam and fly in manually."

He felt the doctor tense beside him. *"Man*ually?" McCoy gasped, horrified.

Sybok noted the reaction and addressed himself to Sulu. "Commander, how often have you done this?"

Sulu turned from the controls to face the Vulcan. "Actually," he answered, with a smoothness Jim silently applauded, "it's my first attempt." He returned to his controls—but not before Kirk caught his eye. Sulu was smugly enjoying Sybok's discomfort, as well as feeling a little nervous about the idea himself.

Sybok stared wide-eyed at Jim, who shrugged. "He's good, really," Jim said. Like Sulu, he took some grim pleasure in the fact that Sybok did not appear reassured. Jim raised his communicator again. "Scotty. On my mark . . . open bay doors."

All aboard the shuttlecraft watched as, on the screen, the massive hangar doors began to part.

Aboard *Okrona,* Klaa and his bridge crew listened to the exchange between the tiny shuttlecraft and the *Enterprise.* Klaa was strapped into his gunner's rig, ready for the instant the starship dropped its shields to bring *Galileo* aboard.

"Kirk!" Klaa threw back his head and howled in triumph. "He's aboard the shuttlecraft! Tarag, alter attack course."

Tarag complied as quickly as he was able. The *Okrona* swung itself around to fire at the *Enterprise*'s underbelly, where the bay doors were parting in preparation for *Galileo 5*'s arrival.

Klaa peered into his targeting scope. The gods were being kind, almost too kind. He could blast James Kirk out of existence this very second, but Klaa realized if he was patient, he could have more than just Kirk—he could have the *Enterprise,* as well. A single undeflected blast right into open hangar doors would rend the ship in two, or at least cripple her beyond all repair.

Klaa's trigger finger twitched slightly on the phaser control. "Stand by to decloak for firing," he told his helmsman, then held his breath and waited for the tiny craft to swim into his target crosshairs.

Kirk raised his communicator to his lips. "Kirk to Scotty—lower shields!"

Scott's reluctant tone came over the grid. "Lowering shields, sir . . ."

Kirk drew in a breath.

"Captain!" Uhura cried. The Klingon vessel loomed threateningly on the screen. "Bird of Prey, bearing one-zero-five-mark-two!"

"Go, Sulu!" Kirk ordered.

Sulu fired the aft thrusters; the shuttle roared to life. As if propelled by a gigantic slingshot, *Galileo* sailed toward the opening bay doors of the *Enterprise*. Pressed against his seat by the sudden acceleration, Jim stared at the sight on the screen. The hangar doors were parting slowly, wider at the bottom than at the top—but not wide enough, it seemed, to permit the shuttle passage. A glance at Sulu's ashen face was confirmation enough.

Galileo was going to pulp herself on the hangar doors.

"My God." McCoy turned pale and tightened his restraints.

"Brace yourselves!" Sulu shouted. "I'm going to bring her in low!"

Galileo shuddered and began to labor, vibrating as if she might break apart. Even with restraints, Jim was crushed against McCoy; Spock, in turn, was thrown against the captain. Jim struggled in vain to watch what was happening on the viewer, but the screen was a chaotic blur of images.

An explosion rocked the shuttle, followed by the horrible grinding screech of metal scraping against metal. For a moment, Jim thought the craft had caught on the doors and was being torn in half—but the cabin remained intact. They had actually made it into the bay, and the noise was that of the pontoons being sheared off. Jim braced himself for the final collision against the hangar's retaining wall . . . or the Klingon phaser blast that was sure to follow them in.

Klaa gaped in surprise as *Galileo,* in a shocking burst of speed, moved out of his sights and into the safety of the hangar bay. He uttered a curse that shed doubt on the fidelity of Kirk's mother and positioned his weapons directly on the now-closing hangar doors. Klaa still had a chance to blow both Kirk and the *Enterprise* straight to hell. "Bear on *Enterprise!*" he thundered at Vixis.

She answered immediately; she was an excellent strategist and had anticipated Klaa's order. *"Enterprise* targeted."

"Firing!" Klaa squeezed the trigger.

The *Enterprise* disappeared. One moment she was there; the next, gone. Klaa's wasted shot dispersed in the void of space.

"Track her course!" Klaa roared. He could not let Kirk go; he had been humiliated in front of his crew. If he failed now to destroy both Kirk and the *Enterprise,* stories of his failure would circulate throughout the Empire. Klaa the Invincible, vanquished by a human criminal, James Kirk. Not so invincible, after all.

No matter where the *Enterprise* went, Klaa would follow, even if he had to pursue Kirk all the way to Earth itself. Sourly, he detached himself from his gunner's rig and climbed back into his chair. The crew, of course, knew better than to speak to the captain after his ego had suffered such an outrage . . . but after a time, Klaa shook his head and muttered under his breath. He was thinking about James Kirk, and admitting to a certain degree of grudging admiration.

"He is good."

Galileo 5 groaned to a halt.

Kirk waited, dazed, for the annihilating blast that would surely follow. It didn't.

In the briefest of seconds, a sense of gratitude stole over him. The hangar's cargo net must have been activated, preventing the shuttlecraft from slamming against the retaining wall. And the fact that they were still alive meant only one thing: the ship's shields were up, and had responded with split-second timing. She had performed beautifully . . . No, more than that. She had saved their lives. Jim uttered a soundless apology to the *Enterprise*.

Galileo lay smoldering on the deck. Jim struggled free of his restraints, aware that his every movement further crushed McCoy, who lay pinned beneath him. At first he could not see Spock; the Vulcan had been thrown clear of his restraints. A brief scan of the shuttle's interior revealed Spock, tangled in a heap with Korrd and the Romulan woman. Spock was unconscious, but Jim could see no injuries.

Beneath Jim, McCoy moaned.

"Bones? You okay?" Jim managed to get to his feet. The floor tilted slightly to one side.

The doctor made a low growl to indicate that he was alive but not necessarily okay. "I take it back," McCoy muttered. "What I said before about the new ship . . . I take it all back."

Jim judged Bones dazed but unhurt and decided to

check on Spock. There was no time. Nearby, Sybok struggled to his feet. Jim looked around for the nearest weapon and dashed for it. A phaser lay on the deck, only a few feet away—

He didn't make it. When he was halfway there, Sybok rose and aimed one of the primitive pistols at his chest.

"We must change course at once," Sybok demanded.

Jim thought fast. "To do that, we'll have to go to the bridge. I can take you there."

"Very well." The Vulcan gestured at the hatch with the pistol.

Jim pressed the hatch control; luckily, it was still functional. The hatch doors opened easily. Sybok gestured for him to go first. Jim crawled out of the wounded craft and waited for Sybok.

Trying to run for safety was foolish; the huge landing bay was too open, too exposed. Sybok would be able to pick him off handily. Better to wait, and stop the Vulcan before they made it to the bridge.

Sybok followed and gingerly stepped out, steadying himself with one hand. At the point where his balance was most precarious, Jim reached out a hand as if to offer help . . .

And grabbed the pistol.

Sybok pulled it back. Both lost their footing and tumbled to the hangar floor. Amazingly, Sybok kept his grip on the weapon, but could not regain his balance to take aim. Kirk flailed at him. With his free hand, Sybok struggled to hold Kirk at bay.

The Vulcan's strength was incredible, even greater than Spock's; with one hand, he caught hold of Jim's wrist and began to squeeze it. Jim yelped in pain; the Vulcan, if he continued, would crush the bone to powder. Desperately, Kirk continued to try with his other hand to free the weapon from Sybok's grasp, even though he saw little hope of succeeding.

And then, over Sybok's shoulder, Jim caught sight of Spock. Sybok was distracted by the sound of someone crawling out of the shuttle. He turned to see who it was.

Jim let go of the pistol and kicked at it with his entire strength.

The weapon clattered to the floor. Before Sybok could recover, Kirk kicked the pistol again until it skittered over to *Galileo,* and came to rest at Spock's feet.

Spock stared blankly at the weapon in front of him.

Infuriated, Sybok increased the pressure on Jim's wrist. Kirk groaned as Sybok forced him to his knees, then gathered his strength to cry out.

"Spock! For God's sake, pick it up!" His voice reverberated in the huge empty chamber.

Spock snapped to as if awakening from a dream. Obediently, he picked up the weapon with obvious distaste. Sybok freed Kirk and faced his adversary. Kirk sat on the floor, cradling his injured arm, and watched.

Spock raised the weapon. "Sybok, you must surrender."

Sybok smiled faintly and took a step toward his fellow Vulcan. Spock gestured threateningly with the weapon; Sybok stopped. "Perhaps," he said softly, "it's my turn to ask *Qual se tu,* eh, Spock? Or perhaps

Et tu, Brute would be more appropriate." He took another step.

"Do not force me to shoot," Spock said, his tone faintly unsteady.

Sybok shook his head; his voice saddened. "Spock, you and I both know that you can't stun me with that weapon. And I've always been stronger than you. If you want to stop me, you're going to have to kill me."

Spock aimed the pistol at a spot just below Sybok's right rib cage, at his heart.

Sybok continued to advance.

"Spock!" Jim cried. He could see the resolve on Spock's face vanishing. "Shoot him!"

Spock cocked the pistol. In the silence, Jim heard the pellets advance into the chamber.

Sybok began to advance; soon he was a mere arm's length from the weapon's barrel.

Spock's finger tightened on the trigger, then relaxed. The pistol began to tremble very slightly.

Sybok gave a warm smile and put a hand on the barrel. He gently pulled the weapon from Spock, who did not resist. "For a moment," Sybok told him, "I thought you might actually do it."

He turned as his soldiers emerged from the damaged craft with McCoy. The doctor hurried to Jim's side.

"Jim! What the hell happened?"

"What about Sulu and Uhura?"

"They're all right. The hostages—er, diplomats—are bringing them out. What happened to you?"

Kirk did not answer. He could only glare angrily at Spock; the Vulcan did not meet his eyes. McCoy seemed to take note of it, but set about taking care of Jim's wrist and asked no further questions.

Sybok addressed his followers. "Put these two"—he pointed at Kirk and McCoy—"in a holding cell. Spock will accompany me to the bridge."

Spock stiffened and seemed to recover a shred of dignity. "I will not."

Disappointment rippled over Sybok's features. "I suppose you think we're even now," he said, then fell silent for a time as he fought for control. At last, he spoke again. "Then you must join them, Spock."

He turned and was gone.

Montgomery Scott hurried into the landing bay observation booth. Two emotions warred within him: concern for those inside the damaged shuttlecraft, and pride at the way the *Enterprise* had performed. The warp drive had performed magnificently—*Take that, you Klingon bastards,* Scott had thought smugly, as the ship sailed out of the Bird of Prey's firing range—and the shields were in place and working beautifully. Scott checked the booth's control panel and saw that the emergency cargo net had been activated. He felt a renewed surge of pride; he'd overseen its repair not two days before.

Good work, lass. He patted the control panel absently. *Keep it up, and ye'll earn your name.*

He craned his neck to get a quick glimpse through the observation window of the deck below. *Galileo* listed to starboard; the area where her pontoons had been torn away were still smoldering. The landing bay bore the scars of her entry: the metal floor had been scraped and gouged in an almost perfectly straight trail—Sulu's handiwork, no doubt—leading from the hangar doors. It must have been one hell of a bumpy ride home.

Scott checked the damage report. The smoke was from friction and a few overloaded circuits, but those within were in no danger from fire or smoke inhalation. The shuttle's radio was out, too; Scott tried to raise someone and got static for a response.

Normally, medics would have been standing by, but there were no medics aboard; no one save Dr. McCoy had been assigned to the medical staff before the *Enterprise* was forced to leave spacedock. There wouldn't have been time to pick up new personnel anyway, without the help of transporters.

Considering the odd circumstances of *Galileo*'s arrival, there should have been a security contingent present as well—but the entire department—those who had been assigned so far—were with the landing party.

A quick scan of the shuttle's interior revealed twelve aboard, all living . . . exactly the right number. Scott sighed with pleasure and relief, and tabbed the intercom toggle. "Scott to bridge."

Chekov answered. "Are they in one piece, Mr. Scott?"

"Aye, sir. All in one piece, though I'm not so sure about *Galileo.*"

"Excellent work, Mr. Scott. We'll wait for you up here."

Scott beamed at the compliment. "Thank you, Mr. Chekov. Scott out."

He closed the channel. A sudden flash of movement caught his eye and made him look away from the board. He went over by the observation window to watch the drama unfolding on the deck below.

At that very instant, Captain Kirk was struggling with the terrorist leader. The Vulcan held Kirk in a grip that brought the captain to his knees. Scott gasped aloud. Kirk was no match for the Vulcan's strength, of course, but he fought with all he had, and succeeded in kicking the weapon from the Vulcan's hand. It slid across the floor and landed directly at the feet of Mr. Spock, who had just climbed from the wounded shuttlecraft.

Scott made an indignant sound and reached absently for his phaser. It wasn't there, of course—he hadn't thought to bring it. Vainly he looked about for anything he could use as a weapon. But in the starkly furnished interior of the booth, there was nothing suitable. Scott swore in frustration at his helplessness. By the time he found a phaser, the captain and the others might be dead or injured. His second instinct, to call Security, made him swear again.

But it appeared that Spock was about to save the day. Slowly Spock bent down and retrieved the pistol. The army's leader let go of the captain and faced Spock.

Spock took careful aim, but did not fire. The renegade moved closer, closer . . .

Shoot him, Mr. Spock! Scott urged silently.

. . . And lifted the weapon right out of Spock's hand. Spock bowed his head.

Scott gasped. Why had Spock not fired when he had the chance?

Scott shrank back into the shadows to watch unseen.

Others appeared: McCoy and a handful of ragtag soldiers, some of them armed with crude hand-made weapons, others with phasers obviously stolen from their prisoners. The landing party had been captured down on Nimbus, which explained their failure to respond to Chekov's signals.

The soldiers led Kirk, Spock, and McCoy away just as Uhura and Sulu appeared with the three diplomats who had been taken hostage. Shockingly, the hostages themselves were armed and seemed to be guarding Sulu and Uhura. When the leader stepped up to them, Scott crouched down and backed over to the control panel. He located the intercom control and pressed it.

"Chekov!" he whispered hoarsely.

"Speak up, Mr. Scott. What is it?"

"They're getting out of the shuttlecraft. There's something verra funny about these hostages."

"Something funny? Did the landing party manage to recover them? Exactly what do you mean?"

Scott froze. Below on the hangar deck, one of the soldiers spotted him and gave a shout.

Scott wasted no time in making his escape.

"Mr. Scott? Scott?"

No reply.

"Chort!" Chekov swore over the intercom. "What the devil is going on?"

173

Chapter Eleven

SULU WOKE to the sensation of an inhumanly warm hand on his shoulder. He opened his eyes to see the underside of the shuttle's pilot console, and recalled vaguely that he had been slammed against it during the rough landing.

"We're aboard *Enterprise*," he croaked, and turned his head to see the Romulan consul, Dar, crouched beside him.

"Are you all right?" Dar asked. In his dazed state, Sulu was taken aback by her loveliness: sculpted cheekbones and a sharp chin gave her an angular, almost feline beauty. Her eyes were lighter than those of any Romulan he'd ever seen, golden brown flecked with green. He began to smile, then tensed at the sight of the pistol she held loosely at her side as he remembered he was her prisoner. Behind her, the

Klingon ambassador watched, one hand resting on his huge belly, the other holding a pistol trained on Sulu's head. The helmsman sat up cautiously, refusing her offer of help, and rubbed the back of his neck. "Uhura?"

Her voice came from only a few meters away. "I'm all right, Sulu. You?"

Dar moved aside to let him see. Uhura was struggling to her feet with the solicitous aid of Talbot, who managed somehow to keep his weapon pointed at her the entire time and still appear gracious.

"Okay. I think." Sulu rose stiffly. He turned to Dar, his tone icy. "What have you done with the captain?"

"He is uninjured," Dar replied. "Sybok is seeing to him. No harm will come to him, if he cooperates."

Sulu raised a skeptical brow at that but said nothing. Dar motioned for the prisoners to make their way toward the hatch. Sulu and Uhura helped each other crawl out of the craft and step down onto the landing deck.

By the time Sulu made it down, he could see the captain, Spock, and Dr. McCoy being led away by the guards. The Vulcan, Sybok, watched the three leave, unaware of the arrival of more prisoners until General Korrd spoke.

"These two will be useful," Korrd said. He nodded at Sulu and Uhura.

Sybok turned to face them, his features composed in a pleasantly neutral expression.

Just what the hell did Korrd mean by that? Sulu wondered. Were they now going to use them as hostages, as bargaining chips with the Federation? Or did they have something else in mind?

175

"We won't cooperate, if that's what you mean," Sulu said tightly. He gave Sybok a defiant stare.

The Vulcan merely smiled and moved closer to them, barely an arm's length away. He studied Uhura's face intently for a moment, then reached out to touch her face.

"Leave her alone," Sulu said dangerously, though there was little he could do with both Dar and Korrd aiming weapons at him.

Uhura tilted her chin defiantly as she met Sybok's gaze. "It's all right, Sulu. I'm not afraid of him."

But as she looked into the Vulcan's eyes, something happened. For an instant, she looked panicked . . . and then her face went completely slack. Sybok leaned forward and gently placed his fingertips against her temples.

Sulu had seen Mr. Spock do the same thing when attempting a mind meld, but according to Spock, Vulcans *never* did so unless the other person had given permission. What Sybok was doing was a total breach of Vulcan ethics.

"Hey!" Sulu cried, moving toward them with the thought of pushing Sybok away. "What do you think you're—"

Korrd stepped forward and shoved the barrel of his pistol square in Sulu's chest, with such force that it knocked the wind out of him. Sulu watched helplessly as Uhura closed her eyes and fell into a trance.

When she opened them again, it was to witness some interior vision that Sulu could not see. Sybok gently released his grip on her forehead, but hovered close by.

Uhura's expression became one of despair. "No," she whispered, "no, please . . ."

Sybok spoke to her so softly that Sulu could not hear the words.

Uhura shook her head. "No . . ."

"You're hurting her!" Sulu said, but this time did not lunge at the Vulcan. Sybok and Uhura were far too focused on the invisible world to hear him.

Uhura's face contorted as she witnessed an imaginary sight too terrible to bear . . . and then, slowly, her grief seemed to fade, and was replaced by a beatific smile. A single tear coursed the length of her cheek as she looked up at Sybok.

"Thank you," she whispered. "Oh, thank you . . ."

"What have you *done* to her?" Sulu asked the Vulcan accusingly.

Uhura turned to him, her face radiant with love. "Sulu, it's all right. He doesn't want to hurt us; he wants to *help.*"

"Right," Sulu said tightly, and turned away to find the Vulcan staring at him.

Sybok's gaze was compelling and more than a little unnerving, but Sulu refused to look away. It was as if the Vulcan were trying to hypnotize him, but Sulu knew for a fact that, regardless of what had happened to Uhura, no one could be hypnotized against his will. Certainly not Sulu himself; he was not at all suggestible.

And yet he began to feel the present slip away.

"Don't be afraid," Dar said in her low voice. It was the last thing Sulu heard before . . .

* * *

He was on Ganjitsu again.

Young Hikaru Sulu had spent his early childhood scaling the alarmingly steep sidewalks of San Francisco. By the time he turned eleven, his family had moved to the frontier world of Ganjitsu.

Unlike home, Ganjitsu was flat—at least, comparatively—but lovely in its own way. The small village of Ishikawa where Hikaru and his family lived was surrounded by cool, lush forests and running streams. Evergreens transplanted from Earth flourished in the dry, temperate climate. Of all the places the Sulu family lived, Hikaru loved Ganjitsu best. The planet was originally settled by conservationists who passed strict laws restricting the number of settlers and guaranteeing that Ganjitsu would never be developed. Living on Ganjitsu was a lot like camping out; the homes were makeshift, spread out, separated from one another by dense forest. People traveled in skimmers from village to village—on Ganjitsu, there were no real cities—but to get around town, everyone walked.

Hikaru and Kumiko walked six kilometers home from school every day. Weisel's Grocery lay between, surrounded on either side by thick forest. Sulu's earliest memories of Ganjitsu were happy ones . . . very happy, until the pirates came.

Ganjitsu was a sparsely populated border planet in an area of space whose ownership was disputed by the Federation and the Klingon Empire. At first the pirate attacks were rare, and too remote from the tiny settlement of Ishikawa to be a real concern. When they first began occurring, Hikaru loved to listen to stories of the attacks; he thought it all very exciting.

And then the attacks moved closer. Settlers in Ishikawa, including the Sulu family, constructed what makeshift shelters they could, or did their best to fortify their flimsy homes. Even then, the pirates held no reality for Hikaru. They were exciting, dangerous, romantic . . . but not *real*. Those tales of people dying —they were just stories.

Most of the stories he heard from Mr. Weisel. Other than the Sulus, the Weisels were the only bona-fide Earth family in Ishikawa. There were third- and fourth-generation humans from Rigel, like Kumiko's family, a sprinkling of Andorians, and a fairly large settlement of Vulcan scientists whose mission was to catalog the wealth of flora and fauna unique to Ganjitsu. But Mr. and Mrs. Weisel were the only other native Earthers. The silver-haired couple owned the largest business in the town: Weisel's Grocery stocked all the servitors for kilometers around.

But Sulu didn't like Mr. Weisel. He was eagle-eyed and crotchety, with wild gray eyebrows, which Hikaru assured Kumiko were ten centimeters long. Mr. Weisel was always complaining about everything— about the weather, about how long it took to get supplies for the Andorians, about the damn Klingons.

Damn Klingons, they're behind all these attacks. Let them try to lie about this one! Twenty-six killed day before yesterday down in Tamaka. . . .

Damn Federation. The Klingons can kill us all, but will the Federation lift a finger to help us? No, they'll just try to work it out diplomatically. Diplomatically!

Hah! In the meantime, people like us are getting killed. . . .

Mr. Weisel always stared at Hikaru and Kumiko when they came in every Thursday afternoon, as if he expected them to steal something. Hikaru was afraid of the old man. His friend and neighbor, Kumiko, teased him mercilessly about it . . . but Kumiko had been born fearless. Every Thursday when Hikaru and Kumiko went to the store—Hikaru to buy candy, Kumiko to pick up her family's servitor order—Kumiko smiled and boldly said hello to Mr. Weisel, who bared his great yellow teeth and snarled. Hikaru merely gulped and trembled at the sight; to him, Mr. Weisel was far more terrifying than any stories about pirates.

But all the kids loved Mrs. Weisel. Everything about her was soft: voice, hair, eyes. She smiled and gave Kumiko and Hikaru candy when Mr. Weisel wasn't looking.

Then, one Thursday afternoon, the pirates attacked Ishikawa. Hikaru remembered, because he was in Weisel's Grocery at the time, standing in front of the counter.

In fact, he could see the counter in front of him now, touch its cold metal surface.

Hullo, Mr. Weisel, Kumiko said.

Sulu swiveled his head to look at his friend standing next to him: Kumiko, precisely as she looked at fourteen, a skinny dark-eyed girl with a neatly trimmed cap of shiny black hair. She wore the faded khaki work suit of an agricultural worker and challenged the old man behind the counter with a smile. Amazingly, Sulu found he had to look *up* to see her, and all that he saw, he saw through an eleven-year-old child's eyes. Young Hikaru admired her because she was everything he was not: decisive, courageous, outspoken.

Behind the counter, Mr. Weisel grunted unpleasantly in response to Kumiko's insistent smile; Sulu shifted his weight from leg to leg and tried to fade into invisibility. *Helene!* Mr. Weisel called.

The adult Sulu remembered suddenly what was about to happen next. "No!" he cried. "Gods, no, not again—"

Mrs. Weisel emerged from the back of the store with the Sulus' order neatly packed into a box—and with two pieces of candy, Sulu knew, hidden in her left hand. Her cheeks were flushed with pink.

Hikaru, Kumiko, how are you? And your parents?

Sulu smiled shyly and mumbled an unintelligible reply.

We're all just fine, Mrs. Weisel, Kumiko said. *How are you today?*

Just the same, Mrs. Weisel answered. She gave the same answer every Thursday. And, just as she always did, she handed Kumiko the box . . . and slipped Hikaru the candy.

"No," Sulu whispered . . . but he was compelled to take the candy from her plump, soft hand with his own small eleven-year-old boy's hand.

There was a sudden, ominous rumble, like a thunderclap. The floor beneath Sulu's feet shuddered violently.

My God! Mr. Weisel shouted. *What the hell was that? An earthquake?*

Another rumble, louder this time; Sulu had to fight

to stay on his feet. Beyond the store windows, the afternoon sky erupted in a blaze of red.

"Pirates," young Sulu remarked in amazement. His heart began to pound with an oddly exhilarating mixture of fear and excitement; the pirates were really *here,* in dull old Ishikawa, and he, Sulu, was about to have a *real* adventure. . . .

Kumiko dropped the box and stared, openmouthed, through the window as a fire bolt streaked through the sky.

Mrs. Weisel darted out from behind the counter and began to push the children to the back of the store. *Come on. Get to the shelter now. . . .*

The store was one of the better-constructed permanent buildings in Ishikawa; it had a basement, with a real shelter. Hikaru felt safer than he would have in his own home.

I hope Mom knows about this, Kumiko gulped, as Mrs. Weisel trundled them along.

Sulu looked over at her in shock; normally brave Kumiko's eyes glistened with tears. Sulu was amazed. It had never occurred to him that someone might actually get *hurt* in his pirate attack. Sure, people got killed . . . but not anyone he *knew,* not anyone he cared about, not his parents . . .

Mr. Weisel already had the trapdoor to the shelter open. *Come on, come on!* He gestured furiously for them to hurry. Mrs. Weisel pushed the children along.

And then Sulu's eyes were painfully dazzled by a blast of pure white light. Stunned, he fell to the floor. This time the rumble was deafening. Something struck Sulu on the cheek, hard enough to draw blood;

he cried out. And then something struck his shoulder; something else hit his back. Horrified, he realized the store was collapsing around them. The noise increased until Sulu could no longer hear his own screams. . . .

He faded into blackness.

And woke again to the sound of Kumiko's voice, timidly pleading, *Hikaru, are you all right? Hikaru?*

The sky was smudged with thick charcoal-colored dust. At first, Hikaru thought he had been unconscious a long time and that it was night, but he could see no stars through the thick iron-gray clouds. He took a deep breath and coughed until his eyes teared.

Not clouds but smoke. Ishikawa was on fire.

Sulu looked around him. Weisel's Grocery was virtually destroyed; the front half of the building had collapsed into rubble under the pirates' phasers. The back of the store was still standing. Mr. Weisel huddled, hands clasped over his head, by the open trapdoor.

Hikaru, Kumiko begged, *where are you? Are you all right?*

"I'm okay," Sulu reassured her. "I'm right here." His head hurt a little, and his shoulder was bruised and sore, but otherwise he felt all right. He got shakily to his feet. Kumiko sat next to him in the debris, her beautiful hair dull with dust; when she turned toward him, he saw a trickle of blood that went from her temple to her chin. "You're hurt!" he cried, alarmed.

Kumiko touched it and stared vacantly at the blood on her finger, then wiped it on her work suit. *Just a little cut,* she said. *It doesn't hurt much. You're bleed-*

ing, too. See? She touched Sulu's cheek and showed him the blood on her fingers.

Sulu tried to help her up, but she was unable to stand; her left ankle was swelling and darkening to violet.

"Stay here," Sulu told her, a little frightened by her passivity, and the distant look in her eyes. He called out to the old man. "Mr. Weisel? Are you okay?"

Helene! Mr. Weisel shouted, in a sudden spasm of hysteria. *Helene! Where are you?*

"Mr. Weisel, take it easy! I'll find her."

Helene! Mr. Weisel screamed with agonizing intensity, and then fell disturbingly quiet.

Sulu began to look through the rubble. Mrs. Weisel was somewhere nearby; Mrs. Weisel would be all right. After all, the rest of them weren't badly hurt. He began to move slowly, carefully, through the scattered food packs, the smoking debris from the collapsed ceiling, the mangled furniture.

"Mrs. Weisel?" Sulu called.

Mrs. Weisel did not answer.

Over there! Kumiko shouted, and pointed at an overturned storage shelf.

Sulu looked, but saw nothing at first. He frowned and picked his way carefully through the wreckage. And then he saw Mrs. Weisel's hand, peeking out from under the heavy metal shelf. Sulu gasped and cried out.

"Mr. Weisel! She's over here! You've got to help me move this shelf!"

Mr. Weisel was immediately galvanized; he ran, tripping over the twisted remains of the grocery counter and, with surprising strength for an old man, lifted the shelf without waiting for Sulu's help.

Helene! he moaned at the sight of her.

Mrs. Weisel lay, face up and limp, in the debris. For one awful instant, Sulu thought she was dead. A sensation of electric horror traveled down his spine.

And then Mrs. Weisel's eyelids fluttered and opened briefly before closing again. Her pupils, Sulu noted, were the size of pinpoints. A jagged edge of the metal shelving had left a deep gash in her forehead; the skin of her normally pink face was a pale, ugly shade of gray.

Do something! Mr. Weisel screamed at Sulu. *Do something, she's dying!*

For a moment, Sulu could only stare at him in shock, until a courageous and previously unknown portion of his brain took control. He remembered the most basic parts of the first-aid course he'd been required to take in school. He removed his jacket and tucked it around Mrs. Weisel, then found the right-sized box of food packs and gently put them under her feet.

"Stay here," he told Kumiko. "If the pirates come back, try to get into the shelter. I'm going to get help."

She nodded vaguely.

Sulu ran toward the forest. He was not sure at first where he was running, or why. He knew only that he had to help Mrs. Weisel. Without making a conscious decision, he found that he was headed home, to find his parents. They had a skimmer; they would be able to travel into the next town for a doctor.

The late-afternoon sky was dark with thick black

smoke, but the orange-red glow that emanated from deep within the forest enabled Sulu to find his way along the pedestrian trail between his house and the Weisels'. Sulu ran hard along the path until a high wall of flame forced him to stop. The fire leapt atop the huge trees, consuming the high evergreen foliage before climbing down to the forest floor. The pirates' phasers had seared the treetops; the forest was burning from the top down. The heat radiating from it held Sulu back; the smoke stung his eyes and throat and made him dizzy.

Beyond the column of fire, less than three kilometers away, stood his parents' house. Had Sulu's eyes not already been streaming from the smoke, he would have wept. For what seemed like a very long time, he stared, sobbing, at the wall of flame . . . then forced himself to calm.

Along with shrieking, panicked wildlife, Sulu left the trail to thrash through the undergrowth. The column of raging fire was at least a kilometer wide. The smoke thickened, making it more difficult for Sulu to find his way. He ran for several minutes until the column of fire grew small in the distance behind him and then disappeared altogether.

Sulu turned and headed toward what—he thought —was the direction of his house, but in the encroaching darkness and in thick smoke without the firelight to guide him, Sulu headed the wrong way.

A half-hour of frantic running found him in unfamiliar territory. His panic grew. The forest had become a ghoulish tangle of flickering dark red shadows and ominous black shapes. Sulu dropped to his knees and sobbed, unable to guess which direction might lead home. He was utterly, miserably, alone and lost, and it struck him that perhaps *no* direction led homeward; perhaps home had been swallowed up by the fire, and there was no help for him, for Kumiko, for Mr. and Mrs. Weisel.

For a time—the boy could not have said how long—Sulu's mind left him. He remembered nothing of that time save a bottomless void of dark fear. He lay with his face pressed against the pungent evergreen needles that carpeted the forest floor.

What finally made him conquer the terror and struggle to his feet was a single, wordless image: Mrs. Weisel, lying still and ashen-faced in the ruins of the store.

Sulu rose without feeling the sharp pine needles that clung to his clothing and hair. It seemed to him that he had somehow miraculously found the courage that Kumiko seemed to have lost. He began again to run—at a lope this time—steadily and with a sense of purpose. When he was once again forced to detour around the fire, he countered the building panic by conjuring Mrs. Weisel's face in his imagination.

It worked. Sulu remained calm and after a while began to recognize where he was.

He arrived home at last and saw the building still standing and his mother climbing into the skimmer to search for her missing child. Sulu stopped in his tracks. He was several meters away, and with the roar from the burning forest, any sound he might have made was swallowed up.

Yet his mother sensed something. She froze an

instant before stepping into the vehicle, turned, and caught sight of her son, his cheeks streaked with soot, tears, and blood.

At the expression on her face, Sulu burst into tears. . . .

Sulu's father had been traveling to another town and was spared the attack; his mother had attempted to leave her son in the below-ground shelter, but he was too near shock to be left alone. There was nothing to do but take the boy with her.

They flew, skipping high above the flames, through the smoke, to the Weisels' store. The trip had taken Sulu over an hour on foot; they arrived by skimmer in less than a minute.

Kumiko's ankle was broken and she was in shock, but the cut on her head was tiny, not even requiring stitches. Except for the nightmares, which would last well into adulthood, Kumiko would be fine. Mr. Weisel had bruised ribs, and, like Kumiko, was dazed. He crouched, muttering, beside his wife, his voice at once soothing and slightly hysterical.

Mrs. Weisel, of course, was dead.

It was Sulu's first encounter with the phenomenon on a personal level.

"*No,*" Sulu whispered, staring down with revulsion at Mrs. Weisel's body. The ugly cut on her forehead had stopped bleeding, and the blood had congealed, thick red-black. The area surrounding it was grotesquely swollen. Mrs. Weisel's eyelids were not quite closed, so that a small strip of white could be seen; her lips were parted as well, and the very tip of her tongue protruded.

What was most horrible for young Sulu was that

Mrs. Weisel was no longer Mrs. Weisel at all. What remained of her was no longer a person at all, but a thing.

The guilt was too overwhelming for Sulu to cry. He simply stood and stared silently at Mrs. Weisel's body until he felt very, very cold, and began to shiver. . . .

Suddenly Sulu realized that he was no longer a child at all, but an adult reliving the experience . . . and, strangest of all, this time he was not alone. Someone stood *with* him now, someone who was not his mother, not Kumiko, not Mr. Weisel. Sulu could not see the stranger who stood beside him, but he sensed him nonetheless.

The stranger spoke to him.

Look at her, the stranger commanded. *Look at her, and don't be afraid.*

"I killed her!" Sulu cried, averting his face in disgust. "Don't you understand? I killed her! I got lost, took too much time—"

Look at her.

"I can't!" Sulu squeezed his eyes shut. "Please *don't*—"

She was dead before you even left, the stranger said.

Sulu turned sharply in the direction of the stranger's voice, and saw nothing but the night sky glowing a dull orange-red. He still felt the heat of the fire on his face. "What did you say?"

She was dead before you left. Look at her now.

Sulu closed his eyes and remembered . . . and saw Mrs. Weisel's eyelids flutter once, and her chest sink with the expiration of breath. It did not rise again.

She was dead before you left, the stranger repeated. *Even if you had made it home as swiftly as possible, she would not have survived. She was a casualty of the pirate attack, not your childish terror.*

"I shouldn't have—" Sulu began, and broke off. He wanted to say that he shouldn't have gotten lost anyway; a part of him wanted to cling irrationally to his guilt . . . but the stranger had cleanly excised it from him. There was no holding on to it. Sulu imagined it rising through the air, levitating beyond his grasp. . . .

You were a frightened child. Even so, you behaved bravely. You got help for the old man and your friend.

"I . . ." Sulu began, then trailed off helplessly. He stared down at Mrs. Weisel's gray, pinched face. This time he felt only sorrow. She had been a kind person, and the pirates had killed her. It was a bitterly sad thing.

And then even the sorrow rose up and floated away. In its absence, Sulu experienced a deep sense of relief and an odd mixture of melancholy and euphoria. He looked at Mrs. Weisel's body and wept tears that were cleansing and free from shame.

When he finished, he looked up and saw that the stranger's features had become visible in the darkness. Sulu had never seen eyes full of such wisdom, such love.

"Thank you," Sulu told him. "Please, let me repay you for your kindness. I will do whatever you ask."

To Sulu's delight, the stranger smiled.

Chapter Twelve

IN THE BRIG, Spock struggled to master his guilt. Of all emotions, this one proved the most difficult to overcome. Most disturbing was the truth he had to admit to himself: He had not been able to kill Sybok, but it had little to do with Surakian pacifist philosophy . . . and everything to do with the adolescent adoration of a young Vulcan for his older brother. He had thought that, with time, such sensations would fade . . . that his only memories of Sybok would be limited to those of Sybok's crime and banishment.

And yet the memory of Sybok's kindness returned unbidden to Spock, awakening within him fondness and a deep gratitude.

He had been not quite thirteen in Earth terms when Sybok came to live with the family. Sybok was a total stranger, and young Spock, though he tried not to admit it even to himself, was terrified of that first meeting.

For Sybok was a full Vulcan—the son that Sarek had always *really* wanted to have. After all, young Spock reasoned, Sybok was also an adept in the ways of kolinahr, the total transcendence of emotion, and here was Spock, half human, always struggling to master his feelings, already made keenly aware by his peers of his inferior heredity.

Spock fully expected Sybok to reject him as Sarek's rightful heir. He was therefore quite unprepared for Sybok's actual reaction. The older boy's demeanor was far different from what Spock expected of one who had been raised since birth on Gol.

Upon being introduced to his younger sibling, Sybok raised his hand in the Vulcan salute and warmly proclaimed, *"T'hyla . . ."* Brother. And with that single word, gained Spock's eternal loyalty.

Spock blotted the image from his mind and forced himself back to the present, to the brig and to the confusing muddle of emotions that awaited him.

Clearly, the captain's anger had in no way diminished. Kirk paced the length of the small cell while Spock and McCoy sat on the bunk and watched.

Kirk stopped abruptly in the middle of his pacing and wheeled around to confront his first officer. "Dammit! Goddammit! Spock, I simply can't believe it!"

Spock did not pretend ignorance of the cause of the captain's rage. He understood how inexplicable his failure to act must have seemed. As much as he dreaded providing an explanation, however, he knew that now was the time for one. "Captain," he began, calm in the face of Jim's rage, "what I have done—"

"What you have done is betray everyone aboard this ship."

"Worse," Spock agreed before Jim could say more. "I have betrayed you. I do not expect you to forgive me—"

"Forgive you?" Jim lowered his voice and said, quite matter-of-factly, "I ought to knock you on your ass."

"If you think that will help," Spock answered agreeably.

"You want me to hold him, Jim?" McCoy blurted sarcastically. Spock was startled to find the doctor, of all people, defending him against Jim's attack.

Kirk turned on McCoy. "Stay out of this, Bones!" He spoke to the Vulcan. "Spock . . . why? All you had to do was pull the trigger. I wasn't asking you to kill him. I realize you find violence distasteful, but you could have shot him in the leg and stopped him that way. Whatever happened to the good of the many outweighing the good of the one? It's appropriate in some cases!"

"Captain," Spock said earnestly, "had I pulled the trigger, Sybok would now be dead."

"Why?" Jim's eyes were blazing. He waited, fists on hips, for an answer. "Explain."

"As Sybok said himself, he would not stop until I killed him. Even wounded, he would have been a formidable opponent. He will not stop until he has control of the *Enterprise*. Perhaps you have noticed that Sybok is most . . . driven."

Jim spread his hands helplessly. "Spock, we're

talking two hundred lives against one. Whatever happened to the good of the many? Did we talk you out of it too thoroughly?"

"I know Sybok well. He would not kill . . . intentionally."

"He's a madman," Jim said. "Spock, I ordered you to defend this ship."

With regret, Spock realized that the time for total revelation had arrived. He shook his head. "No, Captain," he said softly. "You ordered me to kill my brother."

"The man may be a fellow Vulcan," Kirk replied, "and maybe you were once friends. But frankly, there seemed to be no love lost between you—at least, on your part. That's no reason to—"

Spock cut him off; there was no point in delaying the inevitable. "You did not hear me, Jim. Sybok, too, is a son of Sarek."

McCoy, sitting next to Spock, nearly fell off the bunk. *"What?"*

For a moment, Jim stared, thunderstruck, at his first officer. When he could speak, he said, "He's your *brother* brother?"

Spock nodded.

"Spock, you're joking!"

"I am not."

"Spock, I know every piece of data in your file. Sybok couldn't *possibly* be your brother, because I know for a fact you don't *have* a brother. And giving false information in a personnel file is a Federation offense."

"Technically, you are correct," Spock conceded.

There was little to be gained from explaining that Sybok was *ktorr skann,* an outcast, considered dead by his family; his very existence had been expunged from all public records on Vulcan. "I do not have a brother."

"Then what the hell *do* you mean?"

"I have a half brother."

Jim's anger surrendered to confusion. "I need to sit down." He walked over to the bunk and plopped down heavily next to McCoy.

The doctor was frowning. "Now, Spock, let me get this straight. You and Sybok have the same father, but different mothers."

"Correct," Spock said. Even speaking of the matter was difficult, awkward; he had not spoken his brother's name aloud, had in no way acknowledged Sybok's existence, for more than thirty years. "Sybok's mother was a Vulcan priestess—"

McCoy interrupted. "I thought your father was never married before he met your—"

Spock stopped him. "Legally, he never was. After T'Rea—the priestess, his first wife—decided to devote her life to the priesthood, the marriage was annulled. Such things are permitted members of the priesthood. There had been only one mating cycle, and Sarek was led to believe that the union had borne no fruit. Had he known . . ." Spock paused, then continued. "T'Rea conceived a son and kept his birth a secret. It was not until she died that Sarek learned of his son, Sybok. After that time, he brought Sybok to live with him. Sybok and I were raised as brothers."

Until the elders banished him forever from Vulcan.

"Why didn't you tell us this before?" Jim asked. "At least, when you first recognized him from the hostage tape?"

Because he is a criminal, Spock could have said. *Because I am torn. A part of me is deeply ashamed of what he is, and yet another part yearns to call him brother.* Woodenly, he replied: "I was not prepared to discuss . . . matters of such a personal nature. For that I am sorry."

"Sorry," Kirk said haggardly. "And the *Enterprise* is in the hands of a lunatic. Who just happens to be your brother."

McCoy spoke up with surprising ferocity. "Lay off, Jim. Spock couldn't kill his brother any more than he could kill you. Put yourself in his place. What if it had been Sam?"

Jim turned away, stone-faced.

McCoy persisted. "So if you want to punish him for what he's done, what are you going to do? Throw him in the brig?"

Jim sighed, relenting. "I guess we've got bigger problems to deal with. Such as how we're going to get out of here." He glanced over at Spock. "Spock, I shouldn't have lost my temper. I suppose if the positions had been reversed . . ." He shrugged.

"I quite understand," Spock said.

Jim's lips twisted wryly. "For the record, however, I am still galled that someone else has control of my ship."

"And I," Spock said, "am quite amazed to find Dr. McCoy rushing to my defense."

McCoy grunted. "All that time with your *katra* rattling around in my head must have unhinged me.

196

God help me, I'm starting to see your point of view. I'll just say this, Spock: *you* never cease to amaze *me.*"

"Amen," Jim echoed.

"Nor I myself," Spock confessed. He was quite shocked at the conflicting emotions that had filled him upon confronting his brother: hatred, love, anger . . .

Most surprising of all was gratitude.

It is because of Sybok, after all, Spock thought, *that I am who I am.*

It was because of Sybok that Spock entered Starfleet.

More than thirty years before, Spock had wandered out into the garden in the cool night and discovered his elder brother sitting in the seclusion of the arbor, weeping.

Sybok made no sound. His face was expressionless, not at all contorted; he merely closed his eyes briefly from time to time and let the tears flow down his cheeks without making any effort to contain them.

Spock was horrified. Up to that moment, Sybok had comported himself in the circumspect Vulcan fashion. Spock had great admiration for him, for Sybok possessed a serene confidence that Spock entirely lacked.

To Spock's embarrassment, he gasped aloud at the sight of Sybok's tears. Sybok noted the intrusion and calmly, deliberately, ran both hands over his face and wiped the tears away.

"Forgive me," Sybok said. "Had I known you were in the garden, I would not have indulged myself. I realize you are offended by such a display of emotion." His tone was matter-of-fact and entirely free of shame.

Spock was astonished into speechlessness; he stared, wide-eyed, at his brother.

Sybok came close to smiling—a small, ironic smile —which astonished Spock even further. "I was not raised as you were, Spock. I was taught not to fear emotion."

"I am not afraid," Spock protested. It occurred to him that this might be a lie, but he was young and decided against such intense self-honesty.

"You *are* afraid," Sybok corrected him. "The elders have taught you that emotion is the ultimate evil, and you do not think to question their wisdom."

"Question the elders? But they have acquired much knowledge."

"What if they are wrong?" Sybok asked simply. His expression was implacable.

Spock began to answer indignantly, then decided against it. For the first time in his life, he considered the possibility that the elders might be wrong. The best tactic, he decided, was evasion. He asked Sybok a question.

"Why are you weeping?"

"For my mother," Sybok said. It was the first and last time that Spock would hear him speak of her. "Because she is dead, and I miss her, and because I could not keep a promise I once made to her." Before Spock could ask another question, Sybok said, "You are going to follow in Sarek's footsteps and become a diplomat," he said. It was not quite a question; Vulcan custom dictated that Spock would do so, and, besides, Sarek had always said as much.

Spock nodded.

"Is that what you really want, Spock?"

"Of course," Spock replied . . . and then stopped as the full impact of Sybok's question struck him.

"Is that what you really want? To live and die to please someone else, to live according to tradition simply because that is the way things have always been done? Is that logical, *t'hyla?*"

Spock had no answer then, but from that moment, he began to consider the question in earnest.

Chekov sat in the command chair and puzzled over Mr. Scott's cryptic message about the hostages. He tried vainly to raise someone—anyone—on the hangar deck, but received no reply.

It occurred to Chekov that he was alone on the bridge. With the captain and Mr. Scott gone, and a skeleton crew of mostly repair technicians, there was no one to relieve him of duty. And he was unarmed. He considered going to his quarters to retrieve a weapon, but leaving the bridge unattended, especially after Scott's strange communiqué, went against Chekov's ingrained sense of duty.

No, he could not leave. He would simply wait until he heard from Scott or the landing party. The thought brought the memory of the unpleasant premonition he'd experienced earlier, that something had definitely gone very, very wrong with the landing party's mission. The captain and the others were in trouble, and Chekov had no way of knowing how to help them.

The lift doors snapped open behind him. Chekov jumped out of the chair and whirled around. At the sight of Sulu and Uhura, his nervousness became relief.

"Thank God." Chekov grinned. "I was beginning to worry. Where is the captain?"

His relief vanished as the terrorist leader, Sybok, strode onto the bridge. He was followed by the hostages and several armed soldiers. Oddly, the soldiers' primitive weapons were aimed, not at the three diplomats, not at Sulu or Uhura, but at Chekov alone. Worse yet, Sybok, the diplomats, Sulu, and Uhura were all smiling the same faintly psychotic smile.

Horrified, Chekov took a step backwards and stumbled over the command platform. "He's done something to you," he said to Uhura and Sulu. "What has he done to you?"

Uhura moved toward him, her voice warm and soothing. "It's all right, Pavel. You don't have to be afraid of anything anymore. Sybok will explain it all to you."

"I've already listened to Sybok enough to know he is a liar." Chekov directed a cold glare at the Vulcan, who smiled in return.

Sulu swept past Chekov and took his seat at the helm. He began to program in commands.

Aghast, Chekov turned to him. "Sulu, what are you doing?"

Sulu smiled serenely; his attention never wavered from the helm. "Plotting our new course."

"New course? You have no authority!" Chekov faced Sybok angrily. "What have you done to my friends?"

"Pavel," Sulu said gently behind him, "I'm doing what I think is right. Listen to what Sybok has to say. For my sake. Please."

Suddenly Sybok was standing before him, close enough to rest a hand on his shoulder.

"I don't want to force you," Sybok said.

The bridge suddenly faded. Chekov was aware of nothing but the Vulcan's dark eyes. They seemed incredibly ancient, wise . . . and strangely sad.

"I don't understand," Chekov protested weakly. His own voice sounded very far away.

"Each of us hides a secret pain," Sybok told him. Pavel felt the touch of a feverish hand on his brow, though the Vulcan never moved. "Share yours and gain strength from the sharing."

It would be some time later before Chekov realized that Sybok had spoken to him in Russian.

Kirk's anger sublimated itself in the need to escape. Inside the brig, Jim balanced precariously on Spock's shoulders and loosened a circuitry panel. McCoy watched with a notable lack of interest from his place on the bunk.

"Captain." Spock held Kirk's ankles in a firm grip. "May I reiterate that this entire attempt is quite useless?"

Instead of sliding away smoothly, as it should have, the panel cover broke off in Jim's hand. "Shut up, Spock," he answered pleasantly. "I'm trying to find a way out of here, and I think I'm onto something." He reached out to touch the partially exposed panel of glowing circuits.

"Unwise," Spock said.

Jim touched the panel. The resulting shock knocked him to the floor. Spock staggered backwards and barely managed to keep his footing.

McCoy was instantly beside the captain. "You all right, Jim?"

Kirk opened his eyes. "Yes. I think." He raised his head off the floor and glowered at the Vulcan. "You could've at least warned me."

"He did, Jim." McCoy helped him to his feet. "You know, I want to take back all that nasty comment I made about this ship. After all, the shields worked, the hangar doors worked. Hell, even the brig works."

"Now it has to work," Jim said crossly. He rubbed the spot on the back of his skull where it had struck the floor. "I don't care what anyone says. There's got to be a way out of here."

Spock clasped his hands behind his back. "This brig is a completely new design, Captain. A flawless one. It is escape-proof."

"The designers *always* claim the brig's escape-proof, Spock. What makes you think this time is any different?"

"The designers tested it on the most intelligent and resourceful individual they could find. He failed to escape."

McCoy shot Jim a look. "This sounds pretty suspicious to me, Jim."

Kirk narrowed his eyes. "This . . . resourceful individual. He didn't by any chance have pointed ears and an unerring capacity for getting his shipmates into trouble, did he?"

Spock considered the question thoughtfully. "He *did* have pointed ears."

"Well, Spock, maybe you couldn't find a way out by yourself, but the three of us together can accomplish it."

"I doubt it." Spock's tone was matter-of-fact.

"Here, help me up again." Jim reached for the Vulcan's shoulder—and stopped. Outside the cell, a monitor screen on the security terminal flickered and came to life with an image of Sybok standing on the bridge flanked by Chekov, Uhura, and Sulu.

"My crew," Jim said bitterly. He stepped as close to the brig entrance as possible without touching the glowing force field that kept them prisoners. "The bastard's brainwashed my crew."

"Brave crew of the starship *Enterprise*," Sybok intoned dramatically. "Consider the questions of existence: Who am I? Why am I here? Does God exist? These are the questions all beings have asked since they first gazed at the stars and dreamed.

"My Vulcan ancestors were ruled by their emotions. They felt with their hearts, made love with their hearts, believed with their hearts. But modern Vulcan philosophy has stripped away emotion, leading to imbalance and unhappiness. Suppress *all* emotion, Surak insisted. To suppress hate, you must also suppress love.

"Is this truly wisdom? We know no more than our ancestors did about our beginnings. We still grope in darkness, seeking answers to our questions. Unless we are guided by our hearts as well as our intellects, we shall never find them.

"Our ancestors believed in a place where all these questions of existence could be answered. Modern dogma, of course, tells us this place is a myth, a fantasy concocted by misled fanatics. But even in legend one can always find a kernel of truth." Sybok leaned closer to the screen, his eyes blazing fiercely. "I tell you that it exists! My sisters and brothers, we have been chosen to undertake the greatest adventure of all time—the discovery of Sha Ka Ree."

"Fascinating," Spock whispered. By now he stood next to the captain. "I suppose he believes he has found it."

"Found *what?*" Jim was baffled.

"Sha Ka Ree. The reason Sybok left Vulcan." Spock turned his attention back to the screen.

"Just a dad-blame minute," McCoy said. "What the hell are you two talking about?"

Sybok spoke again. "Our destination: the planet Sha Ka Ree. It lies beyond the Great Barrier at the center of our galaxy."

His image faded into darkness.

"Bless my soul," the doctor remarked sarcastically. "Sounds to me like we're headed for the Promised Land."

But Kirk drew back, alarmed. "The center of the galaxy?"

"Apparently he intends to take the *Enterprise* there." Spock looked at him knowingly.

"But the center of the galaxy can't be reached!" Jim said. "Even a schoolchild knows that! The radiation is too intense. No probe has ever returned from there."

"Quite true." Spock's expression was thoughtful.

"What the hell does he mean? What *is* the Great Barrier?" McCoy demanded.

"An accretion disk," Spock explained, "bordered by an area which is densely populated by stars."

"An ah . . . a what kind of disk?" McCoy asked.

"A ring which lies approximately thirteen light-years from the galactic center, and consists of dust and molecular gases. The dust in the ring is hot, heated by an unknown energy source in its center, which radiates an enormous amount of high-energy X rays and gamma rays. Current research indicates that the energy source is at least ten million times more luminous than Earth's sun."

The doctor frowned. "Well, what the heck *is* it? A giant star?"

Spock shook his head. "Unlikely. The accretion disk is rotating about the center, which means the object at the center possesses gravity—such enormous gravity that its mass must be roughly two million times greater than that of Sol."

"Two million times," Jim marveled. "That'd be *some* star."

"Indeed. But there is not enough gas or dust present to account for more than a fraction of the mass. This has led to two theories: one, that a singularity—either a neutron star or a black hole, compact but incredibly dense and exerting incredible gravitational force—is at our galaxy's center."

"And the second theory?" Jim asked.

"A white hole. A 'creation machine,' if you will." Spock paused. "Of course, this is sheer speculation."

No one spoke for a few seconds. And then McCoy said, very hesitantly, "And ... this source ... is what Sybok's looking for?"

Spock gave a single curt nod.

"Great." The doctor's tone was sarcastic. "And he's gonna take *us* into the middle of *that?*"

"He's mad." Jim's anger had been reawakened.

"This starship simply isn't constructed to withstand that sort of intense radiation, nor is her crew. He may be your brother, Spock, but he's mad."

The Vulcan's tone was calm, but there was a faintly troubled look in his eyes. "That thought has occurred to me as well; certainly his actions and beliefs are bizarre by any standards. And yet Sybok possesses the keenest intellect I have ever known. He is better versed in the theories I have just named than I; indeed, his training was in astrophysics. As a scientist, I am skeptical about his claims, but at the same time I am curious to know his rationale. So little is known about the galactic center. Perhaps he really has discovered something that explains the legend of Sha Ka Ree."

"Spock!" Jim snapped. "My only concern right now is getting my ship back. When that's done and Sybok is in *here,* the two of you can debate Sha Ka Ree until you're green in the face. Until then——"

Jim broke off and frowned at the tapping that came from the back wall of the cell. He turned. "What the hell is *that?*"

Spock tilted his head and listened. "I believe it is a primitive form of communication known as the Morse code." He moved over to the wall and knelt down to rest a hand on the spot from which the sound emanated.

Jim crouched next to him. "You're right, Spock. Morse code was required knowledge at the Academy, but I'm a little out of practice."

The message ended; Jim waited for it to be repeated. "Let's see . . . that's an *S,* isn't it?"

Spock nodded. "The next letter is a *T."*

"A," Jim translated. "N, D . . . end of word."

"Stand," McCoy said. "So what kind of message is that?"

Kirk shushed him. "It's not finished. A new word now: B, A—"

Spock finished: "C, K."

"Back," the doctor said, pleased with himself for solving the riddle. "Stand back."

Kirk and Spock looked at each other in horror.

A panel from the wall exploded into shrapnel. Jim lunged for cover, but not soon enough to avoid getting showered with debris.

When Jim opened his eyes again, he saw Scott's head and shoulders poking through the opening. He stared, stunned, at the engineer.

"Well, what are you waiting for?" Scott scolded them. "Don't you recognize a jailbreak when you see one?"

Scott led them through the labyrinthine bowels of the ship. The fact that the *Enterprise* was in the hands of a group of unwashed hooligans offended him beyond words. After all, he had virtually rebuilt the entire ship with his own two hands; she was now his as much as her predecessor had been, perhaps even more so.

Scott crouched down as he led the three escapees into a narrow ventilation shaft.

Behind him, Mr. Spock spoke. "We can trust no one, Captain. You saw the mental condition of the hostages. Sybok is capable of doing the same thing to every person aboard this vessel."

"They looked like religious converts," McCoy remarked in a subdued tone. "Completely brainwashed. I don't mean to pry, Spock, but I thought mental control was illegal or something on Vulcan. In poor taste, at least."

Spock answered reluctantly. "Both. It is considered a breach of personal ethics and one of the most heinous crimes imaginable."

"We've got to stop him as soon as possible," the captain said. "We've got to send a distress signal."

"How?" McCoy asked. "We'll never make it to the bridge."

Spock replied, "It is possible to override the bridge communications board with the emergency signaling apparatus in the forward observation room."

"The only problem is," Kirk said, "it's up there . . . and we're down here."

There was a solution, of course. Scott thought for a moment, then turned his head to look back at them. "You might be able to reach it by means of turbo shaft number three."

"Oh, no." McCoy shook his head vigorously. "You're not getting me in any turbolift shaft. That's dange—"

Scott silenced the doctor with a scornful look and a wave of his hand. "It's closed for repairs, so there's no danger of being crushed by the lift, if that's what you're worried about, Doctor. But it *would* be a long and dangerous climb."

For reasons Scott did not understand, McCoy's tone turned ironic. "Actually, some of us get off on long and dangerous climbs."

Kirk ignored him. "Scotty, get the transporter

working. If we make contact with a rescue ship, we'll need it."

"Aye, sir. You can count on me. I'll get right on it."

"Before you go," Kirk said. "Which way to the turbo shaft?"

Scott pointed. "Head down this tunnel and make a right at the hydrovent, then a left at the blowscreen. You canna miss it."

Kirk smiled and shook his head. "Mr. Scott, you're amazing." He and the others turned and headed in the opposite direction down the shaft.

Scott allowed himself to revel in his sense of accomplishment as he made his way down the long, dark shaft toward the transporter circuits. What the captain had said was undeniably true: He *had* accomplished a miracle, after all; why, he had overhauled the *Enterprise* almost single-handedly.

"Nothing amazing about knowing my way around," he muttered to himself. "Why, I've fixed just about everything aboard her that can malfunction. I know her now like I know the back of my own hand."

He was so caught up in his prideful reverie that, as he rounded a sharp corner, he forgot to duck.

And knocked himself out cold on a low-hanging pipe.

If there was one thing in life he hated more than transporters, Leonard McCoy reflected, it would have to be heights. He had to tilt his head all the way back to gaze up at the turbolift shaft; claustrophobically narrow, it stretched up into the darkness, seemingly to infinity.

And the only way up was a narrow emergency ladder.

Even Jim seemed a little taken aback by the idea of climbing up there, but he covered his uneasiness, as he always did, with forced enthusiasm. "Look at it this way, Bones. At least we'll get a good workout."

McCoy grimaced sourly. "Or a heart attack."

Jim ignored him and began to climb. McCoy balked, then shot a glance at Spock, who gestured for the doctor to go ahead. McCoy sighed and began to climb.

Look at it this way, he told himself. *At least you're not last, so you won't get left behind if you're too slow. You're in the middle, the safest place to be. If someone's at the other end, Jim'll find out about it first, and if I lose my grip, Spock will break my fall.*

It didn't help much, but McCoy kept right on climbing. He tried to stay below the heels of Jim's boots, but in a matter of minutes Jim was several meters ahead of him . . . and McCoy was sucking in air like a dying fish. The air in the shaft had little oxygen in it; McCoy's arms began to tremble with fatigue.

"Jim," he gasped. "Slow down! This is going to take me forever."

Jim was unsympathetic. "You were the one who told me I had to exercise more, as I recall. You should learn to take your own advice, Doctor." He peered down at McCoy, then suddenly stopped climbing. "Where's Spock?"

Struggling against vertigo, McCoy cautiously glanced down between his boots. Below, the shaft disappeared into blackness. Spock was nowhere to be seen. Had the Vulcan fallen without so much as a sound?

A soft *whoosh* descended upon them from above; McCoy looked up, startled. Spock eased slowly down the shaft, sporting the levitation boots he'd used at Yosemite. The Vulcan floated down to Kirk's level and hovered there.

"I believe," he told Kirk and the doctor, "that I have found a faster method."

Jim grinned. He stepped off the ladder and held on to Spock's neck; they slowly descended until they were beside McCoy.

"C'mon, Bones," Jim called. "All aboard."

McCoy clung stubbornly to the ladder and shook his head. "Not me. You two go ahead. I'll wait for the next car. The three of us'll never make it. Spock'll have trouble levitating with only one passenger, much less two."

"Don't be ridiculous." Jim was beginning to sound exasperated. "We can't split up." He paused, then said craftily, "Well, maybe we should. We'll just leave you here. There's no time for Spock to come back for you. But you can climb up yourself, if you insist, and meet us up on deck later."

That did it. McCoy took one last fearful peek at the dizzying blackness above and below him, then squeezed his eyes shut and took hold of Jim's neck.

"Oh, hell. Here goes. . . ."

He made it. McCoy opened his eyes; amazingly, they did not fall . . . but they began to sink steadily downward.

"It would appear that the doctor was correct," Spock admitted. "The levitation boots cannot support our combined weight."

"Thanks a lot," McCoy snapped. "That's a great comfort. I can see it on my tombstone now—'Leonard H. McCoy: He really was right.'"

"It's all those marsh mel—" Jim began . . . and stopped as soon as he saw what awaited them in the shadows below. McCoy followed his gaze.

"There!" Sulu cried, pointing up at them.

At first, McCoy smiled, relieved . . . and then he saw that the search party Sulu led was composed, not of *Enterprise* crew members, but of Sybok's soldiers. McCoy caught a glimpse of the expression on the helmsman's face and realized with a shudder that Sulu really wasn't Sulu anymore.

"Spock!" Jim hissed. "The booster rockets!"

Spock hesitated. "Captain, if I activate them, we will be propelled upward at an unpredictable speed. If we collide with the shaft ceiling, we could be injured . . . perhaps killed."

"Great," McCoy muttered bitterly. "Caught betwixt the devil and the deep blue sea."

"Fire the boosters!" Kirk ordered, in a tone that made Spock comply immediately.

The boosters hurled them upward; the ladder whizzed by at vertiginous speed. McCoy cried out and clung to Jim and Spock for all he was worth.

They stopped with a sickening lurch.

Timidly, McCoy opened his eyes. Sulu and the others had disappeared into the darkness below. The doctor's head was reeling, but he was alive and uninjured. So was Jim, though the captain looked as pasty-faced as McCoy felt.

Spock was entirely unruffled by the event. "I am afraid," he announced, "that I overshot our mark by one level."

"What the hell," the doctor said shakily. "Nobody's perfect."

Spock carried them to the exit. McCoy clambered out first, and was gratified to find that they were in the corridor directly outside the forward observation deck.

Once inside the observation deck, Spock crossed over to the communications console and activated it. He turned to Kirk. "Emergency channel open, Captain."

Jim stepped up to the console. "To anyone within the sound of my voice: this is Captain James T. Kirk of the Federation Starship *Enterprise*. If you read me, acknowledge."

Several moments passed, and then a burst of static crackled through the grid, followed by the faint sound of a feminine voice.

"Enterprise, this is Starfleet Command. We can just barely read you. Over."

Encouraged, McCoy exchanged grins with Jim. Kirk raised his voice as he spoke into the grid.

"A hostile force has seized control of our vessel and put us on a direct course with the Great Barrier. Our coordinates are zero-zero-zero, mark two. Request emergency assistance. Acknowledge."

"Acknowledged, *Enterprise*. We are dispatching a rescue ship immediately."

"Roger, Starfleet. Kirk out."

"Starfleet out."

Jim closed the channel and exchanged a hopeful look with his friends.

"Thank God," McCoy breathed reverently. "Thank God."

Aboard *Okrona*, Vixis leaned over the subspace transmitter at her station. "Starfleet out."

Her accent was flawless; the humans had been completely fooled. Triumphant, she looked over her shoulder at her captain.

Klaa's face was that of one obsessed; without turning from her gaze, he barked an order at the helmsman. "Tarag! Plot course zero-zero-zero, mark two."

Vixis had feared as much. Klaa had no choice now but to kill Kirk, or lose face before his entire crew. Yet Vixis understood quite well the risks of nearing the Great Barrier: draw too close, and the high levels of radiation would penetrate the shields, killing all aboard *Okrona* . . . if the incredible temperatures did not kill them first by superheating the ship's hull.

"Captain," she said tentatively, "that course will take us directly into the Great Barrier."

The fire in Klaa's eyes told her that he was willing to risk it . . . and more.

"Where Kirk goes, we follow," he growled, and stomped back to his chair.

She dared say no more. But her admiration for her captain dimmed somewhat. Klaa was indeed brave— brave enough to risk his life, his ship, and all aboard her—but not brave enough to risk the contempt of his crew.

Vixis sighed and watched the star pattern change on her viewer as *Okrona* came hard about and swooped after her prey.

Chapter Thirteen

SCOTT WOKE to a dull headache and the realization that he was in sickbay. He struggled to sit up and found he could not; restraints held him back. He fumbled for them—and discovered they were not restraints at all, but Uhura's arms.

"Easy, Scotty," she soothed, and stroked his forehead. Even under her light touch, his skin felt tender and bruised. "You had one heck of a knock, but you're all right now. You're back with us."

He relaxed and blinked up at her. He hadn't the vaguest notion how he had come to be in sickbay; the last thing he remembered was that he had been walking through a ventilation shaft, going to fix the transporter . . . The transporter was somehow very urgent.

"The captain—" he began, then stopped, confused. The captain had wanted him to fix the transporter, but for some reason he felt he shouldn't tell Uhura . . .

And then he remembered Spock's words: "We can trust no one, Captain. You saw the mental condition of the hostages. Sybok is capable of doing the same to every person on board. . . ."

There was something faintly unnatural about Uhura's tender smile, about the vague euphoria in her eyes. Scott decided to test her. He groaned theatrically and raised a hand to his aching temple.

"Uhura, I had the strangest dream. I dreamt a madman had taken over the *Enterprise*."

Uhura laughed softly. It was a pleasant, gentle sound, but it made Scott's flesh crawl. "Dear Scotty," she said, still smiling as she shook her head. "He isn't a madman."

"He's not?" Scott asked with false innocence as he tried his best not to appear sickened by her answer.

She laughed again. "What ever gave you that idea? Sybok's different . . . amazing, unlike anyone I've ever known. He's helped Sulu and Chekov, too—put us in touch with feelings we've always been afraid to express." She laid a hand against Scott's cheek and gave him a loving look.

Scott blushed as thoroughly as he would have if Uhura had been herself. "I . . . er . . . Uhura, I have to repair the transporter." When she frowned quizzically at him, he added, "After all, where we're going, we'll need it." He gently freed himself from her grip and got off the exam table.

She sighed with disappointment, but she let him go. "I suppose you're right. It's just that there's so much I want to tell you."

"Of course." Scott comforted her with a pat on the shoulder. "Maybe when I'm a wee bit stronger and the transporter's working. I dinna think I could take it in my present condition." *Or yours.*

"Perhaps a little later?" she asked hopefully.

"Later," Scott reassured her, and headed for the exit before she changed her mind.

Sybok blocked the doorway, accompanied by two armed soldiers.

"Mr. Scott." The Vulcan's expression was benevolent, but Scott sensed the presence of something sinister. As the Vulcan took a step forward, Scott stepped back into sickbay. The door snapped shut behind them, over the guards. "Where are you headed in such a hurry?"

Scott's expression hardened; he did not answer.

"He's going to fix the transporter," Uhura volunteered cheerfully, to Scott's dismay. "After all, we'll probably need it when we . . . when we get to wherever we're going."

"I see." The Vulcan folded his arms across his chest in a manner that was curiously reminiscent of Mr. Spock. "How very interesting. Unfortunately, I don't think it would be wise to fix the transporter just yet. It seems the captain and his two friends have escaped— with help." He turned to Scott. "You wouldn't happen to know anything about that, would you, Mr. Scott?"

"Aye, that I would," Scott said with utter contempt and a proud tilt of his chin.

"I thought you might." The Vulcan's tone was

amiable. He nodded at Uhura, who seemed to understand; she headed immediately for the door.

On her way, she paused to lay a hand on Scott's forearm.

"Trust him, Scotty. Don't be afraid. You'll understand everything when it's over."

The doors opened, and Uhura stepped outside with the guards.

Scott found her words less than reassuring. He was alone with the Vulcan now; Sybok moved closer to him, but Scott refused to cower or back away from him.

"I suppose ye'll try to brainwash me now," Scott said.

Sybok appeared faintly amused. "I don't brainwash anyone. I merely show people how to share their pain and transform it into a source of strength. I can show you now." He stepped forward until he was close enough to touch the engineer.

"I'm not in pain," Scott retorted coldly. "If anyone's in need of psychological help, you—"

He stopped, confused. For a brief, almost imperceptible instant, the Vulcan loomed vast in Scott's field of vision. Scott felt a twinge of panic, the very same panic he had experienced when, long ago, Mr. Spock had touched his mind in order to protect him from a delusion. The panic arose from his fear of opening his mind to the unknown, to another's control. It brightened like a flare, then dimmed. The sharp features of the Vulcan faded to reveal . . .

Sickbay, but somehow changed. It was, Scott realized with a resurgence of fear, the room on the old

219

ship, as it had looked roughly a year ago, when Dr. McCoy had worked grimly to save the life of a fourteen-year-old cadet trainee.

Scott looked down at himself and gasped. The front of his uniform was damp, stained with blood. Peter's blood.

Scott sagged against the glass, pressing a hand against it to steady himself, to be closer to his youngest nephew. His palm left behind a red smear.

"Peter," he moaned softly, finally daring to raise his head and stare through the glass. "Lad, I canna bear to lose you again."

Cadet Peter Preston had been on a training mission aboard the *Enterprise* when it was fired on by the starship *Reliant*, pirated by Khan Noonian Singh. As a result of the attack, the *Enterprise*'s engine room had suffered severe damage. Cadet Preston had remained faithfully at his post, long enough to keep auxiliary power from failing and the *Enterprise* from being destroyed, and long enough to inhale enough poisonous coolant gas to ensure his death.

Scott found himself reliving the dreadful moment when Kirk had appeared in sickbay to witness Peter's final agony.

Scott closed his eyes. Even so, he could still see the pity and sorrow etched on the captain's face, the horrible expression of defeat McCoy wore as he glanced up and shook his head.

Coolant poisoning, McCoy said. Other words followed, words too awful for Scott to register.

The engineer drew close to the boy's bedside, and touched his forehead.

Peter's skin burned his hand. The fever resulted

from exposure to the intensely radioactive gas. Dr. McCoy had done what he could to stop the hemorrhage, but the damage to the cell walls was too great; thin pink-red blood oozed from the boy's nose and mouth.

Scott wept. During the last few days before his nephew's death, he had disciplined Peter in response to what Scott perceived as flippancy. In retrospect, he realized he had overreacted, had singled the boy out for punishment in an effort to make clear that he would show no favoritism to his young nephew.

"If only I could have *told* you," Scott sobbed. "But you were gone so quickly, there wasna time."

Peter opened his eyes.

Next to Scott, the captain leaned over and spoke to the dying boy: *Mr. Preston.*

Peter's voice was faint, almost too faint for Scott to hear. He spoke, not to his stricken uncle Montgomery —Scott doubted Peter even knew he was there—but to his captain. *Is the word given?* he whispered.

A shadow passed over Kirk's face, but his tone was sure. *The word is given.*

Aye, Peter said, and died.

Scott collapsed to his knees and did not rise this time. In his attempt to teach the boy discipline, he had made the final days of Peter's life miserable.

And Peter would never know the depths to which his uncle regretted the fact.

Yet as Scott wept into his hands, he experienced a peculiar awareness: he was not alone. Even though Peter and Dr. McCoy and Captain Kirk had all faded away, another remained, touching Scott's mind in much the same way Mr. Spock had touched it.

"Only a child," Scott sobbed. "If I hadna been so hard on him . . ."

He would still have died, a distinct voice answered in Scott's mind, but the voice was not his own.

Scott gazed up into Sybok's eyes. They seemed ancient, fierce, blazing and, paradoxically, infinitely loving.

Share your pain with me and gain strength from it, his eyes said. The message was delivered in a manner beyond all language; but when Scott recalled the incident later, he would be convinced that Sybok had spoken to him in Scots Gaelic.

Peter was an intelligent boy.

"Yes," Scott whispered. The thought of Peter's brilliant mind, lost forever, only intensified his sorrow.

He understood the reasons behind your actions, Sybok told him. *Peter knew you acted out of love.*

Scott dared to allow himself a small ray of hope. "Peter . . . understood?"

A silent *yes. There was no need to tell him. Peter remained at his post, not out of fear of your reaction, but because of his sense of duty. He would have done the same in any case. You in no way contributed to his death, Montgomery.*

Scott bowed his head. The horror of Peter's death began to fade; Scott felt the overlay of guilt and grief being gently stripped from him, much as one might undress a child. Scott searched his heart and found a melancholy fondness for Peter . . . and a new and growing joy.

He peered up at the Vulcan with love and admiration, and was reminded of a legend he'd been told as a child.

"You're a sin-eater," he whispered to Sybok.

He had said it with the most sincere gratitude, but Sybok's eyes flashed with such pain for an infinitesimal fraction of a second that Scott felt sorrow. And then the Vulcan's eyes were calm once more, full of love and wisdom.

"God bless ye," Scott told him, and rose to his feet. He still wept, but not from sorrow. "Forgive me for thinking ye had evil intentions."

Sybok conveyed a single, wordless impression to Scott's mind. The engineer nodded, realizing the utter lack of need for apologies.

"Then what can I do, Sybok, to express how grateful—"

The Vulcan smiled and answered him aloud. "The captain has ordered you to fix the transporters, and so you shall. But first, there is a far more important task that demands your attention. It concerns the safety of everyone aboard this vessel."

"Name it. Give the word, and I'll see that it's done."

"The shields. Their basic structure must be altered radically before we reach the Great Barrier, so that they will offer considerably more protection."

Scott tilted his head skeptically. "Begging your pardon, but if there were a way to boost the shields, *I'd* know about it."

Sybok seemed amused again. "Do you trust me, Mr. Scott?"

"Aye, that I do," the engineer replied passionately.

"Good. I will give you a formula so that you can

make the appropriate adjustments to the shield design. The transporter will have to wait."

"Aye, sir," Scott replied. And after the Vulcan gave him the formula, he went to work joyfully.

Her duty shift ended, Vixis headed down the dark corridor to her quarters.

She was deeply agitated, torn between her admiration and attraction for Klaa and her duty as first officer of the *Okrona*. Klaa's insistence that *Okrona* follow the *Enterprise* into the Barrier—and certain destruction—taxed Vixis's loyalty beyond its limits, for it indicated that the captain's arrogance had become megalomania.

There were no regulations in the Empire's service that allowed her to simply relieve Klaa on the grounds of incompetence; it was assumed that irresponsible captains would be the victims of assassination or exile by their own crews.

Action would have to be taken before *Okrona* reached the barrier, but Vixis was reluctant to act, not merely because of her loyalty to Klaa but because she knew Klaa to be a formidable enemy, mad or not.

If she did succeed in killing him, there remained the task of convincing Command of the need for such a drastic measure. At the moment, Klaa had many influential supporters—supporters who would be swift to avenge his murder.

These thoughts troubled her as she arrived at the door to her quarters and called out her private access code. The computer lock recognized her voice and the sequence, and permitted her access.

The door slid open to reveal Morek.

Vixis was startled to see him there, but only because she did not think him shrewd enough to override the security on her quarters. She remained in the doorway and eyed him coldly.

"Morek. How did you get in?"

She did not ask why he had come; she was not in the habit of asking questions for which she already had answers.

"Unimportant," Morek replied. He smiled at her; his eyes were small and glittering in the semidarkness. "Enter."

He stepped back to permit her entry. He was not completely ignorant, at least; he understood that Klaa probably monitored the corridors—and that the jamming devices installed in Vixis's quarters made it safer to discuss topics such as the captain's assassination.

The door closed behind them. Vixis uttered a soft command; the room brightened, causing Morek to squint.

"Speak, Morek," she said, impatient to be done with it.

"You know why I have come," Morek began, looking to her for confirmation.

She scowled without answering.

Uncertainly, he continued. "As you can see, I have discovered a means to override the security on the officers' quarters." His tone became wheedling. "Few women in the Empire have managed to attain the rank of captain, Vixis. If you were to take Klaa's ship, you would be much honored."

And the target of Klaa's friends and family, she finished bitterly. Aloud, she said, "Do not try to flatter me, Morek, when we are speaking of murder."

Morek's expression darkened with anger. "The alternative is to become victims ourselves, of Klaa's insanity. Are you willing to die to soothe his ego?"

"No," she said reluctantly.

Morek stepped closer, close enough for her to feel his moist breath on her face. He touched her shoulder, then ran his hand slowly down the length of her arm. Repelled, she pulled away.

"I am first officer, Morek. The captain heeds my advice. I hold your rank—and your life, if I so choose—in my hands. Remember that before you dare touch me again."

His arm dropped to his side. She saw a flicker of rage cross his face before he gained control of himself and adopted a servile expression.

"I ask forgiveness," he said. "But for your sake and the sake of the crew, I ask you—do not allow *Okrona* to be destroyed to appease a madman."

"I would never allow it," she responded coldly. "What do you suggest, Gunner?"

"Go to him. I have seen the way he looks at you, Vixis. Go to him, distract him . . . and I will see to the rest."

Vixis studied Morek's crude, thick features carefully and saw deceit written there. Morek ranked one grade below her; with the first officer and the captain gone, *Okrona* would be his to command.

How convenient for you, Morek, to find the two who stand in your way together.

Yet if she was careful, perhaps there was a way to rid

herself of Morek . . . and of Klaa, if necessary. She altered her expression to make it appear that she had considered Morek's plan carefully and decided it was the only viable solution to their problem.

"When?" she asked finally. They would approach the barrier in a matter of hours.

Morek smiled at her. "Tonight."

Chapter Fourteen

McCoy's RELIEF at the promise of being rescued by Starfleet was short-lived. As he, Jim, and Spock prepared to exit the observation deck, Sybok and his soldiers confronted them.

Spock's half brother smiled faintly at the startled looks on his prisoners' faces. "I trust your message was received?" He appeared entirely unconcerned by the fact that Starfleet would soon be in pursuit.

Jim was right; he is *mad,* McCoy decided. Besides, he'd never met anyone, human or Vulcan, who smiled quite as much as Sybok.

Spock said nothing. Jim stepped forward angrily, which caused the soldiers to cock their weapons and take aim.

"You can put us in the brig again," Jim said hotly,

"and I'll do everything in my power to escape again. I won't stand by while you take the *Enterprise* into the Great Barrier. And if you kill me, then Starfleet will stop you. Go ahead and commit suicide if you want, but do it without my ship and my crew."

Sybok's smile faded at last. He gestured for his troops to lower their weapons—which they did, grudgingly—and focused his full attention on Kirk. His voice held no trace of anger, only concern.

"What you fear is the unknown, Captain Kirk. The people of Earth once believed their world to be flat, but Columbus proved it was round. They said that humans would never reach out into space, but they reached far further than anyone ever believed possible. They said no vessel could ever travel faster than the speed of light . . . until warp speed was discovered.

"The Great Barrier represents the ultimate expression of this universal fear of the unknown. It is no more than an extension of personal fear."

Jim's face and voice hardened. "That's insane. Fear has nothing to do with it. We're not talking about psychology; we're talking about physical *fact*. Intense gravitation and intense radiation bombardment will hurt you whether you admit their existence or not, whether you're afraid of them or not. Enough people have died proving it."

Sybok did not, as McCoy expected, react with anger; instead, his expression saddened, and his response was surprisingly gentle. "Captain, I so much want your understanding and respect. Will you hear me out—or are you afraid?"

"I'm afraid of nothing," Jim said, with such conviction that McCoy almost believed him.

Sybok turned to his soldiers. "Wait outside."

One of them, clearly the second-in-command, began to protest. "But Syb—"

"Do it, J'Onn."

Reluctantly, the soldiers withdrew. As the door to the corridor snapped shut behind them, Sybok stepped toward his prisoners. "Come."

McCoy saw the ripple of doubt pass over Jim's face and knew exactly what the captain was thinking. Sybok was unarmed; if the three of them could manage to overpower him . . .

But the guards were right outside, a shout away. Sybok intended no violence; perhaps it would be better to play along for a while and await the arrival of the rescue ship. The alternative was to risk getting killed by a blast from the soldiers' crude guns.

McCoy read all of this on Jim's face in no more than a second. For a minute, he was honestly worried that Jim might choose to risk death, as he so blatantly had at Yosemite.

"Lights dim," Sybok commanded, and immediately the deck darkened so that the stars shining through the huge observation window brightened to dazzling intensity.

Sybok ignored Spock's reproachful gaze. "I'm sure you have many questions." His manner was warm and confidential, like that of a professor eager to share his knowledge with a handpicked group of exceptional scholars. "Here, with the stars for our backdrop, we shall seek the answers together."

McCoy tensed in his chair. Sybok's voice was deep

and full, his intonation melodic, his eyes compelling. It would be all too easy to slip into a trance. . . .

The captain, at least, was still frowning.

"Sha Ka Ree," Sybok said reverently. "Translated into Standard, 'the Source.' Call it what you will—heaven, Eden. The Klingons call it Qui'Tu; the Romulans, Vorta Vor. Every culture shares this dream of the place from which creation sprang. For us, that place will soon be a reality."

Only not quite in the way you hoped, McCoy thought, but he held his tongue.

Kirk's tone was hostile. "The only reality I see is that I'm a prisoner on my own ship. You've brainwashed my crew, manipulated them somehow. And now you're obviously trying to do the same thing to us. What is this power that you use to control others' minds?"

Spock shifted uncomfortably next to McCoy.

Sybok drew back as if he had been slapped. "I don't control minds," he said, with a trace of defensiveness. "I free them."

"How?" McCoy demanded, before Jim could ask. "In my professional judgment, these people were brainwashed."

Sybok regained his composure. "Not at all. I simply make them face their pain and draw strength from it. Once that's done, fear cannot stop you . . . for its purpose is merely to help you avoid pain."

Spock shifted his weight again. Jim caught his discomfort and asked, "Spock? Is he telling the truth?"

"As he sees it," the Vulcan replied, with more than a hint of irony. He did not meet Sybok's eyes. "It is an

231

ancient Vulcan technique, forbidden in modern times. I am not at liberty to reveal much more . . . except to say that it *was* misused by many to impose their will upon others."

"Sounds like brainwashing all right," McCoy said.

Sybok looked sharply at the doctor, then closed his eyes and concentrated. "Your pain, Dr. McCoy, is the deepest of all."

McCoy jerked back, caught off guard. "What?"

Sybok opened his eyes. They seemed very wide, very deep; McCoy felt swallowed up by them. "I can feel it. Can't you?"

Leonard . . .

The voice was hauntingly familiar. It seemed to emanate from within McCoy's own skull. Startled, he looked over at Jim and Spock to see if they had heard, but his two friends were staring curiously back at him.

Leonard . . .

With heart-wrenching certainty, McCoy recognized the voice. "No," he whispered savagely. "No, this is some kind of horrible trick."

Sybok, Kirk, and Spock melted into the darkness. McCoy was utterly alone.

Leonard, the voice implored, full of pain and love.

The walls throbbed with energy; images swirled, danced, coalesced. McCoy saw that he was no longer in the forward observation room of a starship, but in an intensive-care hospital room.

"My God." Terrified, McCoy covered his face with his hands. "Don't do this. Please don't do this."

When he dared to lower his hands, he saw a pale white-haired figure, wasted, skeletal, lying on a life-support bed in a white room. The white was blindingly intense, stark, dazzling; it pained McCoy's eyes. Snowblind, he looked away.

Down at the foot of the bed was a small terminal displaying a readout on the current patient. Black characters on a white background.

The top line read: McCOY, DAVID A.

The color of death, McCoy knew, was not black, but white . . . brilliant, blinding white.

Leonard, the old man begged. McCoy forced himself to look down at the pale, waxy face, aged and twisted by pain. It was not the way he wanted to remember David A. McCoy, but it was the way he remembered him far too often.

Three months before, David McCoy had been a square-shouldered, hale man of eighty-one who still had an active family practice in Atlanta. He hadn't even thought of retiring when he learned he had pyrrhoneuritis.

A disease imported from the colony worlds, so rare that Leonard had to look it up to understand that his father had been given a death sentence. The worst part about the disease was the pain. Peripheral nerves were affected at first; as they flared and died, muscle function was lost. Death came when the damage to nerves serving major organs became too great.

For those afflicted, death never came soon enough. Within one month, McCoy's father was a cripple. Within two, he was unrecognizable. During the last three months of his life, David McCoy, a slender man like his son, lost fifty-four pounds.

Somehow, Leonard found his voice. Surprisingly, it

was steady and reassuring. "I'm here, Dad. I'm right here with you." He clasped his father's fragile hand, paper-thin flesh against bone.

David stared up with sightless sky-blue eyes; the disease had already destroyed the optic nerves. *The pain. Just stop the pain . . .*

"We've done everything we can do, Dad." McCoy choked on the words. "Try to hang on."

David McCoy was on total life support; he had brain function, but little else. His heart, lungs, and kidneys had failed days before. He was receiving massive doses of painkillers, but they were not enough, and nerve blocks were ineffective for those suffering from the disease. There was only one way to end his father's suffering.

"I can't help him!" McCoy cried raggedly at the radiant stars overhead. "I can't do anything to help him!" He screamed it so loud that his throat was instantly raw.

A calm voice in his head spoke. His conscience . . . or was it Sybok? *You've done all you can. The support system will keep him alive.*

"You call this alive?" McCoy asked haggardly. "Suspended between life and death by a bridge of pain?"

His father tried to whisper something. McCoy bent close to the old man's parched bluish-gray lips.

Release me. . . .

David turned his face toward the life support machinery. He could not see it, but his mind was still sharp; he knew it was there. He fumbled in its direction.

Release me. . . .

There was no doubt in McCoy's mind about what his father was asking him to do. He recoiled in horror. "I can't . . . but how can I watch him suffer like this?"

Sybok, the voice of conscience again. *You're a doctor.*

"I'm his *son!*"

David cried out in silent agony; Leonard could bear no more. With trembling fingers, he reached out and shut off the life support systems one by one, then gently gathered his father into his arms. The older man's body felt cool and feather-light; he stared blindly up at Leonard, then drew a single, sighing breath and died.

McCoy held the body for several minutes. It seemed suddenly foreign and utterly empty, so devoid of the bright spark that had been David Andrew McCoy that his son had no difficulty believing his father was gone.

Sybok stood at his side. *Why did you do it?* His tone was gentle, without a trace of condemnation.

"To preserve his dignity. You saw what he had become." McCoy felt his throat tighten in response to what he knew would follow.

Sybok's voice was almost inaudible; McCoy was unsure whether he had spoken aloud or in McCoy's head. *But that wasn't the worst of it, was it?*

McCoy began to shiver violently. "No." It was at once an answer and a plea. "No, please . . ."

Share it, Sybok told him. *Share it and be free of it forever.*

McCoy gently laid his father's body against the pillows and bowed his head. "Not long after . . . they found a cure. A goddam cure!" His voice broke.

If you hadn't killed him, he might have lived.

The doctor sobbed bitterly. "No! I loved him!"

You did what you thought was right.

"Yes."

You must release this pain. . . .

The hospital room darkened and was gone. McCoy was standing once again on the forward observation deck.

He wept until he was exhausted. And then something strange occurred. It was as if someone else were absorbing his grief and replacing it with joy. McCoy felt an incredible surge of relief. The memory of his father's horrible suffering and death remained, but now McCoy remembered it through the eyes of an objective observer. Sybok had told the truth; McCoy felt suddenly strong, able to bear this sorrow . . . and more.

He understood now why the Vulcan smiled so often. Gratefully the doctor glanced at his savior; Sybok was speaking.

"This pain has poisoned your soul for a long time. But now you've taken the first step. The other steps we'll take together."

"Thank you," McCoy whispered, wiping at stray tears. "Thank you." He smiled up at the Vulcan.

Spock observed the unfolding drama between McCoy and his dying father with growing distress. Not only had he been forced to witness something that should have remained private, but he had been dismayed at the degree to which Sybok had strengthened his natural telepathic powers. Violating a person's mind was a criminal act . . . but to do so and then project eidetic images of that violation for others to witness was monstrous.

Spock found himself grieving with McCoy, not only for his father's death but also at the grievous invasion of the doctor's privacy.

And now Sybok turned to Spock.

Spock regarded him with something very much like loathing.

"Each individual is unique," Sybok continued.

"I hide no pain," Spock said coldly.

Sybok smiled. "I know you better than that, Spock."

"Do you?" Spock challenged. He could struggle mentally against Sybok's invading mind, but the most likely outcome was that Spock's mental defenses would be permanently damaged and Sybok would no doubt be the eventual victor. Better, Spock decided, to risk a temporary loss of face than endure such damage. "Go ahead," he told Sybok. "I shall not resist you."

"Spock," Jim said next to him. The captain's face was lined with concern. "Don't."

"It's quite all right, Captain." Spock faced his brother. "Proceed."

The lights dimmed. Somewhere in the darkness, a woman screamed. Out of the blackness, sounds and images formed: the insistent throb of ceremonial drums echoed against the high stone walls of a cave. Crude torches illuminated the scene and threw shadows of a woman in labor against the walls. It was a scene from Vulcan prehistory, starkly primitive, and for a moment, Spock was confused. Then, from deep within his consciousness, long-buried memories rose.

Like the ceremonies of marriage and burial, the Vulcan ritual surrounding birth had remained intact over the millennia. Even the logic of Surak had failed to strip the Vulcans of their dark and ancient rites.

Jim turned to his friend, perplexed. "Spock, what *is* this?"

"I believe," Spock said calmly, "that we are witnessing my birth."

Sybok appeared before him, holding out a hand. "Come. If you are truly unafraid, let me lead you into the past."

Spock rose and went with him. In the far reaches of the cave, Spock recognized the young human female lying on the rough pallet as his mother. Beneath her ceremonial robes, Amanda's distended stomach lifted; her contorted face shone with perspiration. At her feet, a Vulcan high priestess intoned the ancient rites of birth. Spock recognized her as the regal T'Lar, the priestess who had fused Spock's body and spirit after his death.

How appropriate, Spock thought, *that she who attended my second entry into this life also attended me at the first.*

At Amanda's side stood Sarek, Spock's Vulcan father, who watched the proceedings with uncomfortable reserve.

Because of T'Lar, Spock realized, *he does not show his concern for my mother.* Even more than Sarek's apparent detachment from the proceedings, Spock was struck by how young his parents appeared; Sarek's hair was jet black, Amanda's golden brown, neither with a trace of silver.

Amanda screamed; the drums quickened to a climax—then stopped abruptly as the child was born. A sound: an infant crying.

T'Lar picked up the child and presented it to the father. Sarek stared at it without joy.

So human, he said. Spock thought he detected a trace of disappointment in the father's tone. Sarek took the infant and gently handed it to his wife. Amanda cradled it next to her, and traced a finger along its tiny pointed ears. She glanced up at her husband.

Neither human nor Vulcan, but ours.

Jim watched the proceedings with growing anxiety. "Spock . . ." He laid a tentative hand on his first officer's shoulder, but the Vulcan remained mute. Angrily Jim turned on Sybok. "What have you done to my friend?"

Sybok's expression was serenely satisfied. "I've done nothing. Your friends . . . this is who they are. Didn't you know that?"

The question caught Jim off-guard. "No," he said blankly. "No, I suppose I didn't."

"Now learn something about yourself." Sybok drew closer.

Jim avoided meeting the Vulcan's eyes. "No! I refuse."

McCoy emerged from his solitary reverie and laid a comforting hand on Kirk's arm. "Jim, try to be open about this." There was a vagueness in the doctor's eyes that was unsettlingly familiar. . . .

The hostage tape. Caithlin Dar's eyes had looked exactly the same.

Brainwashed, all right, McCoy had said then.

Jim realized that he was on the verge of losing his two best friends to a madman. He pulled away from McCoy. "Open about what?" He almost shouted it. "That I've made the wrong choices in my life? That I went left when I should've gone right? I know what my weaknesses are."

The very thought made images shimmer and swirl in the shadows: *Enterprise,* as her fiery hull streaked through the sky toward Genesis like a falling star as she plummeted to her death. *David, my son, my own flesh and blood, dead before I had the chance to really know him. Lost chances with his mother, Carol* . . . "I don't need Sybok to take me on a tour of them."

"Jim," McCoy pleaded, his eyes dulled by euphoria, "if you'd just unbend and allow yourself—"

"To be brainwashed by the con man? You said it yourself, Doctor, remember?"

"I was wrong," McCoy countered. "This 'con man' took away my pain! No psychiatrist in the universe has ever—"

"Dammit, Bones, you're a doctor. You know that pain and guilt can't be dispelled with the wave of a magic wand. They're things we carry with us—the things that make us who we are. If we lose them, we lose ourselves. I don't want my pain taken away. I don't want to forget David and Carol . . . and losing the *Enterprise.* I *need* my pain."

"Jim, you've got to listen—" the doctor began, but he was interrupted by a hailing whistle, followed by Uhura's voice emanating from the communications console.

"Sybok, this is the bridge." Her pitch rose a half-octave in excitement. "We are in approach of the Great Barrier."

Beyond the observation window, the starlight was fading, swallowed up by a bright reddish pink glow.

Sybok's face brightened with anticipation. "Captain Kirk, I'm afraid you'll have to remain here. Spock . . . Doctor . . . come with me." He headed confidently for the exit.

McCoy took a step toward the exit, then stopped and looked uncertainly back at Kirk and Spock. The Vulcan remained next to his captain and did not stir. Jim gave his first officer a look of gratitude mixed with a sizable amount of relief.

Sybok reached the exit before realizing he was alone; he turned to regard his half brother with puzzlement. "Spock? Aren't you coming?"

"I cannot go with you," Spock replied with utmost dignity.

Sybok stared at him in disbelief. *"Why?"* There were traces of petulance and hurt in his voice.

"My loyalty is to my captain."

"I don't understand . . ."

"You are my brother, but you do not know me," Spock said. "I am not the outcast boy you left behind. Since that time, I have found myself and my place in the universe . . . here, among my shipmates. My life is here, aboard the *Enterprise.*"

McCoy listened to this speech intently; his eyes seemed to clear. He returned to take his seat next to Spock and Kirk. "I guess you'd better count me out, too, Sybok."

Kirk smiled at him; guiltily, McCoy averted his gaze. "Sorry, Jim. It's just that—"

"You don't have to explain, Bones. Besides, it doesn't matter." Jim touched his shoulder. "You're here now."

To Jim's surprise, Sybok regarded them not angrily but with honest affection. "The bond between the three of you is strong, very strong, but the ultimate victory will be mine." He headed for the exit; the doors slid open to reveal his soldiers waiting patiently in the corridor.

"Wait!" Kirk called.

Sybok paused in the open doorway and looked back at him.

"We'll never make it through the Great Barrier," Jim said, in a desperate attempt to reason with the Vulcan. "As a scientist, you must know that. The shields—"

Sybok interrupted him. "But if we *do*"—he smiled mysteriously—"will that convince you that my vision was true?"

"Your vision?" With a sinking sensation, Jim realized what was coming next.

"Given to me by the One," Sybok said boldly, "who waits for us on the other side." He watched their surprised reactions with relish.

"You *are* insane," Jim told him.

"Am I?" For an instant, honest doubt flickered in Sybok's eyes, only to be replaced by a fiery look that could have been confidence . . . or utter madness. "I'll see you on the other side."

The doors closed behind him.

Chapter Fifteen

VIXIS PATTED THE PHASER concealed beneath her belt and pressed the buzzer on the captain's door. The doors snapped open so abruptly—as if anticipating her arrival—that she had to force herself not to jump. Her nerves were frayed, the result of being constantly alert, for she could trust no one: not Klaa, certainly not Morek.

"Come," Klaa called gruffly.

She entered; the door closed behind her. Klaa sat at his desk, his dark eyes focused intently on the terminal monitor, his expression smug, almost gloating. Vixis searched his face for traces of insanity, but found none.

She stepped before the desk and waited for the captain to acknowledge her presence.

A full minute of silence passed before he glanced distractedly up at her. "Ah. Vixis." He gestured at a chair across from his. "Sit."

She sat. Klaa appeared distracted, intent . . . but not mad.

"Well?" He interlaced his fingers and rested his hands on the desk, then leaned forward, inviting her to speak.

Vixis collected herself. She had considered her actions and their consequences most carefully; if it was necessary for Klaa to die, then he would die by her own hand, not the hand of a dishonorable creature like Morek.

"I came to warn you, Captain."

"Of what?" His eyebrows lifted slightly, but he did not seem particularly surprised. She got the impression he was—indeed, they both were playing carefully scripted roles.

"A plot against your life. A certain member of the crew—"

"Morek," Klaa interjected.

"Yes. Morek is concerned that *Okrona* will be destroyed when we enter the Great Barrier." She paused. "It is a valid fear. He sent me here to distract you, at which point he intends to strike. I have no doubt he means to kill me as well and then take command himself."

"So." Rage flickered across Klaa's features, then faded, replaced by an expression of gratitude. "It is all as I expected, Vixis. I appreciate your loyalty. You will be rewarded."

She smiled thinly. Even if Klaa really was mad, she

knew he would be grateful to hear of Morek's treason. If she found it necessary to assassinate the captain in order to protect the ship, it would be far easier now that she had gained his trust.

"Morek thinks he has set a trap for me," Klaa said, "but he is about to spring the one I've laid for him. Congratulations, First Officer. You have passed the test."

He swiveled the monitor so that Vixis could see the graphic on the screen: a representation of the *Enterprise,* enclosed inside a fantastic web of glowing filaments that formed miniature dodecahedrons, all fitted together in several complex layers.

"The *Enterprise*'s shields," Vixis remarked, gazing at the screen in wonder. Their structure was unlike that of any shields she had ever seen. Somehow, Klaa had used *Okrona*'s scanners to gain access to them.

In a flash, she understood Klaa's motives. She knew that he had behaved irrationally in order to test his crew, that he had forced Morek to reveal his disloyalty in order to be rid of him legitimately, without giving Morek's relatives cause to seek vengeance.

And she knew that, all along, Klaa had studied the unusual design of *Enterprise*'s shields.

Vixis regarded him with infinite admiration. "Shrewd, my captain. Very shrewd."

He smiled faintly, then returned his attention to the screen. "Some hours ago, the *Enterprise*'s shields underwent a dramatic alteration. Tarag called it to my attention. I have entered the new design into our computers; he is working now to restructure *Okrona*'s shields as well." He nodded at the screen. "These shields were invented by a genius. Somehow the Federation has stumbled upon a way to protect a ship from the increased radiation in the Great Barrier."

"But no one has ever entered the Barrier," Vixis protested. "How do we know the shields will hold?"

"*Enterprise* will enter the Barrier first," Klaa said firmly. "If she is destroyed, we will turn back."

Vixis stared at the terminal in amazement. "But, Captain, how did you—"

"How did I get past the security on the shields' structure?" Klaa finished for her. "In their haste, the *Enterprise* crew neglected to affix a security code. Apparently they think they have discouraged us from following."

"It could be a trick."

His confidence did not waver. "If it is, those aboard *Enterprise* will die, either from radiation or *Okrona*'s phasers."

She stared in silence at the amazing spectacle on the screen.

Klaa watched her for a time. When he spoke again, his voice was low and soft. "First Officer, if I had insisted on taking *Okrona* into the Barrier unprotected, you would have killed me, yes?"

Her heart began to beat faster, but she fixed her gaze on him fearlessly and said, "Yes."

He smiled faintly, pleased. "That is as it should be." And he rose and stepped out from behind the desk.

She glanced up, uncertain what to expect; she rested her hand on the hidden phaser.

Klaa reached out to touch her face, and gently drew a fingertip over the soft skin between her jawline and neck.

"Morek expects you to distract me, does he? We must not disappoint him."

She rose and embraced him.

Vixis woke to darkness and confusion.

A sound roused her—the sound of a door rushing open. For an instant of complete disorientation, she could not have said *which* door, or even where she was.

She struggled to sit up. As she did, her arm brushed against warm flesh: Klaa.

She remembered. She was in the captain's quarters, on Klaa's bed with the captain beside her, and the black figure in front of them, backlit by the dimly illuminated corridor, was Morek.

Vixis tensed with fear. In the doorway, the dark figure raised a weapon, clearly intending to kill them both.

Klaa spoke softly into her ear. "Do not be afraid. We are safe—"

A bolt of red pierced the darkness and imprinted itself on Vixis's retinas, blinding her. For an instant she thought she had witnessed her own death. With the bolt came a cry of pain, anger, and defeat. The sound and light reverberated throughout the small cabin, then faded quickly.

She was still alive, though the sound of Morek's death cry still reverberated in her ears and she saw nothing save a streak of dulling red, framed by darkness.

"Well done, Tarag!" Klaa exclaimed; his breath was warm against the skin of her neck.

Her vision cleared. Beyond the doorway of the

captain's quarters, Tarag placed his phaser on his belt and saluted. "I am grateful, my lord."

The door snapped shut.

Vixis released a great sigh and sank back into Klaa's arms. She was not captain of the *Okrona*, but perhaps that was to her advantage—for with the discovery of the new shield design and the death of James Kirk, Klaa would be the Empire's greatest hero . . . and Vixis, as his first officer and paramour, would share in his glory.

Seated at the helm, Sulu stared in awe at the fierce and beautiful sight on the main viewscreen. *Enterprise* had entered the area of giant starclusters known as the Great Barrier. The bridge glowed with the reflected brilliance of a thousand stars as the ship made her way through areas of stellar birth, through expanding blast waves from suns dying in glorious explosions.

Sulu himself felt poised on the verge of fear. He trusted Sybok utterly. But at the same time his rational mind told him that while the *Enterprise*'s shields might withstand a single phaser blast from a Klingon Bird of Prey, they would not withstand the enormous onslaught of radiation from the galactic center.

Sulu watched as his hands, amazingly steady, held the ship on course. *I'm mad,* he told himself, yet for some reason he could not veer from the programmed heading. He did not want to. Sulu glanced back at the Vulcan, Sybok, who sat in the command chair, staring intently at the dazzling display of light and color on the screen. Next to Sybok stood the three diplomats, all of them focused on the sight as well. The Romulan,

Dar, looked exactly the way Sulu felt: moved, humbled . . . and frightened, but too enthralled by what was happening to try to stop it.

We're all *mad,* Sulu thought, and looked back at the screen. Behind him, Dar gasped softly.

The screen suddenly dimmed. Directly before them, a great black thundercloud of gas and dust reared its head.

Sulu's rational mind knew that it was simply an accretion disk, an accumulation of stellar matter, and yet, for no comprehensible reason, the sight of it filled him with panic. He was convinced that the cloud was sentient, *evil* . . . and for an instant, he was on Ganjitsu again, and the black cloud was no longer stellar dust but smoke from the burning forests of Ishikawa. Sulu glanced at Chekov for reassurance, but Chekov's brown eyes widened with terror at the sight of the dark specter confronting them.

"Behold the veil of darkness," Sybok said. He spoke with the authority of a prophet. "Behold fear, in all its ugliness."

Sulu averted his eyes, unable to bear the sight.

"Look," Sybok commanded, "and see what lies *beyond* . . . beyond the fear."

Sulu quailed . . . and then, as he had done so long ago in the forest on Ganjitsu, he gathered himself. Through an act of sheer will, he forced himself to look. Through tiny gaps in the dark cloud, he saw flashes of intense brilliance, of incredible, blinding blue-white fire.

"Fear blocks the light within," Sybok intoned. "A light brighter than ten million suns. Master your fear . . . and free the light within."

The viewscreen went blank.

"Radiation levels were off the scale," Chekov said, gazing down at his console. "The circuits have overloaded. We have no instrument readings."

Sulu turned to face the Vulcan. "They say no ship can survive it," he said, feeling a slow trickle of fear. His outward calm surprised him.

Sybok stood up. "I say they're wrong. The danger is an illusion. Go beyond it. Full ahead, Mr. Sulu."

Sulu paused, recalling the mindless panic that had seized him in the forest of Ishikawa . . . and how the thought of Mrs. Weisel had given him the strength to find his way home. He was thinking of her when he programmed Sybok's order into the helm's computer.

"Full ahead, aye," Sulu said.

Enterprise leapt into the abyss.

"The new shields are now operative, Captain," Vixis reported from her station.

"Excellent," Klaa said. "If all goes well, we will soon have an opportunity to test them. Activate."

"Activating."

Klaa's gaze lingered admiringly on his first officer for an instant. On the bridge, her demeanor—which had been forthright and delightfully unrestrained in the privacy of his quarters—was once again consummately respectful and efficient. He had done well to trust her.

"Captain!" Tarag cried excitedly. *"Enterprise* has entered the Barrier, and her shields appear to be holding!"

Klaa jumped up from his seat and strode over to the

helm, where Tarag sat next to Morek's conspicuously vacant chair.

Okrona's main viewscreen displayed an awesome vision: *Enterprise,* bombarded by a flux of visible energy and light that pulsed brilliant spectral colors like an insane aurora borealis.

"Amazing," Klaa whispered. The sight evoked within him an intense excitement. The chase was on; he would follow *Enterprise* into the unknown, destroy her, and return not only a hero but a discoverer as well. At the same time, he was filled with wonder and an awareness of his own insignificance compared to the cold, vast beauty of the cosmos.

"Captain!" Tarag exclaimed again. *"Enterprise* has disappeared! Our scanners have lost track of her."

Klaa stared at the huge and terrible specter of the Barrier, then glanced at Vixis. Her expression only served to underscore the uncertainty Klaa felt.

He looked back at the viewscreen and made a decision.

"Follow," he told Tarag.

On the forward observation deck, Jim Kirk stood with his friends and watched in helpless rage as *Enterprise* sailed into the Barrier. Starlight streamed through the viewing window; when it reached an unbearable degree of luminosity, Jim turned to Spock, who stood beside him. The Vulcan still gazed out at the dazzling panorama; Jim caught a glimpse of filmy nictitating membrane as it flashed in the Vulcan's dark eyes.

"He's really going to do it," Jim said tightly. He

paced a few steps forward, then pivoted and paced a few steps back. He paused to glance at the two possible exits—one leading out to the corridor, the other to the ventilation shaft. Both were guarded on the other side by Sybok's soldiers . . . and while Spock's brother might have reservations about killing, Jim was certain the Nimban homesteaders did not.

Behind Spock and Kirk, McCoy sat glumly, one elbow on the communications console, with his chin propped on his fist. "What I want to know is," the doctor said, "where the hell is the rescue ship?"

It had the ring of a rhetorical question, but Spock took it upon himself to reply.

"Unknown," the Vulcan said, turning at last from the view. "Perhaps no ship was close enough to respond, or perhaps our communication was intercepted."

Jim stopped in midpace. "Worst-case scenario: the Klingons intercepted it, but even *they're* not crazy enough to follow us here." He paused. "Spock, how much time before the shields give way?"

"Impossible to be precise, Captain, as the radiation levels are fluctuating greatly. Even if I had access to instruments that could measure the precise amount of radiation to which *Enterprise* has been exposed—"

"Get to the point," Jim snapped. "I'd like to hear the answer before we die."

Spock raised a brow in mild surprise and said, "There is no chance that the *Enterprise*'s shields will survive passage through the accretion disk. Bombardment levels will increase significantly."

"Just tell me it'll be fast," McCoy said softly. "Just tell me I don't have to . . ." His voice faltered.

Spock glanced questioningly at him. "You were saying, Doctor?"

"Dammit, Spock." McCoy looked away, and said in a low voice, "I didn't want to have to see you—you know. See it happen to you again. Once is enough."

For a moment, Jim feared that the Vulcan would press McCoy for an explanation, but Spock questioned him no further. Instead, the Vulcan nodded at the observation window. Jim followed his gaze and saw the approaching darkness in the form of a huge, slightly irregular ring. *Interstellar dust,* Jim's rational mind told him, but the sight of it repelled him; a more ancient part of his nervous system recoiled in fear at the sight of the malignant black mass. It was ugly, evil, and in the back of Jim's brain, a hysterical voice told him that this thing would destroy them all.

"The thermal radiation, combined with the high-energy X and gamma rays should—" Spock broke off abruptly. His voice rose with puzzlement. "Quite frankly, Captain, there is absolutely no logical explanation as to why the ship has withstood it thus far. According to the laws of physics, we should not be alive."

McCoy's tone was faraway. "Maybe Sybok was right."

Jim looked at the doctor sharply. "Maybe he was—but I can't let him take that chance with *my* ship, *my* crew. Spock, maybe we can create a diversion before it's too late."

The Vulcan appeared skeptical. "There are eight soldiers outside in the corridor and another five guarding the ventilation shaft. I do not believe that—"

"I won't just stand here waiting to die along with my entire crew!"

"Jim, aren't you listening?" McCoy asked. "We should already be dead . . . but we're not."

At that precise moment, *Enterprise* sailed into darkness.

The room went black. Jim held his breath and waited, grateful for the darkness. McCoy had voiced a terror that Jim had felt as well: he had seen his first officer die from direct exposure to high levels of gamma radiation. It was not a sight he cared to witness again . . . or experience himself.

Shows how right you were about dying alone . . .

The presence of Spock and McCoy should have been some consolation, but Jim felt totally isolated, unable to open his mouth and speak a final word of comfort and friendship. The darkness filled him with unfamiliar blind panic.

"Bones," he whispered, reaching out in the darkness and catching hold of nothing. "Spock . . ."

Brightness streaked through the dust ring like lightning through a roiling thundercloud. The brightness flashed and grew. It seemed as though *Enterprise* had been caught in the midst of an incredible electrical storm, but she made her way through the turbulence as smoothly as if she sailed through empty space.

The cloud thinned and parted to reveal not the black hole Jim had feared but an area of utter calm, like the peaceful eye at the center of a hurricane.

In the midst of this serene spacescape a single planet rotated around a single white dwarf star. The planet was touchingly beautiful, as beautiful as the dust cloud had been hideous.

"My God," McCoy whispered reverently. "He was *right*. Sybok was right."

Awestruck, Jim stepped forward and rested his hand on the antique ship's wheel. For a moment he stared, mesmerized by the sight before him. Then, inexplicably, his attention was drawn to the bronze plaque attached to the wooden spokes of the wheel. On the plaque was engraved the *Enterprise* charter. Jim's gaze fell upon one phrase: TO GO WHERE NO MAN HAS GONE BEFORE.

He looked away, moved. His mind could not accept what was happening . . . and yet his heart accepted it gladly.

"Are we dreaming?" The doctor's voice shook with emotion.

"If we are," Jim replied, "then life *is* a dream."

Of the three, Spock seemed the most stunned by what had transpired. His mask of self-control had vanished; he half frowned in open amazement at what lay beyond the observation window. "Fascinating," he whispered. "Captain, I am at a loss to explain it. We should not have survived. And . . ." His voice trailed off. He struggled to regain his composure, then forced himself to continue. "This small solar system cannot be the source of power. Logically . . . logically, the source simply cannot be here."

"Spock," McCoy said, smiling at the vision of beauty before them, "I believe it's high time to stop worrying about logic. I don't think it's important anymore."

"Illusion?" Jim asked his first officer.

Spock considered this. "Possibly. The bridge's sensors would be able to tell us. But even Sybok is incapable of influencing all our minds to this extent."

"Then we'll go to the bridge," Jim said, "and find out."

McCoy spoke, still unable to look away from the sight. "If it's an illusion, I don't want to know. Besides, the guards aren't gonna let us walk out of here."

"They might, if we invite them along."

On the bridge, Chekov started as his monitor screen crackled back to life. The main viewscreen lit up with a breathtaking sight: a planet with swirling white clouds. At the command console, Sybok rose and spoke in an awed whisper.

"Sha Ka Ree." A smile as beautiful and luminous as the planet before them crossed his face. The diplomats stood beside him, their faces aglow with ecstasy.

Dar laughed. It was a sound of release, of infinite joy. "Vorta Vor."

"Eden," Talbot breathed.

They turned as the lift doors opened to reveal Kirk, Spock, and McCoy, flanked by soldiers.

Jim faced Sybok calmly. "We come in peace. About the ship . . ."

Sybok still smiled. "You were right to come here. The ship needs its captain." To Jim's surprise, he stepped down from the command chair and gestured for Kirk to take his place. "Perhaps now you believe me, Captain Kirk, when I say I mean no harm to the *Enterprise* and its crew. My mission has been fulfilled. I now return control of your vessel to you, with my deepest thanks and apologies."

Kirk took an eager step toward the conn, then hesitated. "No special conditions?"

"No conditions," Sybok answered happily.

"What makes you think I won't turn us around?"

Grinning, Sybok arched a brow in a striking imitation of Spock. "Because, James Kirk, you too must know, and you must understand. A starship's purpose is to explore the vast mysteries of space . . . and now *Enterprise* is poised on the verge of a great mystery, a great frontier—no, not great. The *greatest* frontier of all."

Jim looked about at the bright, hopeful faces of his crew.

"Mr. Chekov," he began.

The navigator responded excitedly before the captain had a chance to ask the question. "Aye, Captain. Instruments back on line."

"Radiation levels?"

"Enormously high passing through the dust ring, sir, but the shields held. There is a source of incredible power emanating from the planet—not electromagnetic, not thermal or radioactive. It's something I've never seen."

"Dangerous?"

"Doubtful, Captain." Chekov glanced briefly over his shoulder to show Kirk a dazzling smile. "Probably far less dangerous than the Barrier we just passed through." He looked back down at the readout. "The atmosphere below is ninety-three percent nitrogen; the rest is oxygen and a few trace gases. Entirely breathable. And the temperature is a comfortable twenty-five degrees centigrade." He smiled again. "Perfect weather for shore leave, sir."

Sybok watched the two of them expectantly.

Kirk made his decision. "Then if we're going to do it . . . We'll do it by the book. Chekov, take the conn. Sulu, standard orbital approach. Uhura, is the transporter fixed?"

"Not yet, sir. Mr. Scott's working on it."

"Then alert the shuttlecraft crew to stand by. Sybok, Spock, and Dr. McCoy will come with me. The rest of you will remain on board until we've determined what we're dealing with."

He turned to Sybok, who stood gaping at him with a joyous expression.

"Well, don't just stand there," Jim told him. "God's a very busy person."

Chapter Sixteen

SPOCK PILOTED the backup shuttle *Copernicus*. Jim sat between Sybok and McCoy and stared out through the visor as the shuttlecraft entered the planet's atmosphere. For an instant, the view was obliterated as they descended into the swirling clouds, which parted abruptly as if swept aside by an invisible hand.

Intrigued, Jim leaned closer to the shield. The terrain below was varied: verdant and lush as a rain forest near lakes and streams, breathtakingly Spartan near the highest mountains Jim had ever seen. The entire panorama seemed to glow, awash with primary colors of unearthly brilliance.

"Like Yosemite," McCoy said half under his breath, "and *then* some."

"Different," Jim said. The landscape was a glorious riot of shape and color, ranging from the pale pastels and low growth of a seascape to the intense, vibrant shades of jungle and forest.

"Captain," Spock said. There was an uncharacteristic note of urgency in his voice.

Jim looked up to see the Vulcan remove his hands from the controls . . . which continued to move, guided by some invisible force. Clearly amazed, Spock glanced back at Jim.

"I am no longer in control of the craft," Spock said.

"There!" Sybok cried excitedly. He stretched out an arm and pointed at the scenery below. "That's it!"

Jim looked. Beneath *Copernicus,* in the far distance, a series of blue-violet peaks formed a perfect circle— too perfect to be the product of natural accident. The mountains stood equidistant, and were of nearly identical height and shape. Jim was oddly reminded of Stonehenge.

Copernicus descended gently on her own, under Spock's watchful gaze, and came to a rest several meters outside the ring of mountains.

Before Spock could tend to them, the engines switched themselves off; the exit hatch opened. Jim rose and went over to a storage compartment. He riffled through it and found a communicator, which he slipped onto his belt. He was about to pick up a hand phaser . . . when he felt someone's eyes on him. He turned.

Sybok was watching with sad disapproval.

"Captain," he said, "do you really expect to find Klingons here?"

Jim thought about it, then smiled. "Force of habit." He put the phaser back and shut the compartment.

Sybok was first out, followed by Jim and the others. Before them, the closest of the ancient, rugged peaks rose into the clouds.

Sybok tilted his face up to the sky, his expression one of childlike wonder. "Amazing! The land . . . the sky . . . This is the place of my vision, just as I knew it would be." He walked with slow, rambling steps; Jim forged past him into the narrow passageway between the bases of two mountains.

On the *Enterprise* bridge, a miracle occurred.

The main viewscreen flickered, then came into abrupt focus, no longer showing the lone planet in its distant orbit, but the landing party as they made their way through the narrow passage.

"What the—" Sulu exclaimed.

Caithlin Dar stared at the screen, quite unable to believe what she was seeing. "Look!" She touched Talbot's arm.

Talbot glanced up with his pale gray eyes—now that he had released his pain, with Sybok's help, Talbot's eyes were very clear, very gentle. At the sight before him, his lips curved into a wide grin. "Now *that's* what I call Paradise!"

Even Korrd was smiling. "Qui'Tu," he corrected Talbot.

"You can call it whatever you bloody well like," Talbot told him, slapping the Klingon's shoulder. They both laughed.

At their reactions, Commander Uhura swiveled in her chair to see what the excitement was about. Her large eyes widened; she stood up, leaving the communications board unattended, and crossed over to the helm for a better view of the screen. "How did *that* happen? Who's transmitting the visual of the planet surface?"

The helmsman, Sulu, shook his head slowly as a smile spread over his face. "No one from the landing party, that's for sure."

"Whoever's doing it, it's beautiful," Chekov whispered. He and Sulu rose and stepped around to join Uhura in front of the helm. The three of them exchanged joyous smiles before fixing their gazes back on the screen.

"Where's Mr. Scott, your engineer?" Caithlin asked suddenly. "Shouldn't he see this?"

Uhura turned to her with a smile. "That's a nice thought. He's in the transporter room. I'll give him a call."

She moved back to her station, almost stumbling on her way because she dared not look away from the unfolding scene. She leaned over, so familiar with her board that her fingers found the toggle for the transporter room without her having to look. Eyes still focused on the screen, she said, in an urgent tone, "Scotty?"

"Scott here." The engineer sounded infinitely weary.

"Scotty, you've got to get up here and see this."

"In a minute," Scott answered unenthusiastically. "I have no time right now. The captain told me to get the transporter working, and I'm not about to let him down."

"It's important! You've got to—"

The engineer interrupted her. *"Nothing* is as important as getting the transporter in working order. I've already put it off long enough. Scott out."

He cut off the communication.

Uhura looked over at Caithlin and sighed. "I tried." She joined Caithlin, Talbot, and Korrd to marvel at the view on the screen.

Behind them, the unattended defense station at the helm blinked, then emitted a low warning beep as the graphic of a Klingon Bird of Prey appeared on its console screen. A warning flashed: KLINGON VESSEL IN QUADRANT. RECOMMEND ACTIVATION OF DEFENSE SYSTEMS. AWAITING COMMAND.

No one was there to respond.

Joyfully, Sybok made his way into the center of the mountain circle. All that he had seen—the single planet orbiting the star, the glorious landscape, the impossibly perfect ring of peaks—all of it was exactly as it had appeared in the vision T'Rea had shown him.

His heart was filled with wonder and gladness at the vision made real, but there was one small spot of dark grief: T'Rea could not share his joy.

In the center of the ring was a roughly hewn crater; the effect was that of a natural amphitheater. Sybok scrambled down into its rocky bowl.

Herein lies the One . . .

His heart was beating wildly by the time the others joined him. Spock was taking it all in with his usual reserve. Sybok laughed fondly and addressed his younger brother.

"Spock," he whispered, inspired to quiet reverence by their magnificent surroundings. "Don't you understand? We are here, you and I, in Sha Ka Ree!"

Spock wore a noncommittal expression. He stood beside his friends and continued to study their surroundings warily. In reply, he lifted the tricorder that dangled from a strap around his neck and scanned the bowl of the crater. The device hummed softly.

"Fascinating," Spock said, more to his captain than to his brother. "The force seems to be emanating from a point several kilometers below the surface of this crater. The readings are—" He frowned at the instrument as it emitted a single distressed beep and fell silent. Spock pressed several controls without success. "Readings were off the scale, Captain. It appears the energy flux has damaged the internal mechanisms of the tricorder." He looked up, his expression puzzled.

"Of course it broke your tricorder, Spock." Sybok smiled. He needed no more proof. All they had to do now was await the manifestation of the One.

The others waited, somewhat uncomfortably, with him.

Several moments of silence passed . . . moments during which Sybok's joyous anticipation metamorphosed into impatience, then disappointment, then despair. When he could bear the awful silence no longer, he cried out, beseeching the One of his vision. "We have traveled far," Sybok shouted, "many light-years, in a starship . . ."

His voice broke. He fell to his knees, bowed by a grief far blacker than the one he had known at his mother's loss.

Behind him, the captain spoke into his communicator. *"Enterprise,* this is Kirk."

"I will not leave," Sybok whispered. He lowered his head.

Someone laid a hand on his shoulder. Sybok glanced up and saw, to his astonishment, Spock.

His younger brother's expression was, as always, restrained, but Sybok saw the unmistakable compassion in Spock's eyes. In the midst of his anguish, Sybok felt a small ray of warmth.

His brother's tone was quietly consoling. "Perhaps," Spock said, "the energy—"

The crater rumbled mightily, drowning out the sound of Spock's voice. Sybok pitched forward as the ground under him rocked.

A shadow fell over the amphitheater as the sky darkened from an onrush of jet-colored clouds. The rock beneath Sybok's hands and knees shuddered; next to him, Spock lost his footing and fell. The earth began to undulate, swelling and rippling like a storm-ravaged sea. An enormous earthquake, Sybok thought —until the impossible occurred.

Along the outer perimeter of the crater, a pillar of sheer rock ripped its way through the barren surface, and hurtled skyward. Sybok held his breath and waited, uncertain what would happen next; these were not the sights T'Rea had unveiled to him.

Another pillar reared up, crashing its way through the rocky ground, into the sky. Another. And another, and another . . . until the crater's basin was encircled by gigantic fingers of stone.

Sybok watched as the fingers interlaced to form a shrine, a crude cathedral of rock. Abruptly, the earth ceased its torment—but the ground in the center of the shrine began to glow a dull, deep red. As Sybok watched, the earth melted, and the molten rock began to swirl in spiral motion. There came the rushing sound of a mighty wind.

The energy flux Spock had detected deep beneath the crater's surface was pushing its way to the surface.

"The One!" Sybok cried in triumph as he scrambled to his feet—but the words were swallowed up as a brilliant beam of pure force exploded out of the vortex and burst upward in an erupting geyser of light. Particles of energy flew outward onto the four bystanders. Sybok's skin tingled electrically where the sparks struck him. Blinded by the raw beauty of the beam, he shielded his eyes with his arm and staggered back against Spock and the others.

A voice spoke—a voice that Sybok thought he knew, but his glad recognition was tainted with a small, dark particle of doubt.

"BRAVE SOULS," the voice boomed, with infinite power, infinite grandeur. "WELCOME."

Remarkably, the doctor recovered first. "Is this the voice of God?" McCoy asked in a hushed, respectful tone.

As if in answer to his question, the shaft of light throbbed; the dust within it began to swirl and form shapes. Sybok lowered his arms and watched the light perform a dance of incredible, enticing beauty.

Within the maelstrom of pure force, eidolons were born. Sybok recognized one of them instantly: Khosarr, the ancient Vulcan god of war, fierce and hawklike of countenance, muscular and strong, with long black hair tied with a green thong and allowed to stream down his naked back. He was dressed in a green mesh loincloth, and he carried a shield of green—dark green, the color of war. On Vulcan, nothing that lived was green, save blood.

Khosarr's compelling form pulsed, whirled, and took on new shape, becoming that of his warrior consort, the goddess Akraana.

The image died and was reborn again as the red goddess of fertility, Lia. Sybok stared, mesmerized. These were the deities that peopled the legends his mother had taught him as a child. He forced himself to look away, at the others beside him. The humans watched with expressions of utter bedazzlement; Sybok wondered what images they saw in the swirling display. Even Spock stared, openly enthralled.

Unnoticed, Sybok smiled at his companions. He did not know what he had expected to encounter . . . but he had never dreamed of this.

He looked back to see the goddesses and gods coalescing into the One. Sybok perceived the One as having Vulcanoid features, neither male nor female. The Being's face and form glowed, illuminated from within. Remaining inside the perimeters of the energy shaft, it directed its gaze at the four travelers. It addressed Sybok first.

"DOES THIS BETTER SUIT YOUR EXPECTATIONS?"

Sybok stood speechless, too overwhelmed by ecstasy to speak. When at last he found his voice, he whispered, *"Qual se . . . tu?*

The Being smiled radiantly at him. "IT IS I, THE ONE, THE SOURCE OF ALL."

Sybok released a single sob of joy and bowed his head.

The One spoke. "THE JOURNEY YOU TOOK TO REACH ME WAS NOT AN EASY ONE."

"It was not," Sybok replied softly. "The Barrier stood between us, but we managed to breach it."

"MAGNIFICIENT." The Being glowed approvingly. "AND YOU ARE THE FIRST TO FIND ME."

"We seek only Your infinite wisdom," Sybok said humbly.

"AND HOW DID YOU BREACH THE BARRIER?"

For the most fleeting of seconds, Sybok felt a tug of doubt: Why would the Almighty ask a question to which It knew the answer? But in the joy of the moment, he pushed the doubt away. "With a starship. It took me years to perfect the shield design so that the Barrier could be crossed, but I persisted."

He noticed from the corner of his eyes that James Kirk reacted strongly to the statement. In the glory of the moment, it hardly seemed important.

"Ah." The One brightened considerably, so that Sybok shaded his eyes again. "AND THIS STARSHIP . . . COULD IT CARRY MY WISDOM BACK BEYOND THE BARRIER?"

"Yes! It could, yes!" Sybok was utterly seduced by a glorious vision of his destiny. He alone had been chosen to reveal the One to the galaxy. He closed his eyes and heard the beguiling whisper of his mother's voice.

Shiav . . .

"I SHALL MAKE USE OF IT."

Sybok laughed with joy. "It will be your chariot!"

Jim Kirk had heard just about enough. Politely, he

raised his hand, like a cadet trying to get the instructor's attention. "Excuse me."

The Being, who appeared to Jim as a benevolent, white-haired human male, ignored him in favor of addressing the enraptured Sybok.

"IT WILL CARRY MY POWER TO EVERY CORNER OF CREATION."

"Excuse me," Jim repeated, this time more insistent.

The Being—Jim refused to think of it as God—regarded Kirk with annoyance. Jim smiled his best conciliatory smile. Whatever it was, it was enormously powerful, and he did not want to anger it. "I just want to ask a question: What does *God* need with a starship?"

Instead of an answer, the Being spoke again to Sybok. "BRING THE SHIP CLOSER."

"You didn't answer my question," Jim said, a little irritably. If the Being was unable to reach the ship from this distance, it couldn't be all that powerful. "What does God want with a starship? I mean, if you're omnipotent, why don't you cross the Barrier yourself?"

"Jim," McCoy whispered sharply. The doctor looked scandalized. "What're you doing?"

"I'm just asking a simple question," Jim said aloud.

Spock nodded in support. "An extremely logical question, Captain."

"Thank you."

The shimmering dust in the energy beam began to swirl faster. Jim realized that he had made it angry, but he stood his ground. The Being—whatever it was—was not coming aboard the *Enterprise.* Not without a fight.

The Being's benevolent smile began to sag. "WHO IS THIS CREATURE?"

"Who am I?" Jim scoffed. "Don't you *know?* Aren't you supposed to be God?"

The sky overhead began to darken; thunder rumbled faintly. The smile had left the Being's face.

With growing dismay, Sybok glanced from the Being to Kirk and back. "Please," he beseeched the Being. "Do not be angry. He merely has his doubts."

The Being scowled at Jim. "DO YOU DOUBT ME?"

Jim shifted his weight, uncomfortable with the confrontation, but certain of its necessity. "I need proof. I'm captain of the *Enterprise,* and if you're going to commandeer my ship, I—"

McCoy clutched his shoulder. "Jim, maybe it's not such a good idea to ask to see his I.D."

It was too late. The Being's face darkened with righteous anger. "THEN HERE IS THE PROOF YOU SEEK."

A blast of brilliant energy shot from the Being's eyes at Kirk, too fast for Jim to see it coming. With searing force, it struck Jim full in the chest and knocked him to the ground.

The light blinded him. For an awful moment he lay paralyzed, unable to see, unable to catch his breath.

And then his vision cleared and he sucked in a pained, hitching breath. His chest felt as if it had been crushed, though he knew it was probably only bruised. The sharp jolt of pain that came with each intake of breath, however, told him he'd broken at least one rib. He struggled to sit up and saw McCoy kneeling beside him.

Jim looked over at Sybok. All joy had vanished from the Vulcan's face, replaced by shock and uncertainty.

"Why," Jim gasped, "is God . . . angry?"

Sybok turned to the Being. "I don't understand. Why have you done this to my friend?"

"HE DOUBTS ME."

Spock stepped forward to stand beside his brother. "You have not answered his question. What does God need with a starship? Certainly a powerful deity would not need to resort to such a mundane mode of transportation."

Beneath flashing bands of light, the Being's face contorted with wrath.

"No!" Jim shouted.

A second bolt of energy streamed from the Being's eye, hurling Spock to the ground.

Aboard the *Enterprise,* Caithlin Dar stared in mute horror at the scene and leaned against the arm of the empty command chair. Next to her, Korrd growled deep in his throat.

"Dear God," Talbot whispered. "To have come this far only to find—" He squeezed his eyes shut. "Damn. I need a drink."

When he opened his eyes again, he laid a firm hand on Caithlin's shoulder. "Turn away, Miss Dar. Turn away. Don't watch."

Caithlin kept her gaze fixed on the screen. *"How could this happen?* How could he have been so wrong? It was all so *beautiful . . ."*

"Hell always seems heavenly at first, doesn't it?" Talbot's tone became ugly, bitter. "I'm going below for a bloody drink."

But for some reason, he stayed on the bridge.

Sybok's universe was beginning to shatter into a myriad of meaningless fragments, all of them spinning away from each other into utter chaos.

He watched in shocked silence as the luminous Being turned its attention on McCoy.

"AND YOU . . . DO YOU ALSO DOUBT ME?"

McCoy, who had been crouched over his injured friends, rose and faced the Being. He no longer appeared frightened or reverent; his voice shook with indignation. "I doubt any god who inflicts pain for his own pleasure."

The Being's face darkened with fury; it prepared to lash out again.

Sybok spread out his arms and stepped in front of McCoy—not in a gesture of self-sacrifice, but because he felt too bitterly betrayed, too angry to care if the Being struck him down. "Stop! The God of Sha Ka Ree would not do this!"

The Being smiled at him. It was the most hideous expression Sybok had ever seen, full of maleficence, loathing, the deepest contempt. "SHA KA REE? A VISION *YOU* CREATED!"

The sound of its demonic laughter was unbearable; Sybok covered his ears with his hands, trying to blot it out.

"AN ETERNITY I'VE BEEN IMPRISONED IN THIS PLACE! THE SHIP! I MUST HAVE THE

SHIP! GIVE ME WHAT I WANT OR I WILL KILL YOU ALL!"

T'Rea's vision had been nothing more than a delusion, or perhaps a message from this creature. Utterly desolate, Sybok wished now only to join his mother's spirit, to seek the solace of total annihilation.

"Sybok!" Spock shouted.

Sybok looked over at him. Spock sat, shaken but alive, beside the doctor and Kirk. "This is not the God of Sha Ka Ree—or any other God!" Spock cried.

Without responding, Sybok turned back toward the Being. Perhaps there was one small shred of meaning left in the universe—the fact that he loved his younger brother and did not want to see him perish at the hands of this evil entity. Sybok had no one, and life was no longer important to him—but Spock had his friends.

"Reveal yourself to me!" Sybok urged the Being. "I must know the truth! I must see you as you really are!"

The Being's features wavered, changed. When at last they resolved themselves, they were still Vulcanoid . . .

But the face was a sinister likeness of Sybok's own.

Sybok shrank from it, repelled.

His evil reflection laughed scornfully. "WHAT'S WRONG? DON'T YOU LIKE THIS FACE? I HAVE SO MANY, BUT THIS ONE SUITS YOU BEST."

"No," Sybok whispered. "It's not possible." And yet he realized, in one bright and terrible instant of disillusionment, that it was *quite* possible—in fact, obvious. His willingness to deceive himself, his total conceit in believing himself to be the *shiav* of legend. The creature—whatever it was—had instinctively sensed the depths of Sybok's vanity and had revealed it to him.

"BRING ME THE SHIP OR I WILL DESTROY YOU!" the creature demanded; its voice had acquired an unpleasantly shrill edge.

Destroy me now, and be done with it, Sybok almost replied . . . but then he remembered Spock, his brother, and those remaining on the *Enterprise*—Dar, Talbot, Korrd, Sulu, J'Onn, all the others. . . .

Clearly, the creature hoped to gain control of the ship in order to cross the Barrier unscathed . . . and all aboard would be killed.

T'Rea's death no longer had meaning. Sybok accepted this, and knew that if his own death was to have any, he would have to remain alive long enough to ensure the safety of the others. The thought helped sustain him. "The ship—" Sybok began.

"BRING IT CLOSER THAT I MIGHT JOIN WITH IT!" the creature bellowed. "DO IT, OR WATCH THESE PUNY THINGS DIE HORRIBLY."

Anguished, Sybok turned toward his brother. "Spock, what have I done?"

"Sybok . . ." Spock began, and faltered, unable to offer any words of comfort.

"This is my doing," Sybok told him. "My arrogance, my vanity. Save yourselves!"

"No!" Spock protested, rising to his feet and moving toward his elder brother. "Sybok, you mustn't—"

"Forgive me, *t'hyla*," Sybok said. He raised his

hand and saluted his brother in a gesture he had not made in over thirty years. "Live long and prosper. . . ."

Spock raised his hand in the Vulcan salute; his fingertips grazed Sybok's. . . .

And then Sybok turned away from his brother. He faced the Being and drew in a deep breath, summoning all of his power, then looked at his evil distorted image without hope, without joy, without fear. "I couldn't help but notice your pain," he said.

"PAIN?" A ripple of confusion passed over the being's parody of the Vulcan's features.

"It runs deep," Sybok said, feeling an odd stirring of compassion. His words were true; as he probed the outer reaches of the creature's mind, he sensed a loneliness beyond all light, beyond all comprehension. "Share it with me."

He stepped into the swirling beam of power and embraced his enemy.

Chapter Seventeen

W‍ITH M‍CCOY'S ‍HELP, Jim held Spock back as his brother entered the energy shaft.

Spock struggled only for an instant, then was still. "Captain . . ." His voice was hushed, almost a whisper. "Sybok intends to sacrifice himself. He cannot possibly survive the battle. . . ." He fell silent, though Jim got the impression he had intended to say more.

Jim cautiously eased his grip on the Vulcan's arms. His back was to Sybok and the energy-creature; he turned to see the incredible spectacle.

Within the shimmering matrix, two Syboks—the good one and his evil parody—wrestled, merging into one distorted, thrashing body. Abruptly, the good Sybok pulled himself free, and tried to fasten his hands on his evil twin's temples.

Share your pain. . . .

NO.

The evil Sybok began to absorb the good, his bodily tissues melting, flowing around the real Sybok like an amoeba engulfing food.

Jim forced himself to look away from the sight, and back at Spock. He understood very well what Spock had *not* been able to say—that there was no hope of his brother's survival, and that *Enterprise*'s one chance lay in destroying the energy-creature now, while it was distracted.

"Spock," Jim said gently, "are you *sure* about . . . Sybok?"

The Vulcan's expression was wooden; his eyes were focused on the terrible struggle. "Quite certain. Sybok . . . communicated it to me. He understands quite well what he is doing."

"I'm sorry," Jim whispered. He keenly remembered the pain he experienced on the loss of his own brother, Sam, even though Jim had not had to witness his brother's horrible death—as Spock would have to do now.

Reluctantly, Jim raised his communicator to his lips.

"Kirk to *Enterprise*."

"Sulu here, Captain. We can see what's going on down there."

As Kirk watched, the two grappling forms began to whirl, spiraling downward into the bottomless hole created by the being's exit.

"Good," he told Sulu. "I want you to ready a photon torpedo. Prepare to fire on my command."

A pause.

"Aye, sir," the helmsman replied finally. Kirk heard

the faint doubt in his tone. Sulu surely understood what his captain intended—and he knew the torpedo would destroy any chance of Sybok escaping alive.

And if the crew decided their primary loyalty still lay with Sybok . . .

"Arming torpedo," Sulu said. His voice sounded almost normal, like that of a helmsman responding to a routine command from his captain.

Kirk held his breath. Sybok and the demon were chest-deep in the shaft and still swirling downward. Seconds passed; Jim watched as the two of them disappeared into the dark tunnel.

He was glad, at least, that Spock would not have to see.

Sulu's voice filtered through Kirk's communicator grid once more. "We've got a lock on them, Captain. Torpedo armed and ready."

Kirk sighed; his crew was once again his own. "Fire directly into the tunnel, Mr. Sulu."

He could hear Chekov's protests in the background. "But, Captain, that is dangerously close to *your* position."

"Tell Chekov his protest is noted," Kirk said. "Send it down *now*, Sulu!"

Sulu answered: a bolt of red streaked from the sky and descended into the empty shaft.

The Vulcan stared in shock.

"Spock, come on! Let's get out of here!" Jim grabbed his arm and pulled him along, running for cover. McCoy followed a short distance behind.

Far beneath the surface of the crater, the torpedo found its target.

The earth shuddered violently. The stone fingers of the cathedral cracked; chunks of rock fell, narrowly missing Jim and the others. Jim took cover behind a sturdy column of rock.

A searing blaze of light and raw energy erupted from the tunnel, then disappeared, leaving behind smoke and rubble.

Silence. Jim opened his eyes and blinked. His eyes were still dazzled; as they cleared, he squinted, trying to see through the haze of smoke and settling dust. The shaft of light had vanished. In its place, the gaping mouth of the tunnel glowed a dull, angry red, emitting such intense heat that Jim felt as if he were sitting too close to a campfire. Slowly he got to his feet.

Beside him, Spock still crouched beside the column, one hand pressed against the stone, and stared at the glowing wound in the earth. His expression was dazed.

"Sybok . . ." the Vulcan whispered.

Jim bent down and helped Spock to his feet. As he did so, he caught a sidewise glimpse of McCoy. "Bones?"

McCoy appeared beside him, disheveled and covered with dust. "I'm all right, Jim."

An ominous rumble came from deep within the tunnel. Jim cast a worried glance at his first officer. "We've got to get out of here."

Spock gathered himself and gave a single nod of reassurance.

As the rumbling grew louder, the three of them ran together up the side of the crater.

* * *

On the *Enterprise* bridge, the main viewscreen went black, then cleared to a view of the planet. Mute with grief, Caithlin continued to stare at it. The planet that had once seemed so impossibly beautiful had dimmed; its colors were muddied, lackluster.

It was not Caithlin's nature to weep; at any rate, she was too stunned by what she had witnessed to do so.

"It can't be." Talbot had paled. "It can't be."

"None of it means anything," Caithlin whispered bitterly. "None of it means anything at all."

A great warm hand rested on her shoulder; she thought at first that it was Talbot's hand, but this was twice the size.

"Untrue," Korrd said quietly in his bass voice. "Sybok died well, as a warrior should, looking death in the eye. He has saved us and the ship."

Around them, the crew worked feverishly, far too caught up in their efforts to save their comrades to grieve for Sybok. Caithlin watched as Chekov went over to the science officer's station and bent over the hooded viewer; the soft blue-white glow of the terminal readout bathed his face.

"Have you got a fix on them yet?" Sulu asked tersely, rising to look anxiously over Chekov's shoulder.

They at least have their captain and their ship, Caithlin thought. "And what do we have left, now that Sybok is dead?" she asked, unaware that she had spoken aloud. She glanced at the dazed, solemn faces of Talbot and Korrd.

Talbot considered her question carefully, then answered: "We have Paradise."

She wheeled on him, ready to lash out at what she thought was a cruel, thoughtless joke . . . but then she saw that Talbot was quite serious.

On the other side of the bridge, unnoticed and unmanned, the defense station still displayed the graphic of a Bird of Prey, and a message: ESTIMATED TIME OF INTERCEPT: FOUR MINUTES.

The unseen graphic of the ship dissolved; the message flickered and changed into a warning: CLOAKING DEVICE ENGAGED. POSITION UNKNOWN.

Vixis smiled down at the tiny representation of a Federation starship on her terminal monitor, then looked up at the bridge viewscreen, which showed the real *Enterprise* still orbiting the mysterious planet.

"Enterprise defense systems are down," Vixis reported triumphantly, then half swiveled in her chair to exchange smug glances with Klaa. "Captain, they don't even know we're here."

Klaa smiled. "They will." He crossed to his gunner's rig and settled in with relish. "They will."

Accompanied by the captain and the doctor, Spock ran to the top of the crater and through the narrow mountain pass toward the shuttlecraft. He was still dazed by Sybok's death, even more dazed by his own reaction to it. After thirty years, he had expected the emotional barrier erected between himself and his brother to stand. But upon confronting Sybok again, Spock had experienced afresh the pain and betrayal he had felt on learning that his admired elder brother was a heretic. Yet all the bitterness had faded at the moment of Sybok's death. Spock remembered only his brother's kindnesses.

He ran, following the captain; Spock could hear the doctor's ragged gasps close behind them. And more: Spock sensed the malicious entity nearby. Neither Sybok nor the photon torpedo had been able to destroy it utterly.

Kirk reached *Copernicus* first and opened the hatch. The three of them entered, McCoy last, grazed by the lowering hatch as it closed, sealing them inside.

Jim sat and started fastening his restraints. "Spock, get us out of here!"

Spock slid into the pilot's chair and found the thruster controls.

The thrusters failed to fire; *Copernicus* convulsed under the impact of an enormous blow. The entity was trying to force its way inside.

"Do it, Spock!"

Spock tried once more to engage the thrusters; the dials on the shuttle's control console flashed brilliant red, then went dark.

The Vulcan looked somberly at Jim; he had to shout to be heard over the sound of the entity pounding against the shuttle's flank. "Thrusters inoperative, Captain. The entity seems to be damping our power source."

Before Spock could finish speaking, Jim pulled out his communicator. "Kirk to *Enterprise!*"

"Scott here, Captain."

"Scotty! Now would be a good time to tell me the transporter's working!"

Scott paused in a way that indicated it was not.

"She's got partial power, sir," the engineer replied apologetically. "I might be able to take two of you."

The shuttlecraft began to vibrate as if she were trying to tear herself apart. Spock opened his mouth, ready to volunteer to remain.

He was not given the opportunity.

"Beam up Spock and Dr. McCoy," Kirk shouted into the transmitter grid. *"Now!"*

The craft's quaking interior dissolved into the winking shimmer of the transporter beam, then metamorphosed into the *Enterprise* transporter room.

Spock stepped off the pad and crossed to where Montgomery Scott manned the console. "Mr. Scott, send the beam back down."

"Aye, sir." Scott's hands moved quickly to comply.

The ship reeled. Spock watched in amazement as the floor of the transporter room rose abruptly to meet him; the Vulcan staggered forward and fell, dimly aware that the doctor had just been thrown past him. With his peripheral vision, Spock saw the transporter pad rain sparks. It emitted a loud crackle, followed by a small black puff of smoke.

In the confusion of the moment, Spock retained the clarity of mind to realize three things: first, that the *Enterprise* was under attack; second, that she would have to raise shields . . . and third, that with the shields up and the transporter apparently damaged, there was no way to beam Jim Kirk to safety.

Jim waited inside the groaning craft. The rumbling outside steadily worsened; it sounded as though the energy-creature had picked up the shuttle and was trying to shake him out.

Twenty seconds passed, then thirty, then a full minute; Jim began to worry. He flipped open his communicator again. "Mr. Scott?"

Static.

It struck him then that he was alone on the planet surface.

He dismissed the panic and tried again to hail the *Enterprise. Copernicus* was shaking so hard that Jim couldn't keep his hands steady. The communicator almost slipped through his fingers.

"Mr. Scott, you'd better be there."

Static.

"Damn!" Jim returned to the communicator to his belt, trying to think of what to do besides wait.

Mere centimeters behind his head, the thick unbreakable polymer of the starboard hatch shattered into pieces with a dull crunch.

Jim tore off his restraints and turned his head to look.

An arm—Jim did not know what else to call it—an amorphous limb of swirling deep bronze energy, had burst through the hatch and forced its way inside. The creature was pounding an opening in the shuttle's side; within seconds, it would make its way to the very spot where Jim was sitting.

Jim propelled himself from his chair and scrambled to the shuttle's aft hatch. He pressed the emergency exit control. Slowly, over the course of what seemed like eternity, the hatch rose. Jim crouched down and wriggled his way out before it opened completely.

* * *

Spock, McCoy, and Scott arrived on the bridge just as auxiliary control hummed on and the last of the fires was put out. The three diplomats were still on the bridge, huddled quietly together out of the way; their faces displayed shock and loss.

As for Spock, he had managed to achieve singleness of focus. He was prepared to do whatever was necessary to save the *Enterprise,* and Jim Kirk—a singular challenge, considering Mr. Scott's report that both transporter and shields were damaged and temporarily inoperative. Spock would deal with any grief over Sybok's death later, in privacy.

But the doctor was still distraught. As Spock took his place at the conn, McCoy faced him, gripping the arm of the captain's chair.

"What about Jim?" the doctor cried. "We can't just leave him down there!"

Spock did not meet his eyes; he was far too engrossed in the drama unfolding on the bridge. "Doctor, please," he said calmly. "There is no time for arguments."

McCoy surrendered his grip on Spock's chair; his arms fell to his sides and dangled helplessly.

"Commander Uhura, status report."

"Aye, Mr. Spock." Uhura's eyes were clear, as focused as Spock's; any effects of Sybok's mind-meld had vanished. "Klingon captain wishes to name his terms."

"On screen," Spock ordered.

An image flashed on the screen: a smug young Klingon, arms folded across his chest. He sat in the commander chair on the Bird of Prey's bridge as if it were a throne. He wore an expression of triumph, total arrogance that sagged slightly as his gaze met the Vulcan's. Spock got the impression that he was most disappointed to find a Vulcan in command.

"This is Captain Klaa of the Bird of Prey *Okrona*," he gloated in Standard. "Attempt to raise shields or arm weapons and I will destroy you. You are alive for a single reason—the renegade James T. Kirk! Hand him over, and I will spare your lives. My transporter stands ready to beam him aboard."

Spock quite naturally did not believe him; the moment James Kirk was handed over, the *Enterprise* and all aboard her would be destroyed. For the moment, he was relieved the captain was still below on the planet surface; it provided him with the opportunity to stall. "Captain Kirk is not among us," he answered truthfully.

Klaa lunged forward in his chair. "You *lie!*"

"I am a Vulcan. I cannot lie," Spock replied. Not quite the full truth, but it would serve for the moment.

The Vulcan was reminded of a paradox he had once heard the less-than-scrupulous entrepreneur Harry Mudd employ: *I always lie. In fact, I am lying to you now.*

"Captain Kirk is on the planet below."

"Then give me his coordinates!"

Spock experienced a sudden inspiration. It descended on him full-blown, without any attempt on his part at logical deduction. Jim Kirk would have called it instinct and been proud of it.

"Mike off," he said softly, and swiveled in his chair to face the three diplomats. "General Korrd."

Korrd glanced up, startled.

"I am in need of your assistance."

"My assistance?" Korrd asked. "I am of no help to you now."

"On the contrary." Spock inclined his head toward the screen, where a larger-than-life Klaa scowled. "You are his superior officer."

The Klingon shook his head. "You misunderstand. My assignment to Nimbus proves I am in disgrace. I am no more than a foolish old man."

Spock studied Korrd's jowly face carefully. Desperate measures were necessary; Klaa would not wait much longer. Jim's life far outweighed the cost of personal embarrassment.

"Sybok was my brother," Spock said, ignoring the shocked reactions of all those on the bridge. "He sacrificed himself so that we might escape. Are you so willing to see his death become meaningless?"

"Klaa will not—" Korrd began.

Spock had just seen his brother killed; he would not allow the same to happen to James Kirk. "Damn you, sir," he said, his tone deliberate and even, "you will try."

The bridge became oppressively silent as Korrd considered Spock's words. . . .

And then the old Klingon left his friends and moved over to where Spock sat at the command console.

He glowered at the Klingon captain on the viewscreen. "Klaa! This is General Korrd."

The younger Klingon's eyes widened slightly in recognition. "General . . ." He saluted cursorily, but it was clear he considered himself Korrd's equal, rank or no rank.

Korrd narrowed his eyes and glanced briefly at Talbot and Dar, then at Spock, then back at Klaa.

Spock began to wonder if he had made a fatal error in trusting Korrd.

"Klaa!" the general bellowed, switching from Standard to Klingon. *"Jo-ii-chu!"*

All on the bridge stared in shocked disbelief as Korrd's bulky form dissolved into the twinkling shimmer of a transporter beam . . . and vanished.

Simultaneously, Klaa's image disappeared from the screen.

"My God!" McCoy cried. "The bastard's saved himself so the Klingons can destroy us!"

"No," Talbot murmured behind them. "No, I refuse to believe it."

Spock remained silent. Words were, after all, quite useless. They were in Korrd's hands now, and there was nothing the Vulcan could do but sit and stare dully at the darkened screen . . . and wait.

Korrd materialized in the transporter room of the Bird of Prey and was immediately greeted by an armed escort who led him to the bridge. After the spacious, well-lighted Federation ship, the Bird seemed cramped and dim.

Inside the bridge, the first officer—a most attractive female, Korrd noted with a certain amount of lechery —turned from her station to call out excitedly. "Captain, we have located a human life-form on the planet surface below."

"Kirk!" Klaa exclaimed. "I have him at last!" He slapped his hands together and laughed, a sound of pure victory.

Korrd strode over to the command console. The young captain's chair was outfitted with a gunner's rig—a rather obvious display of Klaa's vanity, Korrd noted, a trait he resolved to use to his advantage. Klaa settled into the rig, eager for the hunt.

The first officer smiled dazzlingly at her captain, in a way that convinced Korrd she was more to Klaa than second-in-command. "Success, my lord!"

The atmosphere was charged with excitement. Klaa was a charismatic, persuasive leader, much as Korrd had been in earlier times. The memory evoked a nearly forgotten sensation: the feel of power. Korrd breathed in its scent, basked in it, felt himself grow stronger.

"Fire ph—" Klaa began.

"Captain!" Korrd barked.

All on the bridge turned to look at him; Korrd relished the attention, and the fear in their eyes.

Klaa rose and saluted. "General . . . welcome. You are about to see *Enterprise* destroyed and the criminal James Kirk executed." He grinned arrogantly. "After which I may soon have the pleasure of addressing you as an equal."

Korrd eyed the young upstart coldly. It was impossible to dislike him entirely, for he reminded Korrd too much of himself in his younger days.

"Not so fast, Klaa," he growled. "By virtue of my superior rank, I am commandeering this vessel."

Murder flashed in Klaa's eyes; furious, he gestured toward the guard who had escorted Korrd from the transporter room.

Before the captain could utter a word, Korrd reached for him and lifted him off his feet by his throat. Klaa's face darkened to a deep shade of purple; he made a strangled noise of pure rage.

No one dared come to the captain's aid.

Korrd smiled, giddy with rediscovered power. If he wished, he could take command of *Okrona* and destroy the *Enterprise* and James Kirk himself—and redeem his name totally.

On the screen before him, *Enterprise* hovered, vulnerable and waiting. It was a most tempting prospect.

Korrd eased his grip on Klaa's neck and allowed the captain to collapse into his chair. Klaa wheezed and gulped air noisily while Korrd spoke.

"I have a plan," he told the young captain. "One that will bring much glory and honor. You may claim the victory, Klaa, but for now, *I* have the power."

On the planet surface, Jim scrambled amid the smoldering ruins of the stone amphitheater, searching for a place to hide. At first the energy-creature had appeared as a disheveled, wild-eyed Sistine Chapel God, his long white hair and beard singed and smoking, a ghastly mixture of blood and light streaming from his eyes. Now the creature had reverted to its true form: a pulsating field of energy that glowed a deep, dull bronze. It did not seem as powerful, now that it was separated from the energy shaft that had contained it, but, Jim reflected grimly as he glanced at the battered remains of *Copernicus* in the distance, it was still powerful enough to kill him.

Even in its weakened state, it moved with alarming speed; Jim ran full tilt, then squeezed between two fallen stone columns that lay at the base of one of the mountains.

Apparently unable to squeeze into the space, the

creature reached in after Kirk. Jim pressed his back flat against the mountain; the creature swiped at him, missing him by no more than a centimeter.

There was no place to go except up.

Jim turned to face the mountain and tilted his head back. The view was daunting; the pinnacle's ascent was incredibly steep, at least a seventy-five degree angle.

"Not as bad as El Cap," Jim murmured. He dug his fingers in and began to climb.

There was no time to concentrate, no time to choose the best crevices to support his weight. Jim pulled himself up, grasping with mindless desperation at the rock.

Behind him, the creature roared. It was followed by the sound of stone being smashed to pieces; it was crushing the columns to powder, forcing them out of its way.

Jim climbed. Amazingly, he did not fall. He slipped twice, scraping his hands until they were bloody, and scattering pebbles onto the creature below, who had cleared its way to the mountain and was starting its ascent.

Gasping, Jim made it to the top and looked below. The creature was making its way, slowly, deliberately, up the pinnacle. It paused to regard Kirk, and spoke in a voice that no longer sounded human.

"GIVE . . . ME . . . THE . . . SHIP."

"You're out of luck," Jim said. *And so, for that matter, am I.* "My friends have taken the ship and gone." As he said it, he was gripped by dread; maybe the words were true. The *Enterprise's* sudden silence disturbed him.

Maybe *Enterprise* had been forced to flee to avoid destruction . . . or, far worse, had already been destroyed.

Maybe, for the first time in his life, he was utterly alone.

The creature shrieked; the sound was chilling.

Jim looked around, desperately studying his options as the creature neared. The other face of the pinnacle was a sheer, concave drop to the bottom. The only possible way down was blocked by the creature, now less than a meter away.

Jim's mind reacted with absurd, curious thoughts. He wondered how his life would have changed had he married Carol Marcus; he wondered how Carol would react to news of his death. He found himself trying to picture her expression . . . all the while watching the creature inch closer.

A sound overhead: a ship, slicing through the atmosphere. Kirk glanced up, gladdened, fully expecting to see *Galileo,* miraculously repaired, come to his rescue.

Instead, he saw a Klingon Bird of Prey. It dropped out of the racing storm clouds and strafed the creature with a phaser barrage, forcing it back down the mountain.

As the creature clung, smoking, motionless, the Bird of Prey descended, then hovered over Jim.

In a horrible flash of understanding, Jim knew that Spock and those aboard the *Enterprise* would not have allowed a Klingon ship to come this far, unless . . .

Unless they and the ship had been destroyed. It explained the static on his communicator all too well.

Spock and the crew had remained to save him and had been killed for their efforts.

Kirk cried out, defiant with grief. "So it's me you want, you Klingon bastards! Come and get me!"

The sky wavered, then disappeared in the uncertain sparkle of the transporter beam.

Chapter Eighteen

KIRK FOUND HIMSELF IN unpleasantly familiar surroundings: the transporter room of a Klingon vessel.
Even more unpleasantly, two oversized Klingon
guards seized him, one to an arm, and propelled him
out into the dim, faintly noxious-smelling corridor.

The Klingon Bird of Prey was designed strictly for
battle; the size of its crew and its interior was roughly
one-fortieth that of the starship, which was designed
for exploration. Therefore, it was only a matter of
several steps before the guards arrived with their prize
at the doors to the bridge.

Jim was bitterly disconsolate. The static on his
communicator when he awaited Scott's transporter
beam and the subsequent failure of the *Enterprise* to
rescue him from the Bird of Prey's talons could only

mean one thing: that the ship and all those aboard her had been destroyed.

Jim indulged in an agony of self-recrimination, remembering the instant he had said to Sybok, "What makes you think I won't turn her around?"

He should have done exactly that—should not have permitted himself to slip into the same self-delusion that had gripped his crew. If he had listened to his head instead of his instincts, the ship he had mistrusted at first but that had served him so well would still be whole. Sybok would not have died in the depths of the tunnel. Spock, McCoy, his crew . . . all of them would still be alive.

He had lost everything now—more than David and Carol. He had lost the *Enterprise* again, his crew, and the two closest friends he had in the universe. His grief was overwhelmed by anger—at himself, at the Klingons who had murdered his son and now had killed his friends.

As the bridge doors opened, Jim's rational mind fled. If he was going to die, he would, as the Klingons said, die well. Flanked by the two guards, he walked onto the tiny bridge, intending to lunge forward and throttle the vessel's commander at the first opportunity. At least that way, death would come more swiftly and be more gratifying.

The back of the captain's chair faced him, so that its occupant was not immediately visible. Jim's eye was caught by a surprisingly familiar face off to one side: General Korrd, who stood straight and proud, for the first time in recent days, with his hands clasped behind his back.

Korrd looked Jim in the eye and beamed with pleasure; his expression was entirely devoid of both scorn and ill will. Yet Korrd's presence could only mean one thing: that the Klingons had somehow effected his rescue shortly before destroying the *Enterprise*.

And then Jim saw something even more puzzling: the disgruntled young Klingon standing beside Korrd wore the insignia of a Bird of Prey captain.

Then who the hell was sitting in the command chair?

Kirk stepped toward it; curiously, the guards did not attempt to restrain him. As he neared, the chair swiveled slowly, revealing its occupant.

Jim gasped. "Spock!"

The Vulcan unstrapped himself from what appeared to be a custom-designed gunner's rig and rose with consummate dignity. "Welcome aboard, Captain." Beneath Spock's total restraint, Jim perceived the faintest glint of smugness.

Korrd spoke in booming, guttural Klingon to the guards; they exited the bridge.

"Spock," Jim said, still not quite able to grasp what had happened. "I thought *Enterprise* was destroyed. I thought you were dead, and I was sure *I* was going to die."

The Vulcan's reply was soft. "Not possible, Captain. You were never alone."

Jim was overwhelmed by a rush of affection, gratitude, and relief. Unashamed, he stepped forward and clasped his friend in a hug.

Spock stiffened. "Captain, please. Not in front of the Klingons."

Jim only hugged harder, and laughed until the tears came.

Damned inappropriate, McCoy thought as he stood on the forward deck and gazed through the window at the planet where Sybok had met his death. A reception was in full swing on the observation deck, and McCoy didn't quite understand it.

The Klingon captain, Klaa, and his first officer had come aboard, as polite as you please—never mind the fact that they had just tried to blow the *Enterprise* to kingdom come. Now they were being feted like a couple of VIPs. From what McCoy understood of Jim's sketchy explanation, the reception had been Korrd and Dar and Talbot's idea—something about promoting intergalactic peace—and they'd been able to pull it off largely because Korrd had a brother-in-law named Krell.

It just didn't seem fair. People were drinking, talking, having a good time; McCoy frowned at the sound of clinking glasses and laughter, then glanced worriedly at Spock, who stood at his elbow.

The Vulcan, too, gazed out at the planet. His manner was distant, his expression as coldly controlled as McCoy ever remembered seeing it.

Damned inappropriate. Spock's brother was dead, and here they all were having a party.

Ought to have been a wake, McCoy thought, and took a sip from his glass. He was drinking Thirelian mineral water, out of consideration for Spock. The last thing the Vulcan needed now was to be surrounded by a bunch of drunks.

The doctor had spotted Spock over by the window

and had come over to tell him how he felt—how sorry he was about Sybok, how angry he was that Spock had been forced to attend such a festive occasion, and that there had been no formal memorial service.

But the Vulcan remained aloof. His silence engulfed McCoy; for several minutes the doctor, too, remained silent and stared out the window along with him. When McCoy finally gathered the courage to speak, it was of something entirely unrelated.

"Try this on for size." McCoy had followed Spock's gaze to the distant planet, which now seemed as cold and impersonal as the Vulcan's expression. "Has it occurred to you"—actually, it hadn't occurred to McCoy until that very second—"that the Great Barrier wasn't put there to keep us out, but to keep that thing *in?*"

Spock did not look at him. "It has occurred to me."

"Well," McCoy said, trying rather inanely, he thought, to say something comforting, to make the best of a perfectly rotten situation, "doesn't that imply the existence of a greater power?"

Actually, once he'd said it, it sort of made sense.

Spock turned from his contemplation to face McCoy. "I will say this much, Doctor. We have yet to reach the final frontier."

Awkwardly, McCoy launched into what he really wanted to say. "Spock, if it's any comfort to you . . . what Sybok did for me seems to be permanent. The positive aspect of it, that is. The grief I felt over my dad's death—it's still there, but it's different. It's . . . bearable now. I can think about it and talk about it, something I haven't been able to do for the past ten years." He paused. "I guess what I'm trying to say is

298

that Sybok saved our lives, and for that, I'm grateful. But it's more than that: your brother helped me. He helped us all."

"Thank you, Dr. McCoy," Spock answered simply. He was about to say more when his gaze fell on something behind McCoy. The doctor glanced over his shoulder and saw the consul from Earth, St. John Talbot, approach.

He came up beside McCoy and nodded to each of them. Although others were drinking, Talbot seemed eminently sober . . . and somehow years younger than the man who'd been taken hostage on Nimbus III.

The glazed "hostage look" was gone—McCoy's examination of the crew had revealed no lingering aftereffects from Sybok's mind-meld—replaced by a look of determination.

"Gentlemen," Talbot said graciously. He did not smile; his manner made it clear that he had come to offer condolences to Spock.

At least, McCoy thought with some satisfaction, *someone else here understands what common decency is.*

"Mr. Talbot," Spock replied, acknowledging the fact that the consul had come to speak to him.

"Spock, I speak on behalf of myself and the other delegates. We want you to know that, along with you, we mourn the loss of your brother."

The Vulcan's answer was not at all what McCoy expected. "I lost him a very long time ago, Mr. Talbot."

Talbot lifted one brow slightly to indicate his confusion.

"We were estranged," Spock explained. "In many ways, the recent events have allowed me to reclaim his memory."

"I'm glad for that, at least," Talbot answered warmly. "I remember quite well what you said to General Korrd about your brother's sacrifice. It impressed all of us very deeply. I intend to see to it that Sybok's life and death are honored." He paused. "Dar, Korrd, and I have decided to devote ourselves to improving conditions on Nimbus, to showing our governments that it *can* work. Perhaps someday in the not-so-distant future there will be peace among our peoples. Perhaps we can help Sybok's vision of paradise to become a reality."

Moved, McCoy glanced up at the Vulcan's face. For a moment, the mask slipped. Spock looked—really *looked*—into Talbot's eyes. McCoy felt he saw a communion of souls. He looked away, embarrassed to have witnessed something so private, as Spock said, "Sybok would have been grateful, Mr. Talbot—as I am."

Talbot smiled.

Nearby at the buffet, General Korrd— wearing full diplomatic regalia, and feeling decades younger—set down his half-empty glass of fruit juice and frowned at the daunting array of beverages, already poured and displayed in neat rows. He wanted something stronger.

Not that he wanted to get drunk; Korrd figured that over the past five years or so, he'd consumed enough liquor to last ten lifetimes. No, he wanted to drink a private toast, and fruit juice would not do. But there were a great many beverages to choose from, and many of them were unfamiliar. As a diplomat, Korrd knew enough of Earth's customs to understand that it would be unseemly for him to taste each one.

One of the *Enterprise* crew—from the uniform, Korrd placed him in engineering—was pouring himself a drink and noticed the Klingon's dilemma. The human set his glass down.

"Can I help you?" He spoke English with an accent Korrd was unable to place. His tone was polite enough, but there was more than a trace of cold hostility in his eyes. This was a man with a deep grudge against Klingons.

"Yes, please," Korrd told him, determined to do what he could to ease that hostility. "I was looking for a drink. Something stronger than this." He pointed to the glass of fruit juice. "I want to drink a toast."

The human hesitated; Korrd saw him weigh hatred against kindness. Fortunately, kindness won out; the human picked up a clean glass and gestured at Korrd with it.

"Would you care for a sip of scotch whisky?"

"Ummm . . ." Korrd began, uncertain whether it would be rude to ask to smell it first. But the engineer had already poured a glass and handed it to him; Korrd sensed that a refusal or even a hesitation now would be a grave mistake. In the interests of peace, he raised his glass, Earth-style, at the human. "Would you care to join me in a toast?"

The engineer regarded him skeptically. "That depends on what you're toasting."

"Sybok," Korrd replied. "In my culture, it is a custom to drink in honor of the dead."

The human nodded solemnly as he picked up his drink. "Aye. It's a custom on Earth, too. I'll drink a toast to him." He touched his glass to the Klingon's. "To Sybok."

"To Sybok," Korrd intoned, "a great warrior who died well." He raised his glass to his lips and inhaled the fragrance of fermented grain, a complex, faintly smoky smell. The alcohol content was far lower than what Korrd was used to, but it would serve the purpose. Before he could sip it, the human interrupted.

"Warrior?" His tone was disapproving. "Sybok was no warrior. He dinna believe in violence."

Korrd lowered his drink. "A warrior for peace is no less a warrior."

It was the right thing to say—and besides, Korrd sincerely meant it. The cold mistrust in the human's eyes vanished completely, replaced by warmth. He smiled at Korrd's words. "Aye, that's true. I'll drink to that—and to Sybok." He tilted his head back and drained his glass in one gulp.

Korrd followed suit and smacked his lips with slightly exaggerated relish. "Excellent! What did you say this was?"

The engineer swelled with pride. "Scotch. Single-malt scotch whisky."

"A superior drink," Korrd told him. Not quite the truth, but then, Korrd suspected he would be forgiven this one small lie. It was, after all, told to promote interstellar fellowship. "I will most certainly remember. Might I have a bit more?"

"Absolutely." The human reached for a bottle and

enthusiastically sloshed some liquid into the general's glass, then his own. "Sorry I didn't introduce myself earlier. Chief Engineer Montgomery Scott. To tell the truth, General Korrd, I never thought I'd be drinking with a Klingon."

Korrd clasped Scott's hand. "To quote an old Earth saying, 'Times change,' Engineer Scott. 'Times change.'"

He left Scott beaming. *Korrd, you wily old diplomat,* he congratulated himself. *Between you and Krell, you'll have the entire Klingon Council in your camp again. Can the Federation and the Romulans be far behind?*

To think he owed it to a Vulcan . . .

Korrd spotted Captain Klaa and his first officer, off drinking by themselves in a far corner of the deck.

Glass raised, he walked toward them and boomed in a loud voice, "To the greatest hero in the Romulan and Klingon empires—and the Federation!" As Korrd came up beside them, he threw back his head and polished off the rest of the scotch.

The first officer, Vixis, followed suit and drank with grace and enthusiasm. Many nearby—including Talbot and Dar—heard and raised their glasses in a toast to Klaa. Korrd recalled the old Earth axiom that flattery did little to advance one's cause; in regard to Klaa, this was certainly not the case. Klaa smiled, clearly relishing the attention.

Yet there was a trace of sullenness in his eyes. Korrd noted it and determined to win him over; if his plans for Nimbus were to succeed, he would need Klaa's support. The young Klingon already wielded great influence with the High Command—as much as old Krell himself and, after this latest triumph, perhaps even more.

"But where was the victory?" Klaa asked so softly that only Korrd and Vixis could hear. "There was no battle."

"A victory for peace," Korrd said, reminded again of Sybok, "endures longer than any gained through bloodshed. Think on this, Klaa: Sometimes there is more glory to be found in life than in death.

"If you had killed James Kirk, you would have achieved fame within our empire for a generation, then been forgotten. But now your name will be known not only to Klingons but to Romulans as well, and to all intelligent species within the Federation— and to their children and their children's children, and they will remember you with gratitude. Even more so if you assist us in making Nimbus a success."

"Hmm." Klaa sipped his drink and savored it . . . and the glowing vision conjured by Korrd's words. "You are a very shrewd opponent, General, and very quick to understand another's psychology; it is a quality I can appreciate. I also appreciate the fact that it is your brother-in-law who will make the final decision as to my promotion."

"True," Korrd said with feigned innocence.

Klaa smiled with the admiration of one brilliant strategist for another. "But I will consider what you have said, Korrd. It has the ring of common sense."

Korrd smiled back and, with his free hand, saluted the young Klingon. "Success, Captain."

Klaa returned the salute. "Success . . . General."

Korrd left them and ambled over to where Dar and Talbot were speaking earnestly; he heard just enough to know they were discussing Nimbus again. Dar wore much the same determined, intense look she had worn on the day Korrd first met her. Talbot stood, arms folded, listening to Dar with interest; the Englishman did not bother to hold a glass at all. He looked more fit and sober and animated than Korrd had ever seen him. Dar sipped a clear liquid. Water, Korrd assumed, until he came close enough to catch a whiff of straight spirits.

"It seems you two have changed places," Korrd told them pleasantly.

Talbot chuckled; Dar stopped talking and glanced up at the Klingon with sincere affection. "A human custom," she explained, with a sheepish nod at her drink. "Something called a wake. Talbot explained it to me earlier."

"Wake?" Korrd had never heard the term.

"A . . . a celebration of death," Dar said. "Or rather of the dead one's life. The emphasis is on recalling all that was good." Her expression grew thoughtful. "It seemed to me that since Sybok made this reception possible, we should somehow dedicate it to him."

"A worthy custom." Korrd touched his glass to Dar's with a high-pitched clink. "To Sybok."

"To Sybok," Dar said somberly. They drank.

Talbot watched them. "This is the best way to celebrate death—by appreciating life."

Korrd swallowed his second scotch. The flavor was actually not bad. Perhaps, in the interest of furthering diplomatic relations, he would talk to Krell about arranging the legal importation of the stuff to Nimbus III.

"So," he said, "as Klingon representative, it's my business to know what the two of you were conspiring about when I came along."

Talbot flashed a sudden dazzling smile. "We were just thinking about how far we've come in such a short time."

Korrd nodded, remembering the slow dissolution of his life and wondering where it would have ended had Sybok not arrived. "We certainly have."

"Good heavens!" Talbot exclaimed, with mock astonishment. "Do you realize, Korrd, that we just agreed on something!"

"Gentlemen," Dar raised her glass again, "it's about time."

From a short distance away, Jim Kirk smiled faintly as Korrd threw back his head and bellowed with laughter. The sound reverberated through the observation deck, causing people to stop in midsentence to stare at the old Klingon.

The three laughing diplomats did not at all resemble the people whose file holos Jim had studied en route to Nimbus; these people seemed younger, freer, more animated in their movements and speech, as though their encounter with Sybok had changed them forever.

The reception had been Korrd's idea, one that Jim thought was brilliant. It honored both the recovered hostages and Captain Klaa of the Bird of Prey *Okrona,* their rescuer. Both Talbot and Dar had sworn to get their governments to decorate Klaa as a hero, not only of the Klingon Empire but of the Romulan Empire and the Federation as well. Jim glanced over at the young Klingon, who stood off to one side, conferring with his female first officer.

Klaa seemed to sense that he was being watched; he glanced up and met Jim's gaze. There was a trace of respect and admiration in the Klingon's eyes.

Jim responded with the Klingon salute.

Klaa returned it with a faint smile, then resumed his conversation.

Jim headed over toward the observation window where McCoy and Spock stood. Jim was surprised to see the Vulcan in attendance; he hadn't ordered Spock to appear, and had assumed the Vulcan would still be recovering in private from his brother's death. Yet Spock's expression was more contemplative than grief-stricken.

Jim walked up beside his two friends and followed their gaze to the planet beyond. "Cosmic thoughts, gentlemen?"

"I was thinking of Sybok," Spock said matter-of-factly, without any trace of sorrow. "He was grievously misguided, deluded . . . and yet . . ." His voice faltered, then became strong again. "Even in death, he has brought about great good."

"Amen," McCoy said softly.

"I lost a brother once," Jim said, knowing they would think he referred to Sam. He remembered the barrier of self-pity he'd erected after the loss of the *Enterprise,* after the death of his son, David, and his rejection at the hands of Carol Marcus. For the first time, he saw the depths of his foolishness. He laid a hand lightly on Spock's arm. "But I was lucky. I got him back."

Without changing his expression in the slightest, Spock managed to convey the impression of a smile.

"I thought you said men like us don't have families," McCoy reminded him gently.

"I was wrong," Jim said. His tone lightened. "Speaking of which . . . We still have some shore leave coming to us. I was thinking of going back to Yosemite. Anyone care to join me?"

McCoy studied him suspiciously. "That depends. You going to be doing any more mountain climbing?"

Jim grinned. "No more mountain climbing . . . at least, not for a good long while. I swear."

Epilogue

NIGHT. Jim sat before the blazing campfire and inhaled the intoxicating scents of fresh air, bourbon, and evergreen. Beside him, Spock carefully fastened a marshmallow on the end of a stick and proffered it to McCoy, who took it gratefully.

The Vulcan seemed to have come to terms with his brother's death, although he remained silent and pensive throughout the second half of his shore leave at Yosemite. His solemn face glowed orange with reflected firelight.

"You were saying, Doctor, that your grandfather raised entire fields of melons," Spock began conversationally.

"Say what?" McCoy wrinkled his brow. "What the devil are you talking about, Spock? My grandfather was a *doctor.*"

Jim nudged him in the ribs.

"Marsh melons," Spock prompted.

Revelation dawned on the doctor's face. "Oh, yeah . . ." McCoy nodded vigorously. *"That* grandfather. That's right, grew whole fields of 'em . . . I remember how, when they were ready for picking, the swamps used to look as if they were covered with snow. Lovely sight."

"Indeed." The Vulcan paused. "I trust your grandfather was a better farmer than you are a programmer, Doctor."

McCoy's blue eyes widened as he attempted an expression of complete innocence . . . and failed to achieve it. "Why, Spock, whatever do you mean?"

"The computer program. When I attempted to access information on camping out—as you clearly surmised I would—the data revealed a number of most interesting errors . . . such as the term 'marsh melons.' The next time you attempt such a practical joke, Doctor, I recommend you take the time to also alter the cross-index files."

"I never *touched* the computer," McCoy protested. Both Jim and Spock raised disbelieving brows at that.

"You know me. I don't know a dad-blamed thing about computers. I paid one of the engineering maintenance workers good money to do it." McCoy grinned wickedly. "Sounds like I better ask for a refund."

"You're incorrigible," Jim told him.

"Me? What about Spock? He's the one who dragged this out, pretending to play along!" McCoy retrieved his marshmallow from the fire and popped it into his mouth. "I swear, the two of you—"

"Could drive a man to drink," Jim finished for him.

On cue, McCoy set down the stick, rummaged through his knapsack, and produced the treasured flask. "Give me your cup, Jim."

Jim complied. The doctor sloshed a generous amount of bourbon into Jim's cup and handed it back to him, then filled his own.

"To family," Jim said.

McCoy smiled. "To family," he said, and drank.

Meanwhile, Spock had eaten the obligatory marshmallow and produced his Vulcan harp. He cradled it in his lap and strummed absently, in search of a tune.

Jim stared into the fire for a while.

"Penny for your thoughts," McCoy said. "You seem to be better off this time around. At least I haven't seen you jumping off any mountains."

"It's funny," Jim said, mesmerized by the flames' arrhythmic dance. "Sybok never mind-melded with me, and yet . . . yet I've come to terms with loss, too."

"Sympathetic vibrations," McCoy said, half jokingly.

Jim thought about it for a while. "Or maybe friends." He smiled over at Spock. "Well, are you just going to sit there and pick at it or are you actually going to play something?"

Spock paused to consider the question, then slowly, deliberately began to play.

Jim and McCoy both grinned as each recognized the first few notes of "Row, Row, Your Boat."

The three raised their voices and began to sing.

The Critically Acclaimed
New York Times Hardcover Bestseller . . .
Available at Last in Paperback!

Diane Duane

Ever since 1966, when the very first episode of the
original STAR TREK television series aired, casual fans
and devoted Trekkers alike have been captivated by
the alien Mr. Spock and his enigmatic home planet
Vulcan. Now you can have an in-depth look at
both . . .

SPOCK'S WORLD . . .
**An August 1989 Paperback Release
from Pocket Books**

*FOR AN EXCITING PREVIEW OF OUR NEXT
STAR TREK HARDCOVER, PLEASE TURN THE
PAGE . . .*

Coming in October . . .

Whatever happened to the U.S.S. *Enterprise*™?

STAR TREK®

THE LOST YEARS
by J. M. Dillard

What exactly became of Captain Kirk, Mr. Spock, and the rest of the *Enterprise* crew after their historic five-year mission? How did that mission end? What did they do before they were reunited for the STAR TREK movies? Even the most casual STAR TREK fan finds him/herself asking these questions from time to time . . .

Here, at last, is the book that provides the answers to those questions—a book as anticipated, in its own way, as SPOCK'S WORLD was. In THE LOST YEARS, J. M. Dillard has written her best STAR TREK book to date—and the way she's answered the above questions will excite and delight STAR TREK fans.

THE LOST YEARS . . .
An October 1989 Hardcover Release
from Pocket Books

Turn the page for a special excerpt from THE LOST YEARS . . .

THE MOUNTAINS OF GOL:

140005 V.O.D.
(Vulcan Old Date)

Zakal spent the first half of the night coughing up green-black blood and listening to the wind hurl sand against the side of the mountain fortress. The cavernous chamber was windowless and dark, save for the feeble light emanating from the initiates' room, but Zakal had seen enough sandstorms to picture this one clearly in his mind's eye: a huge, vibrating column of red sand that blotted out the sky until nothing remained but moving desert. Any creatures foolish enough to venture unprotected into the storm would be found the next day, their mummies leached of all moisture, their skin crackling like parchment at the slightest touch.

Around the middle of the night, the stains on his handcloth changed from dark green to bright, the color of a *d'mallu* vine after a rare spell of rain. Shortly thereafter, the healer left him, a sign that there was nothing more to be done, no more easing of pain possible; a sign that he would be dead before sunrise. The relief on her drawn face was all too evident. She was not of the Kolinahru, and had attended her charge with a mixture of loathing and terror. For this was Zakal the Terrible, the greatest of the Kolinahr masters, with a mind so powerful he had twice used it to melt the skin of his enemies into puddles at his feet.

He said nothing to stop the healer from going, merely closed his eyes and smiled wanly. It was fitting to lie here and listen to the roar of the storm on the last night of his life. Eight hundred and eighty-seven seasons* ago, he had been born in a storm like this one, and so his mother had named him Zakal: the Fury, the Desert Storm.

He was drowsing off when an image jolted him awake. Khoteth, lean and young and strong, furling himself in his black traveling cloak, his expression severe, brows weighed down by the heaviness of what he was about to do. Khoteth was crossing the desert, Khoteth was coming for him. Zakal knew this with unquestionable surety, in spite of the three initiates in the next room who stood guard, not over his aged, dying body, but over a far more dangerous weapon: his mind. Even their combined efforts to shield the truth from him could not completely sever his link to the man he had raised as his own son. Khoteth had sensed his master's impending death, and would be here well before dawn.

The new High Master was risking his life by crossing the desert in a sandstorm . . . and oh, how Zakal listened to the wind and willed for Khoteth to be swallowed up by it! He tried in vain to summon up the old powers, but fever and the continual mental oppression caused by the initiates made it impossible. Zakal contented himself with cheering on the storm as if he had conjured it himself. Even so, he knew that Khoteth would complete his journey successfully.

So it was that, a few hours later when Khoteth's soft

*Approximately 276 Earth years.

words drew Zakal from a feverish reverie, they brought with them no surprise.

"Master? I have come."

Outside, the wind had eased, but still moaned softly. Zakal kept his face toward the black stone wall and did not trouble to raise his head. The sound of his former student's voice evoked within him a curious mixture of fondness and bitter hatred.

"Go away." He meant to thunder it with authority, but what emerged was weak and quavering, the ineffectual wheezing of an old man. He felt shame. Could this be the voice of the Ruler of ShanaiKahr, the most powerful and feared mind-lord of all Vulcan? He had known more of the secrets of power than the rest of the Kolinahru put together, but fool that he was, he had entrusted too many of them to the man who stood before him now. He turned his head—slowly, for any movement made him dizzy and liable to start coughing again—and opened fever-pained eyes to the sight of the one he had loved as a son, had chosen as his successor, and now despised as his mortal enemy. "Leave me, Khoteth. I may be your prisoner, but you cannot tell me when to die. There is time yet."

"My name is Sotek," his captor admonished mildly. Khoteth drew back the hood of his cloak, scattering rust-colored sand onto the stone floor. Such a young one—too young for a High Master, Zakal thought disapprovingly—but the responsibility had prematurely etched the first lines of age between his brows. Khoteth's severe expression had eased into one of calculated neutrality, but Zakal could see the emotion that smoldered in his eyes, the one sign of the highly passionate nature Khoteth had been born with. As a child, he had been a true prodigy at the secret arts, devouring everything Zakal dared teach him, always hungering for more. In spite of his own appetite for power, Zakal had early on glimpsed the unpleasant truth of the matter. This child would grow into a man who would surpass his teacher, the greatest of all teachers. If you cannot defeat your enemy, then bring him into your camp. Zakal designated the lad as his successor, for one day Khoteth's abilities would lead him to much more than rulership of a single city. One day, he would be master of all the western towns, perhaps someday even master of the entire continent. And Zakal, the wise teacher and advisor, would have to be content to ally himself with such power if he could not be the source of it himself.

Even with his powerful imagination, Zakal had never thought his protege's incredible talent could be thwarted, wasted, perverted by the simple-minded philosophy of a coward.

"Sotek," Zakal hissed, and raised his head just enough to spit on the floor in Khoteth's direction. The young master did not flinch at the ominously bright green spittle at his boots, but a flicker of dark emotion shone in his eyes. Zakal's thin lips curved upward with irony. So Khoteth was at last afraid of his teacher again . . . as he had been years ago, when he had first confined Zakal here. Only this time it was not mental sorcery that made Khoteth cringe. Lunglock fever made cowards of them all.

Zakal found his breath for an instant. "What kind of name is that for a Vulcan? And what are your followers called now? Sarak? Serak? Sirak? Sorak? And how many Suraks altogether, please? Tell me, how long do you think this can last until you run out of names for your children?" He emitted a wheezing cackle that deteriorated into a coughing spell.

He was far too weak to sit up and so lay, hands pressed tight against his aching ribs, and choked helplessly on the vile fluid seeping up from his lungs. Khoteth watched dispassionately, hands still hidden beneath the folds of his cloak, which would be burned, Zakal knew, as soon as Khoteth left the mountain stronghold.

"How can you bear to see your old teacher like this," Zakal managed to gasp at length, "knowing that they do not permit me to ease my pain?"

"I regret that your pain is a necessary consequence." Khoteth came no closer. "But to permit you access to any of the mind rules would be very foolish."

"Foolish!" Zakal croaked. "Where is your compassion?"

Khoteth's eyes were intense, though his tone remained cool. "I operate according to the principles of logic, not compassion." He struggled to keep a wry smile from curving his lips, and was not entirely successful. "And I know you, Master. You merit no compassion. I have seen you kill without mercy or guilt. Given the chance, you would murder me here and now without a second's hesitation."

The piteous expression on Zakal's face shifted into a harder one. "I would. And that is also why you are here, to kill."

Puzzled, Khoteth raised an eyebrow at him.

"Perhaps," said Zakal, "not to kill my body . . . but my spirit. You have come to deny me the second life."

"You misunderstand, Master." The folds of Khoteth's cloak parted, and with both hands he drew forth a shimmering globe. "I have come to keep the promise I made so long ago."

Zakal's dimming eyes widened at the sight of the *vrekatra*, the receptacle in which his eternal spirit would rest for all eternity. "But Nortakh—" he began, until the heaviness in his chest left him gasping again. Nortakh, one of Zakal's initiates with no particular talent for mental sorcery, had been Khoteth's sworn rival ever since the new High Master chose to follow Surak's teachings. Zakal had been taken prisoner and hidden in the desert so that Nortakh and his followers could have no more access to the secret knowledge. Indeed, Zakal had expected the new High Master to deny him the vrekatra—for to do so was the only way to ensure the secrets would be forever lost, safe from Surak's enemies.

"Nortakh grows more powerful each day." Khoteth brought the glowing orb a step closer to the dying Vulcan. "I will confess that at first I considered setting your katra upon the winds . . . but I am bound to keep my vow to you. And . . . I need all of your knowledge, Master, if I am to defeat him."

Zakal found the strength to taunt him. "I thought the followers of Surak took no action against their enemies. Aren't you supposed to deal peace with Nortakh?"

A slight grimace rippled over Khoteth's serious features. "I will do no physical harm to Nortakh or any of his Kolinahru, but that does not preclude my taking certain . . . precautions. Nortakh must be rendered harmless if Vulcan is ever to be at peace."

Zakal coughed into his handcloth again and idly watched the stain spread through the fabric. "Surak's utopia of peace is a childish fantasy, a refusal to face reality. All creatures must prey on others, and compete among themselves; this is the way of survival, the way of all life. Surak would have us deny what we are." A spasm of pain clutched his chest, making him wheeze. His distress was so desperate, so unfeigned, that Khoteth forgot his composure and, alarmed, moved toward his old teacher, but Zakal waved him back with the bloody cloth. After a moment, he managed to speak.

"Surak will not succeed. His followers will come to their senses, just as S'task did. And S'task was his closest disciple . . ."

"S'task and his followers are leaving Vulcan," Khoteth said quietly, his eyes searching the old master's face for a reaction, "so that Surak may be successful. Even S'task acknowledges the folly of more strife, more wars."

"Leaving Vulcan!" Zakal cried, enraged at the cowardice of S'task and his followers, humiliated that such common knowledge could be kept from him by the three initiated idiots in the next room. The outburst caused another spasm of pain, a hot, heavy fire that shot up from his solar plexus to the back of his throat.

"Twelve thousand are preparing for the journey on the first ship. It is expected that more will follow."

For an instant, Zakal forgot his anger in the face of supreme agony. The achingly heavy fluid in his lungs seemed turned to acid, burning him, eating at him . . . Without the mind rules, he managed for a short time to transcend the pain with sheer hatred. "So . . ." he gasped. "The planet is in the hands of sheep . . . while true Vulcans surrender their birthright. I swear to you—before the Elements—were I free, I would convince S'task to stay and fight. I would kill Surak myself—"

"I know that, Master. That is why I have taken care that your katra does not fall into the wrong hands." Khoteth held out the globe. "It is time."

"No!" Zakal tried to shriek. "I will not be used to help Surak!" But the words came out an indistinct gurgling noise.

Even so, Khoteth understood. "Master," he said sadly, "would you see all of your knowledge scattered on the winds? This"—he nodded at the shining vrekatra—"this is your destiny."

Bitterness filled Zakal's mouth and he began to choke furiously, spraying blood in all direction. In the midst of his desperate fight for air, a ridiculous thought struck him: *I am drowning. I am drowning in the middle of the desert, where there is no water . . .* And in spite of his pain, the irony of it shook him with fevered, silent laughter.

A gentle force propelled him into a sitting position, so that he was able to suck in air. Khoteth was next to him, holding him up, and he was dimly aware that Khoteth was risking his own life to do so. The vrekatra sat at the foot of the bed.

"I can force you, Master," the young Vulcan said. "But I will not. If you wish to join the Elements, I will not prevent you. Your knowledge would be most useful to me, but I can find a way to render Nortakh harmless without it."

And so, Zakal realized, Khoteth had jeopardized his own life not out of a desire to attain the secret knowledge to defeat his enemies, but out of a sense of duty, to fulfill his promise to his old master. And in the midst of Zakal's swirling, dying thoughts, one single, disgusted refrain stood out with perfect clarity: *How did I manage to raise such a fool?*

Eyes closed, Zakal lay against Khoteth's strong arm and used the last moment of his life to consider his options. Attempting a mental takeover of the young master would be foolhardy; the three initiates would prevent it, and even without their help, Khoteth was likely to emerge the victor from such a clash of wills. The choice was simple: utter annihilation . . . or eternal life on the mental plane. Despite his fury at the idea his secrets would be used to further Surak's aims, Zakal was far too selfish to contemplate nonexistence. Perhaps Khoteth had known it, had counted on it, when making his "noble" offer. Perhaps the boy was not as stupid as he had thought . . .

"The vrekatra," Zakal sighed. And as Khoteth pressed cool fingers against the desert-hot skin of his master's temples, Zakal's final thought inside his body was:

I shall have my revenge on you, Surak, for stealing my pupil, my city, my world from me. I shall have my revenge, if I have to wait for ten thousand seasons . . .

Outside, the wind became still.

SPACEDOCK, TERRA
Stardate 6987.31

Jim Kirk sat in the captain's chair on the bridge and watched as Spacedock gradually grew larger, rotating slowly on its axis like some gigantic, burnished metal top. Beyond it, suspended in the void of space, hung a sphere of marbled blue-white: Earth.

The *Enterprise* was coming home.

Impossible not to feel a tug of nostalgia at the sight: It had been no fewer than five years since he last stood on Terra, five years since he last witnessed this very sight—only then, Earth and Spacedock had been receding as the *Enterprise* moved away toward the unknown reaches of space.

Good Lord, Jim remarked silently. *Knock it off before you get maudlin.*

The past few days, as the ship drew closer to its final destination, he'd been alternating between wistful regret and restlessness—he refused to admit that it was fear—yet there it was, full-blown, irrational, waking him in the night to stare up in the darkness. The feeling that what was most important to him— the captaincy, the *Enterprise*—was on the verge of slipping through his fingers.

Not that he would let it.

Kirk ran a finger under the too-tight collar of his dress uniform and promised himself that as soon as the ship was safely docked, he would head for his quarters and deal directly with the source of the anxiety: a certain Gregor Fortenberry, civilian, Director of Assignments at Starfleet Headquarters, more popularly known as the Detailer.

Spacedock loomed a bit larger on the main viewscreen. Jim stared at it, feeling the self-conscious, heightened awareness that came with the realization that this was the *last time* for something. He'd experienced the same emotion—the need to commit every shred of detail to memory, to focus so intently on what was happening that time slowed—his last day at home before leaving for the Academy, and again, his graduation day at the Academy . . .

He stopped the thought; the situation did not apply to this ship, this crew. *Not the last day . . . I'll be back in this chair in a year or so, that's all.* A year or so, and the *Enterprise* would be refitted, recommissioned, and, hell or high water, Kirk would be commanding her. He refused to recognize any other possibility.

"Lieutenant," Kirk said, his gaze still on the screen. "Advise approach control, please."

"Approach control," Uhura said, seated at the communications console behind the captain's chair.

No doubt she had been poised, anticipating this particular order. "This is the U.S.S. *Enterprise,* ready for docking manuever." Her voice was calm, steady as always, but Kirk perceived a trace of the anticipation that permeated the bridge. Even Spock had quit pretending to be busy at the science station and had swiveled in his seat to stare frankly at their destination.

The response signal was strong, clean of interstellar static at such close range. *"Enterprise,"* came the young, masculine voice of the controller, "you are cleared to dock at Bay Thirteen." A pause. "Welcome home."

"Enterprise confirms," Uhura replied, "and thank you. It's good to be back."

Kirk glanced over his shoulder to see her smiling, and smiled himself. It *was* good to be back . . . still, it would have felt better if Jim knew that, while the *Enterprise* spent the next year or so in Spacedock being refitted, another ship awaited him. While he would never feel quite the same pride and loyalty he felt for this ship, his first command, at least there would be a ship; at least he would be out there, in space.

"Mister Sulu. Slow to one-quarter impulse power." Kirk sighed. "Take us home."

"Aye aye, sir. One-quarter impulse power." Sulu's expression was placid, but his dark eyes shone with keen excitement. Like his captain, he wore his formal dress tunic, satin-sheen gold for Command. Sulu appeared to have no regrets about returning home; within a matter of days, he would receive official notification that the promotion Kirk had sponsored him for had been granted, and that he was no longer Lieutenant Sulu, but Lieutenant Commander. It would not be many more years, Kirk reflected, before Sulu captained a ship of his own.

The *Enterprise* slowed as it approached Spacedock and assumed a spiral orbit until it reached the huge hangar doors that shielded Bay Thirteen from the radiation of space. As the ship neared, the hangar doors silently parted; the *Enterprise* glided easily into the massive bay.

Behind her, the great doors closed. Inside, the bay's interior was vast enough to accommodate dozens of starships, and did—some of them, as the *Enterprise* would soon be herself, undergoing refits; others, maintenance; still others, new ships, lay in various stages of construction.

As the *Enterprise* neared Docking Bay Thirteen, the controller spoke again. *"Enterprise, please stand by for final docking procedure."*

"Standing by," Uhura responded.

"Mister Sulu," Kirk said, resisting the desire to jump up and pace until they were safely into port. He wanted no part of the upcoming festivities, wanted only for the docking to be over, for the chance to pressure Fortenberry into reassuring him that the *Victorious* would be his to command. "Activate moorings. Stand by with gravitational support systems."

"Moorings activated, Captain. All systems standing by."

Seated next to Sulu at the navigational console, Chekov did a double-take at the screen, his round, cherubic face reflecting awe. "Captain, look . . ." He emitted a low whistle.

Kirk followed the navigator's gaze to the viewscreen, which showed the blinking lights of Bay Thirteen, and the row of small ports along the bay's upper level. As the ship moved closer, Kirk could just make out the crowds of people pressing against the port, all trying to catch a glimpse of the *Enterprise* as she arrived home at the end of a successful five-year mission.

"Some reception," Sulu remarked *sotto voce,* with a pleased grin.

Kirk did his best to appear unmoved by the spectacle. "Activate gravitational support systems."

Sulu forced himself to look away from the screen

and down at the helm control panel. "Activating now, sir."

"There must be a lot of reporters," Chekov mused, to no one in particular.

"Gravitational support systems locked on, Captain."

"Disengage engines."

At the engineering station, which sat directly opposite Spock, Ensign deRoos, a thin, angular human female, gave Kirk a grim look. "Engines disengaged, Captain."

It seemed to Kirk that the ship sighed as she eased into the bay and then stopped, though someone who knew her less well would not have been able to tell that she was no longer moving.

"Well," Kirk said. It seemed somehow anticlimactic. "So here we are." He leaned down to press the button for the ship-wide intercom.

"Ladies and gentlemen, this is the captain. Let me be the first to congratulate you on a safe arrival home." He paused, confused by his own reaction to arriving home: He should have been exhilarated, or at the very least relieved, instead of this oddly nagging disappointment. And perhaps he wasn't the only one to experience it. The times he had pictured this moment in his imagination, the crew always cheered. But there were no cheers on the bridge, only smiles, and almost—or was he projecting his own feelings onto those of his crew?—reluctance.

He continued awkwardly. "Let me also say that I am proud to have served with you, the best damn crew in the Fleet. My commendations to all of you." Another pause. "Tomorrow at 0900, Admiral Morrow will conduct a review. Until then—let the firewatch festivities commence."

He turned off the intercom and was about to get to his feet when the entire bridge crew—Sulu and Chekov at the helm, Uhura at communications, deRoos at engineering—rose as one, turned to face their captain, and applauded solemnly. All, that is, with the exception of Spock, who nevertheless rose, hands clasped behind his back, his expression grave but managing nevertheless to convey the fact that, although he did not follow the custom, he agreed with the sentiment.

"Not for me," Kirk said, rising. He raised a hand for silence, uncomfortable with the tribute. Modesty, false or otherwise, had nothing to do with it—but the ovation seemed to him misdirected. The applause thinned. "Not for me. For those who didn't make it back with us."

The second round of applause was restrained; this time, Kirk joined in.

Don't miss THE LOST YEARS, coming October 1, 1989 in hardcover from Pocket Books.

COMPLETELY REVISED!

THE STAR TREK®
COMPENDIUM

by Allan Asherman

Here is your official STAR TREK guidebook completely updated for 1989. Relive the voyages of the starship ENTERPRISE with this complete show-by-show guide to the STAR TREK series, including plot summaries, behind-the-scenes production information, and credits for each.

The Compendium is illustrated with over 130 specially selected photographs from each episode. The ultimate guide to one of the most memorable television shows of all time— STAR TREK.

THE STAR TREK® COMPENDIUM
68440/$10.95

Also Don't Miss!
MR. SCOTT'S GUIDE
TO THE ENTERPRISE

Written and Illustrated by Shane Johnson
63576/$10.95

POCKET BOOKS, Department CRC
1230 Avenue of the Americas, New York, N.Y. 10020

Please send me the books I have checked above, I am enclosing $ _____ (please add 75¢ to cover postage and handling for each order. N.Y.S. and N.Y.C residents please add appropriate sales tax). Send check or money order—no cash or C.O.D's please. Allow up to six weeks for delivery. For purchases over $10.00, you may use VISA. card number, expiration date and customer signature must be included

NAME _____

ADDRESS _____

CITY _____ STATE/ZIP _____